PEANUT, BUTTER, & CRACKERS

ON THE TRAIL

PAIGE BRADDOCK

Coloring by Kat Fraser

VIKING

For Leonard –P. B.

VIKING

An imprint of Penguin Random House LLC, New York

First published in the United States of America by Viking,
an imprint of Penguin Random House LLC, 2022

Visit us online at penguinrandomhouse.com.

Library of Congress Cataloging-in-Publication Data is available.

Manufactured in China

ISBN 9780593117491

1 3 5 7 9 10 8 6 4 2

TOPL

Book design by Paige Braddock, Jim Hoover, and Lucia Baez.

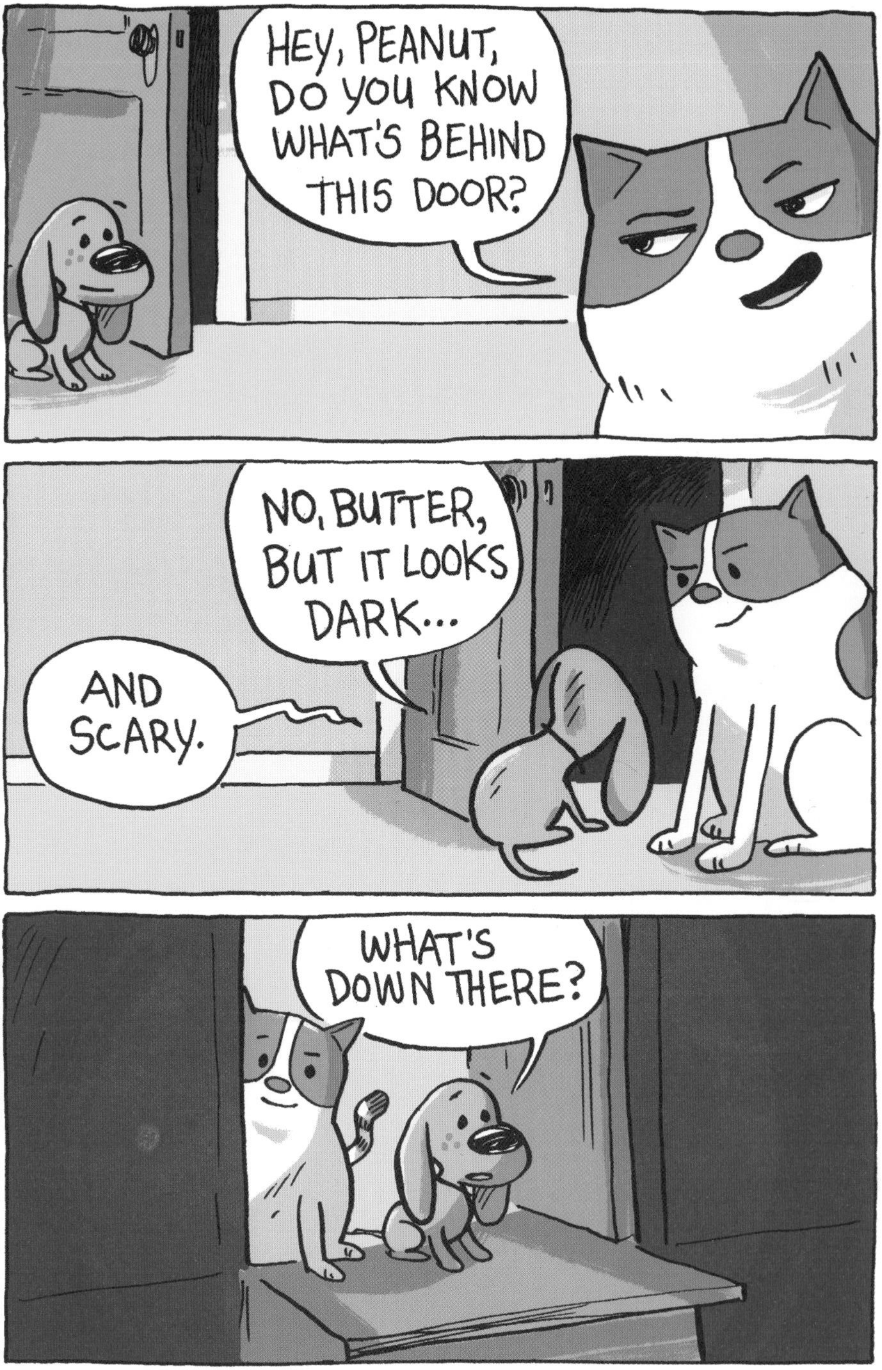
HEY, PEANUT, DO YOU KNOW WHAT'S BEHIND THIS DOOR?
NO, BUTTER, BUT IT LOOKS DARK...
AND SCARY.
WHAT'S DOWN THERE?

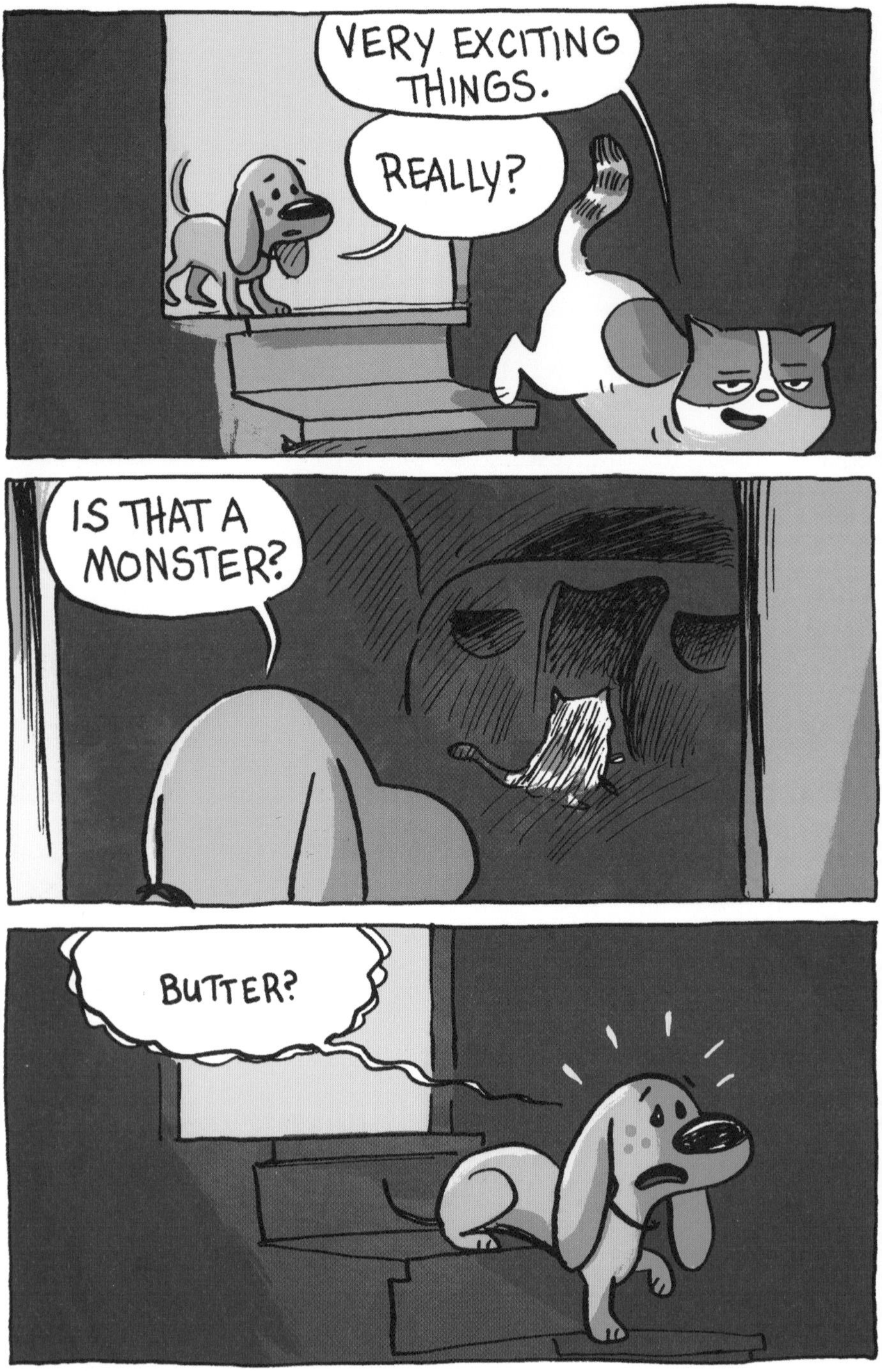
VERY EXCITING THINGS.
REALLY?
IS THAT A MONSTER?
BUTTER?

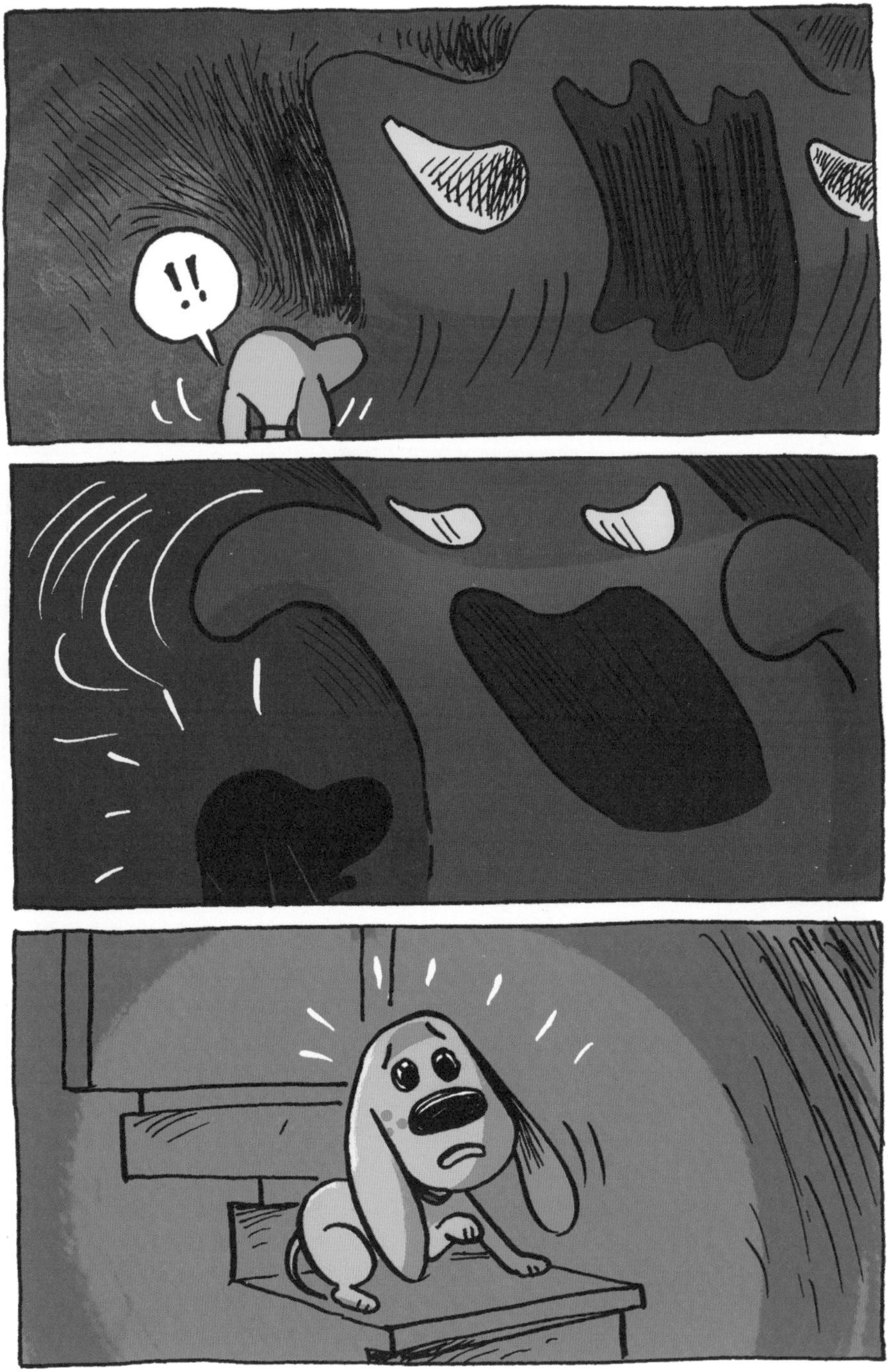
!!

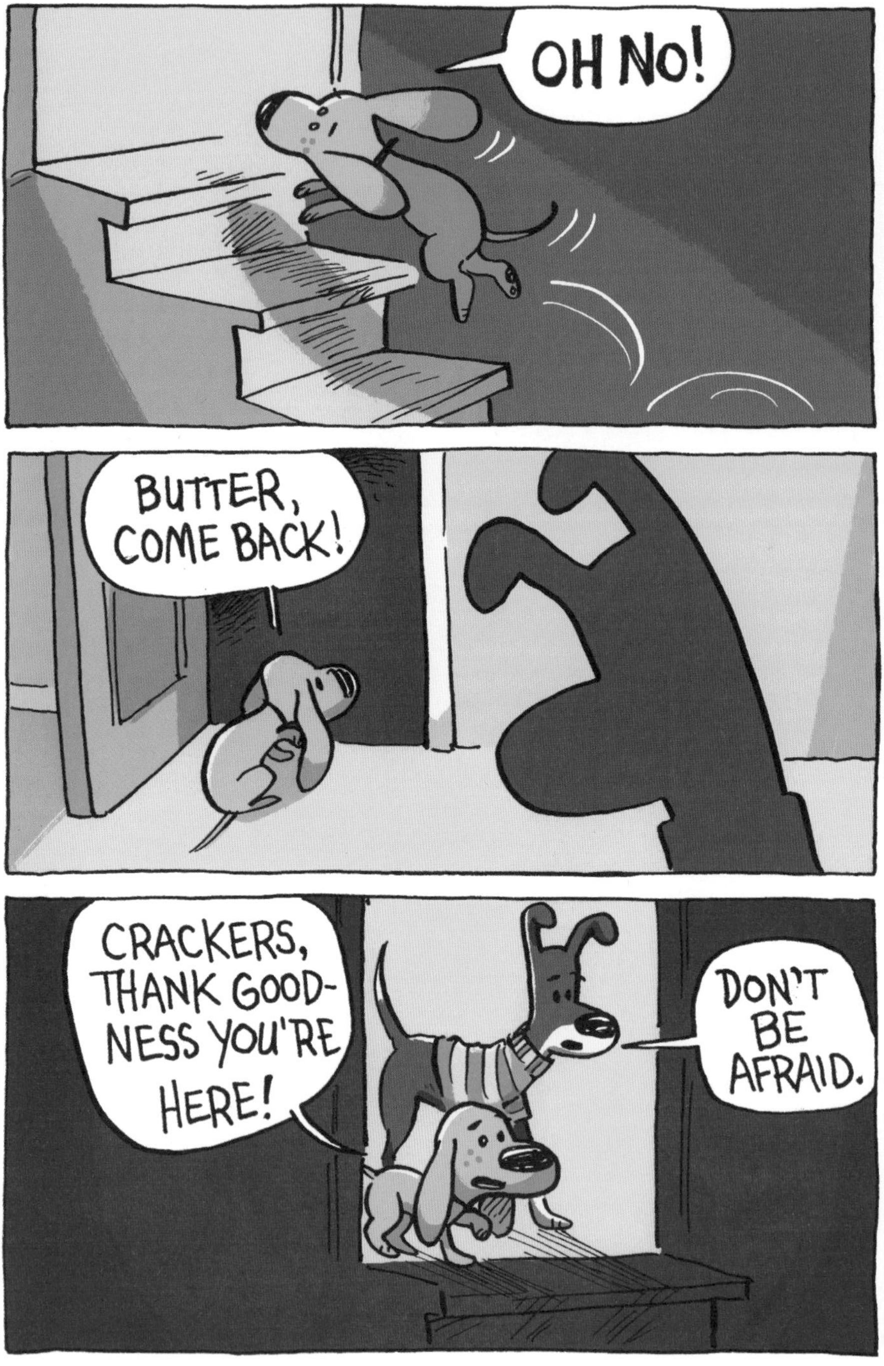
OH NO!
BUTTER, COME BACK!
CRACKERS, THANK GOOD-NESS YOU'RE HERE!
DON'T BE AFRAID.

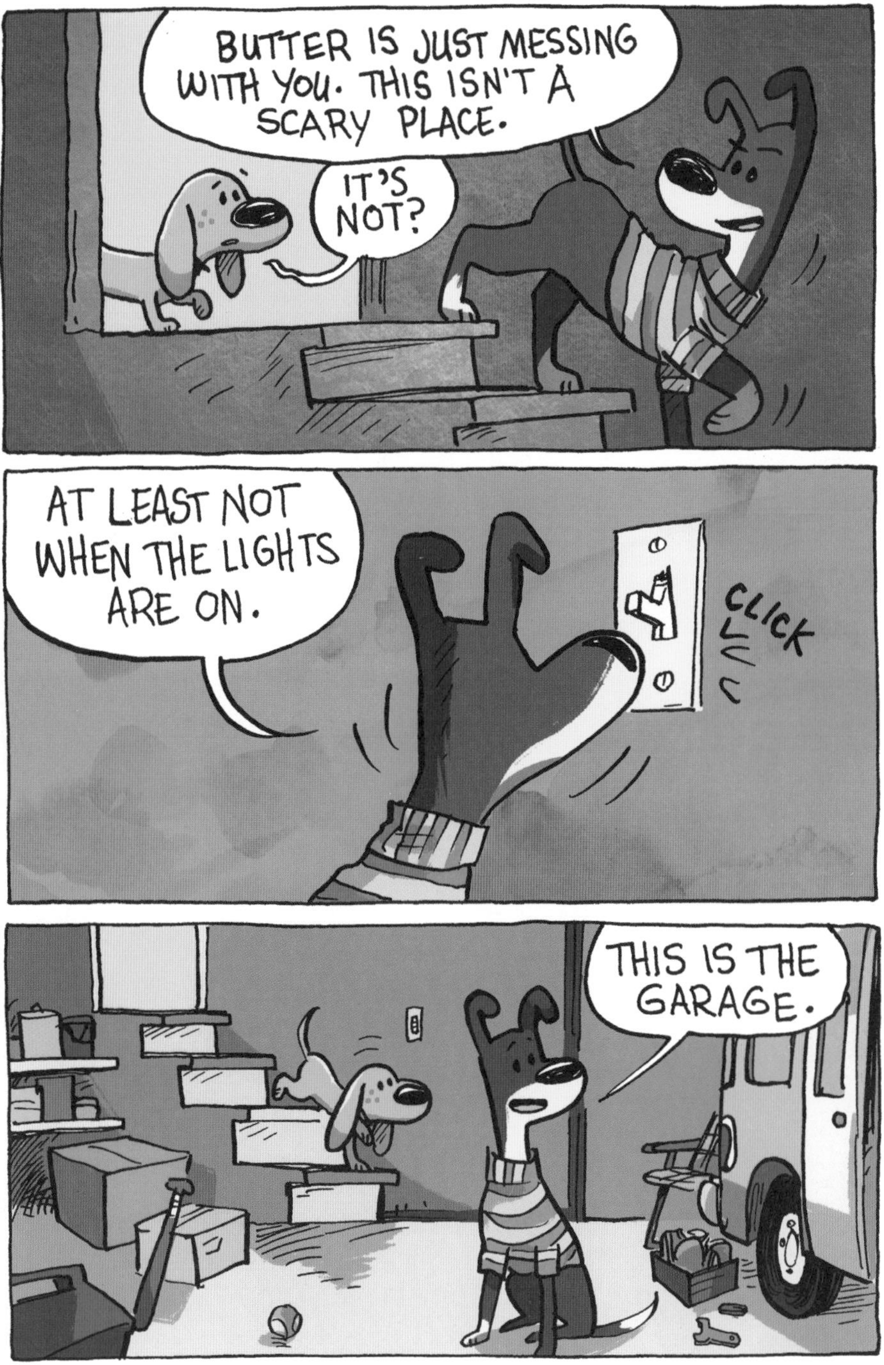
BUTTER IS JUST MESSING WITH YOU. THIS ISN'T A SCARY PLACE.
IT'S NOT?
AT LEAST NOT WHEN THE LIGHTS ARE ON.
CLICK
THIS IS THE GARAGE.

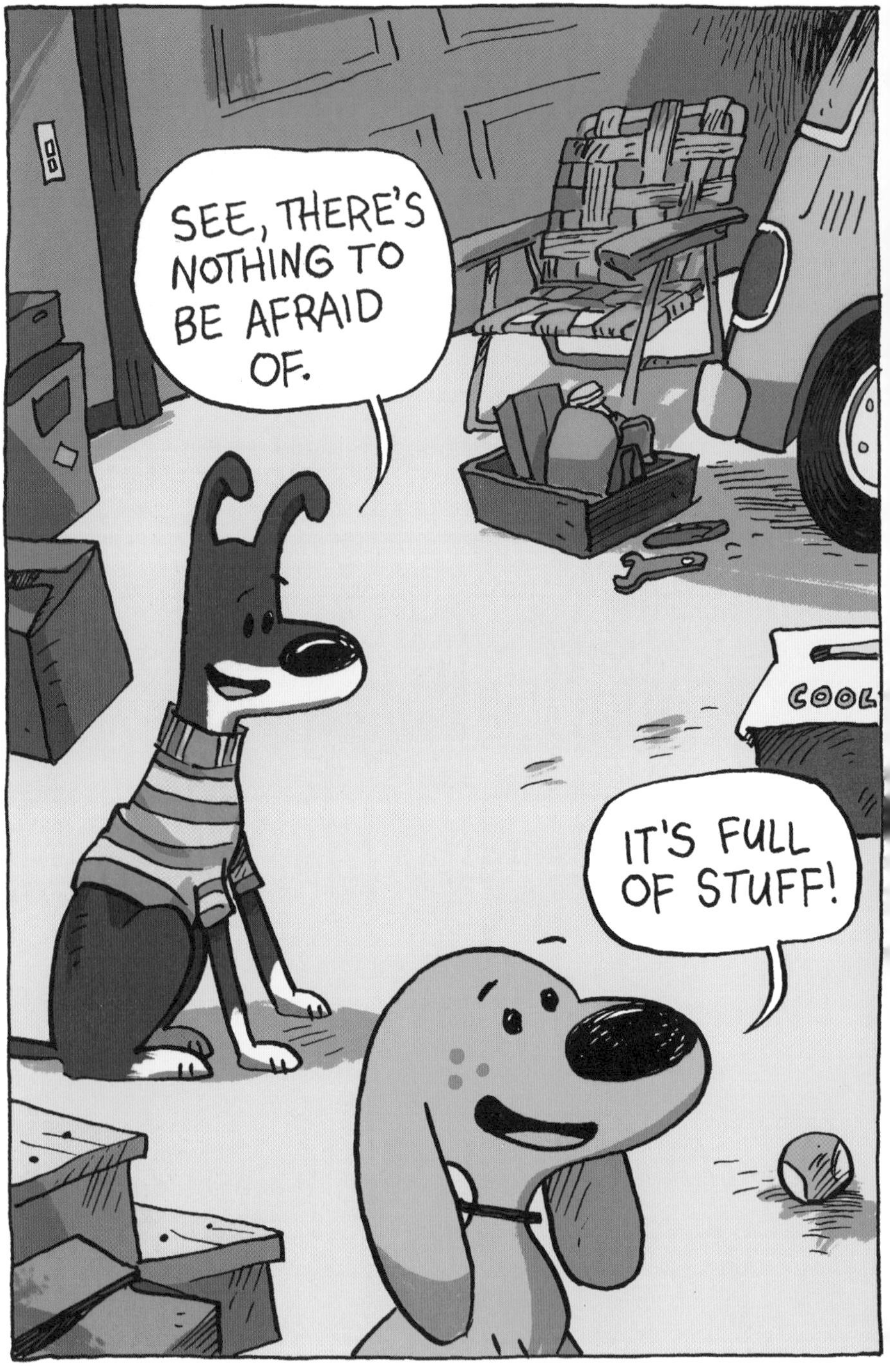
SEE, THERE'S NOTHING TO BE AFRAID OF.
IT'S FULL OF STUFF!
COOL

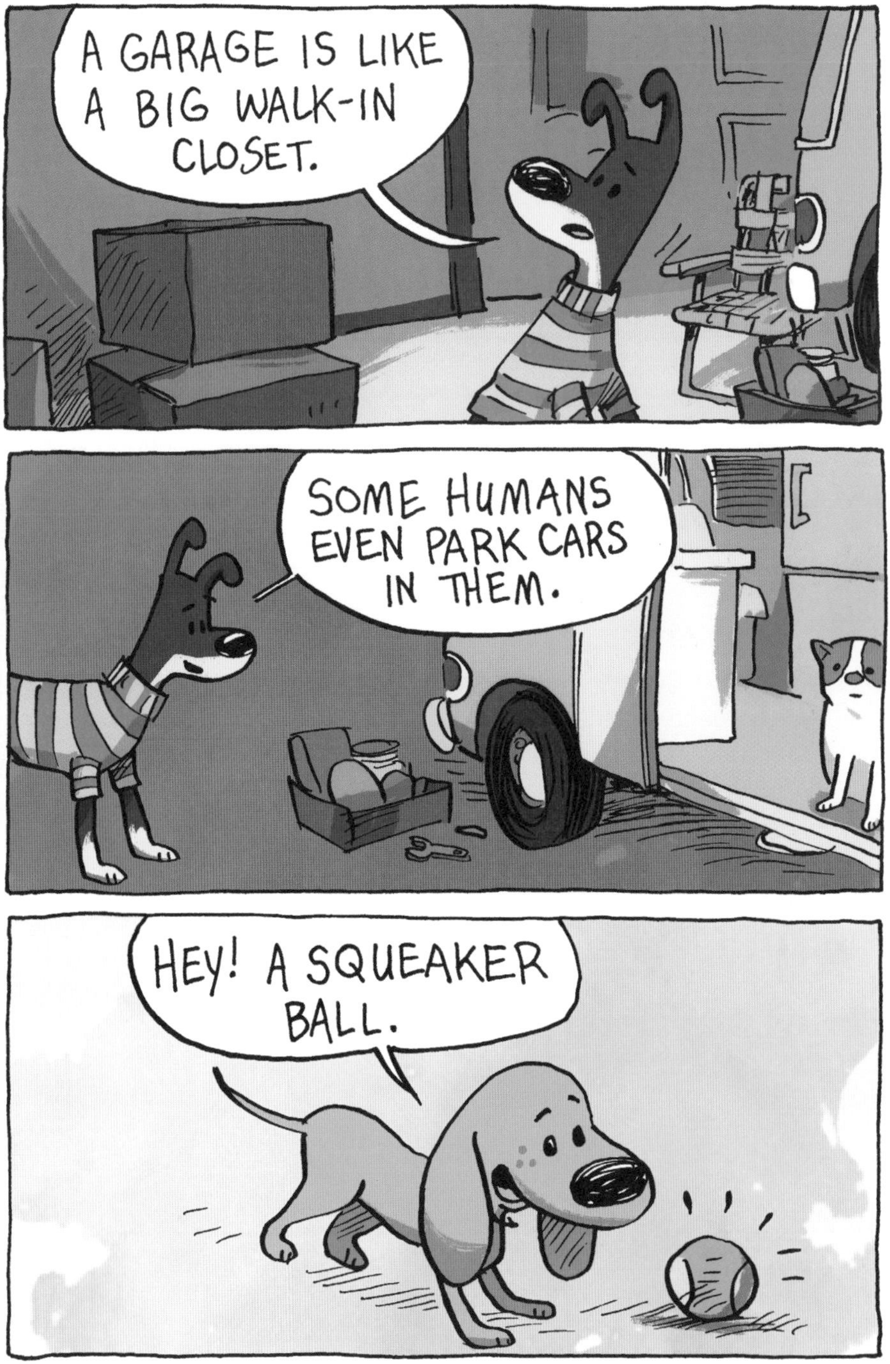
A GARAGE IS LIKE A BIG WALK-IN CLOSET.
SOME HUMANS EVEN PARK CARS IN THEM.
HEY! A SQUEAKER BALL.

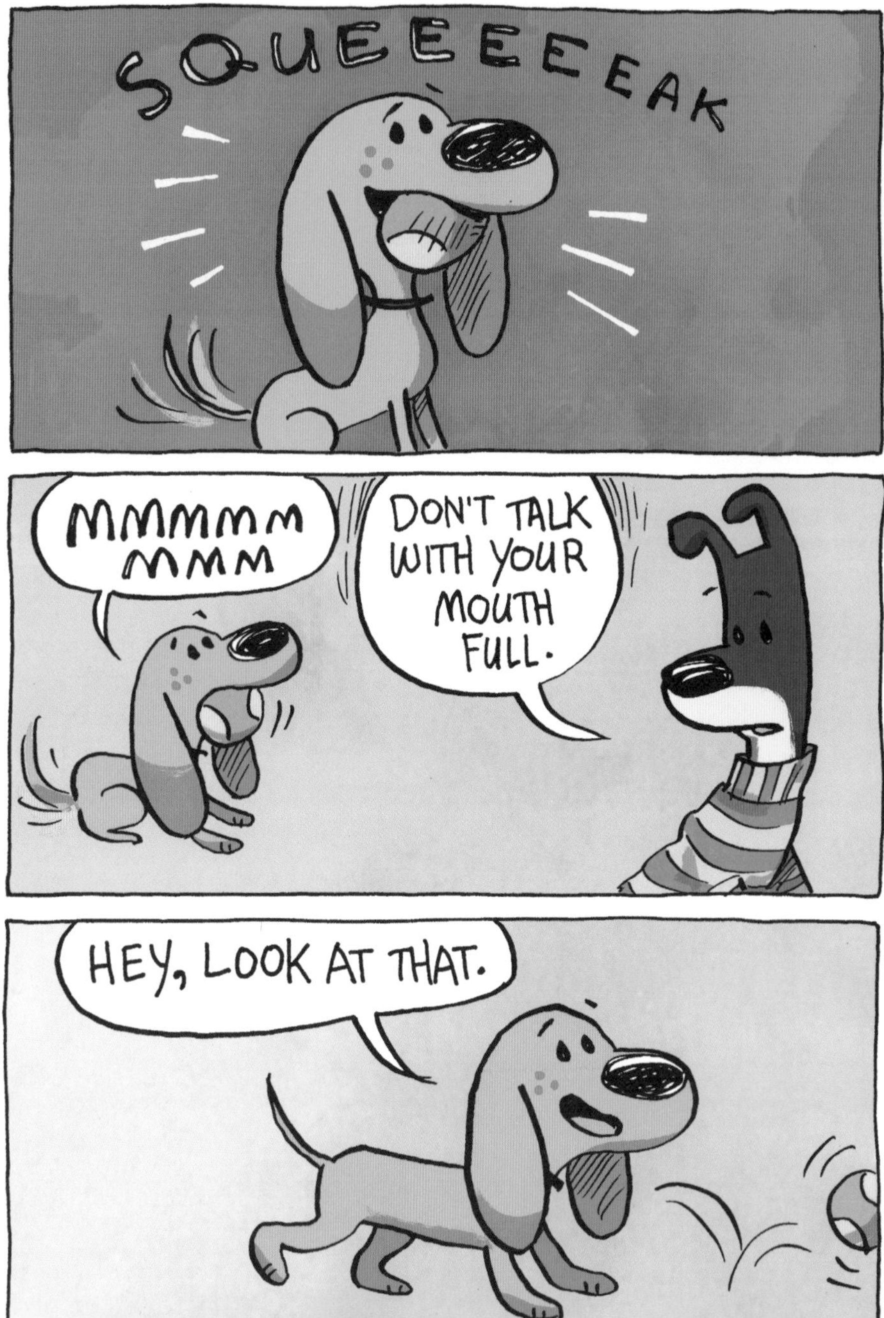
SQUEEEEEEAK
MMMMMM MMM
DON'T TALK WITH YOUR MOUTH FULL.
HEY, LOOK AT THAT.

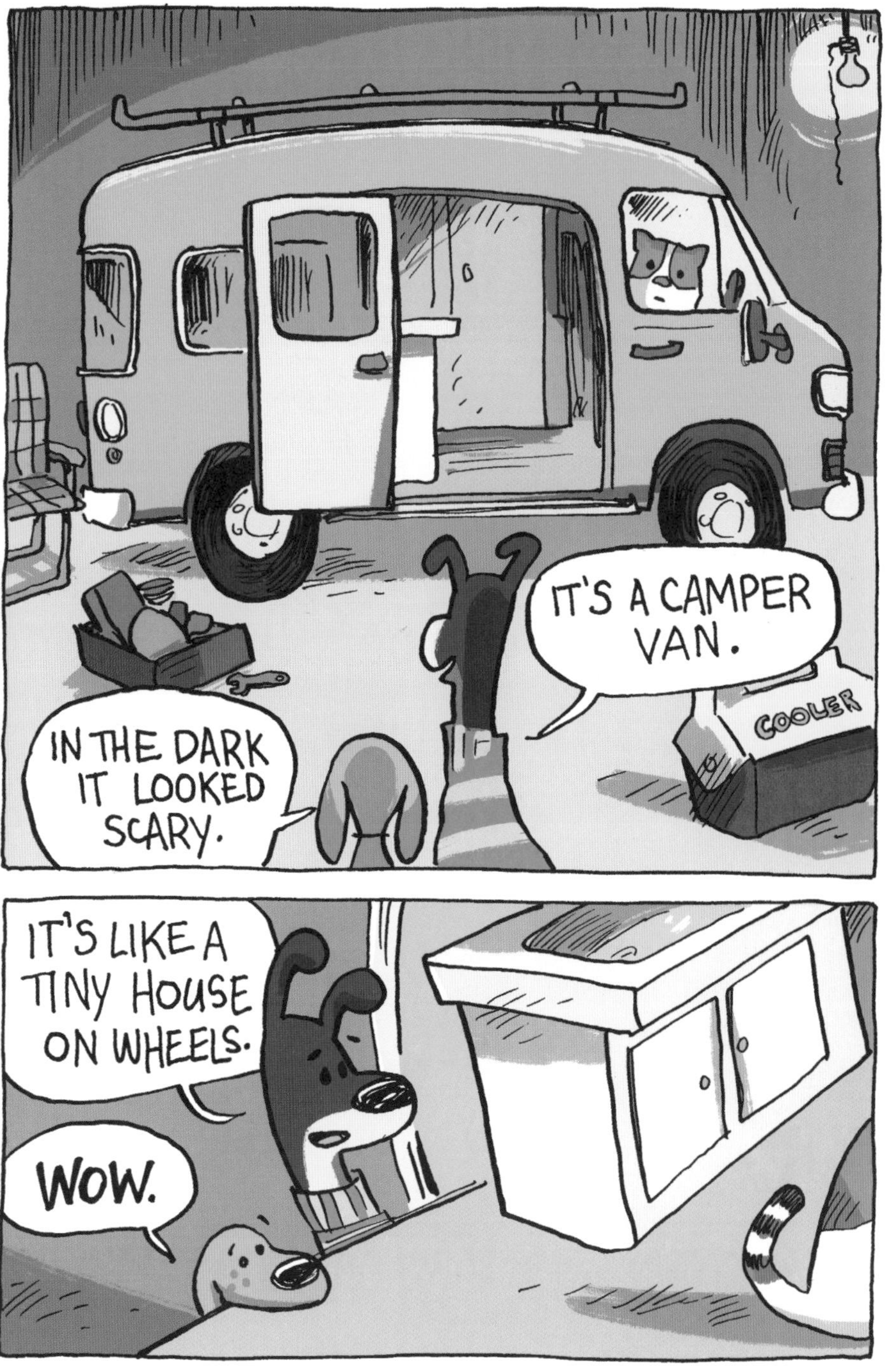

IT'S A CAMPER VAN.
IN THE DARK IT LOOKED SCARY.
COOLER
IT'S LIKE A TINY HOUSE ON WHEELS.
WOW.

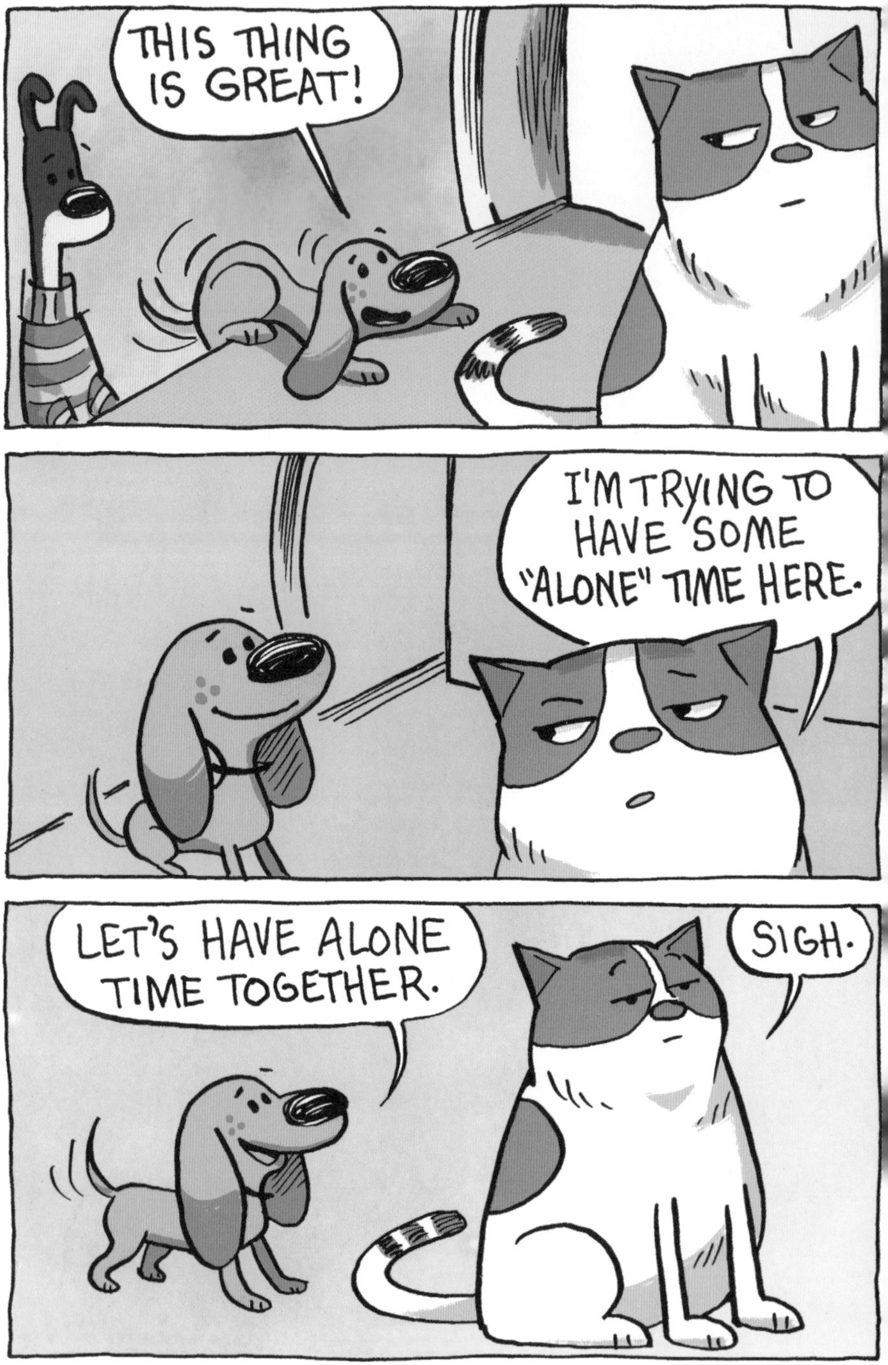
THIS THING IS GREAT!
I'M TRYING TO HAVE SOME "ALONE" TIME HERE.
LET'S HAVE ALONE TIME TOGETHER.
SIGH.

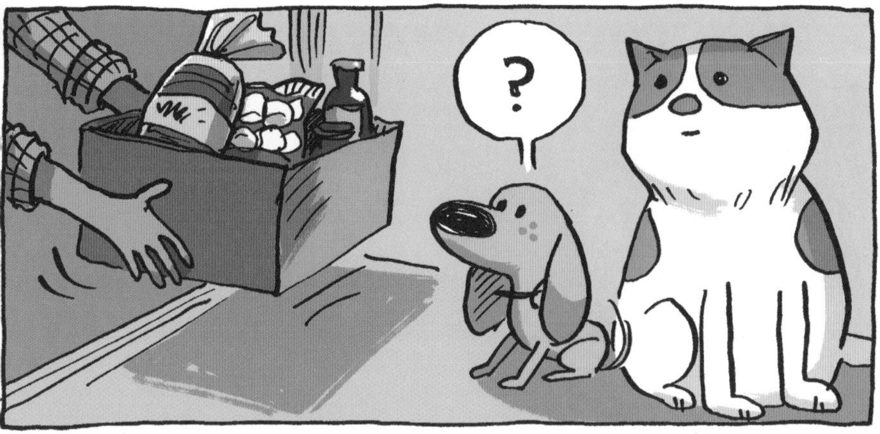
?

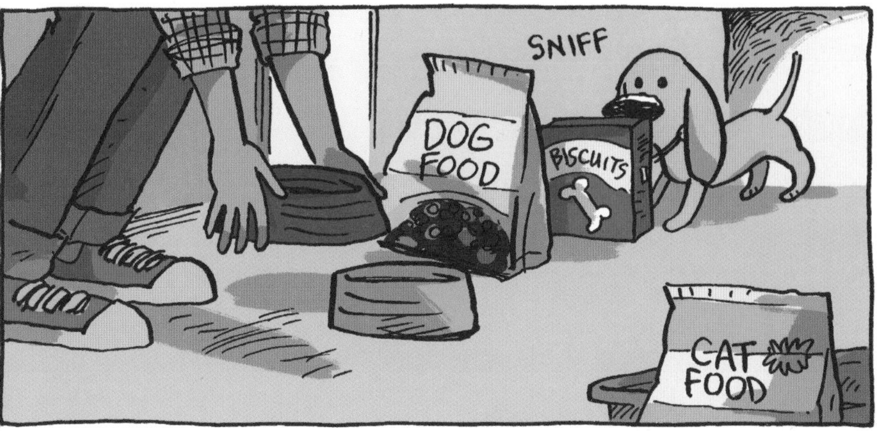
SNIFF
DOG FOOD
BISCUITS
CAT FOOD

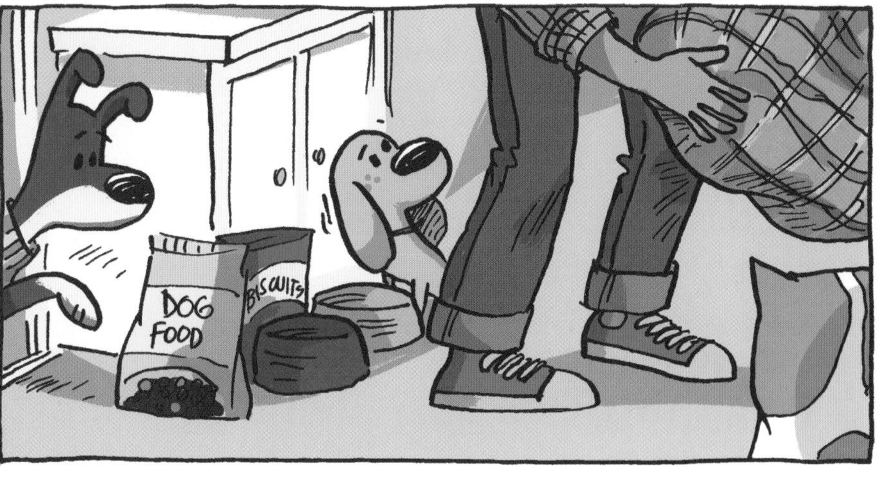
DOG FOOD
BISCUITS

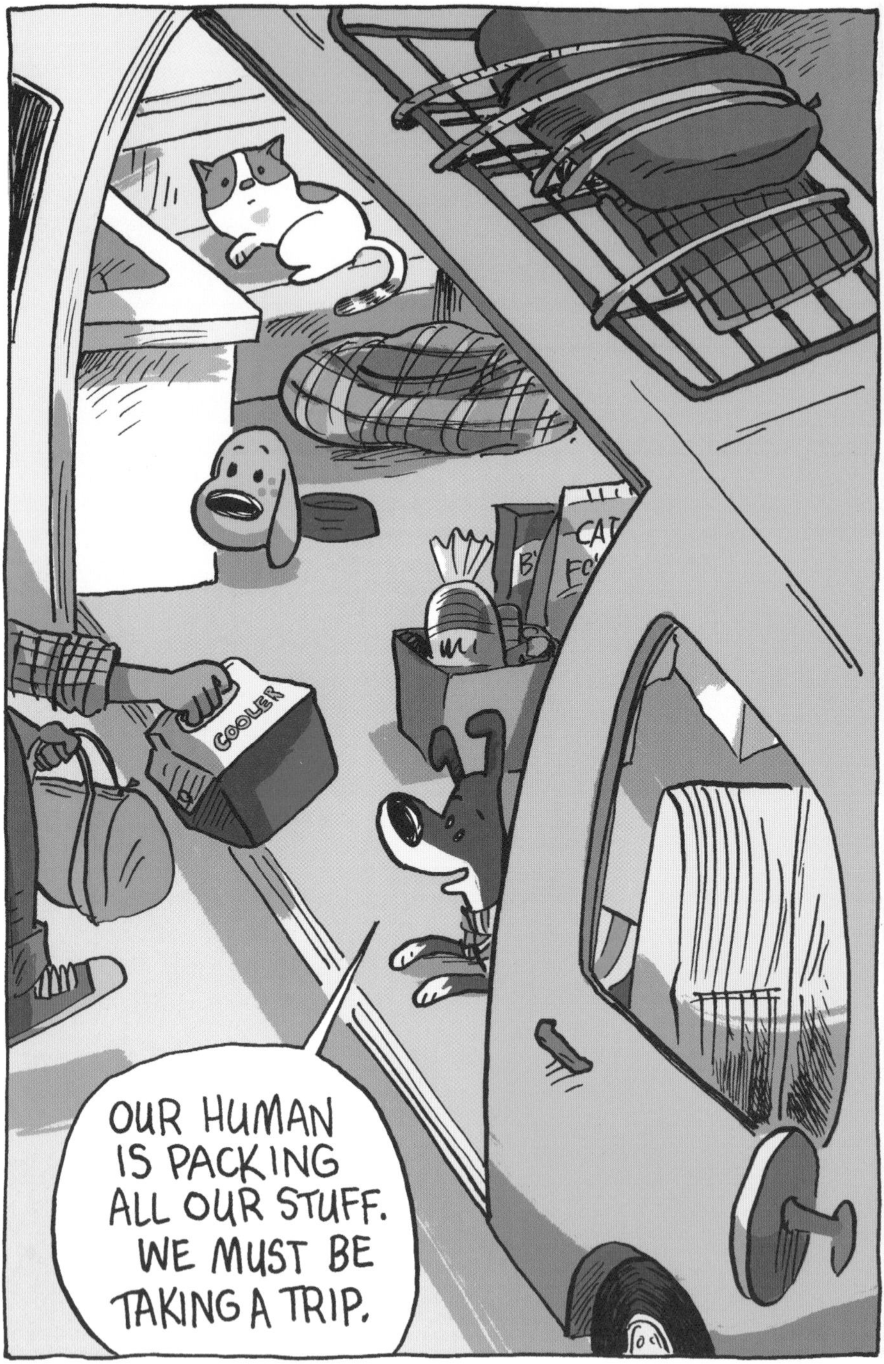
COOLER
OUR HUMAN IS PACKING ALL OUR STUFF. WE MUST BE TAKING A TRIP.

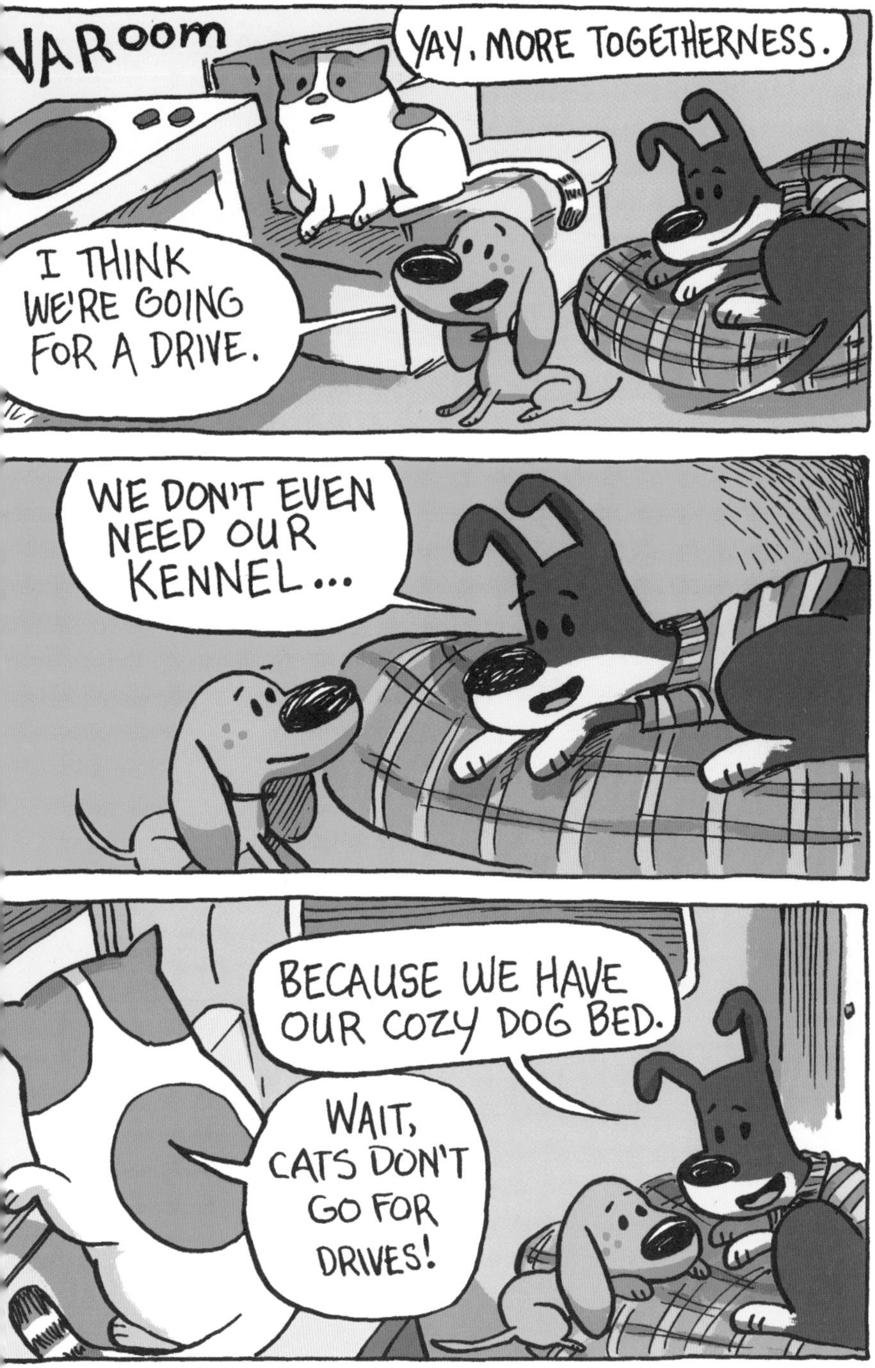
VARoom
YAY. MORE TOGETHERNESS.
I THINK WE'RE GOING FOR A DRIVE.
WE DON'T EVEN NEED OUR KENNEL...
BECAUSE WE HAVE OUR COZY DOG BED.
WAIT, CATS DON'T GO FOR DRIVES!

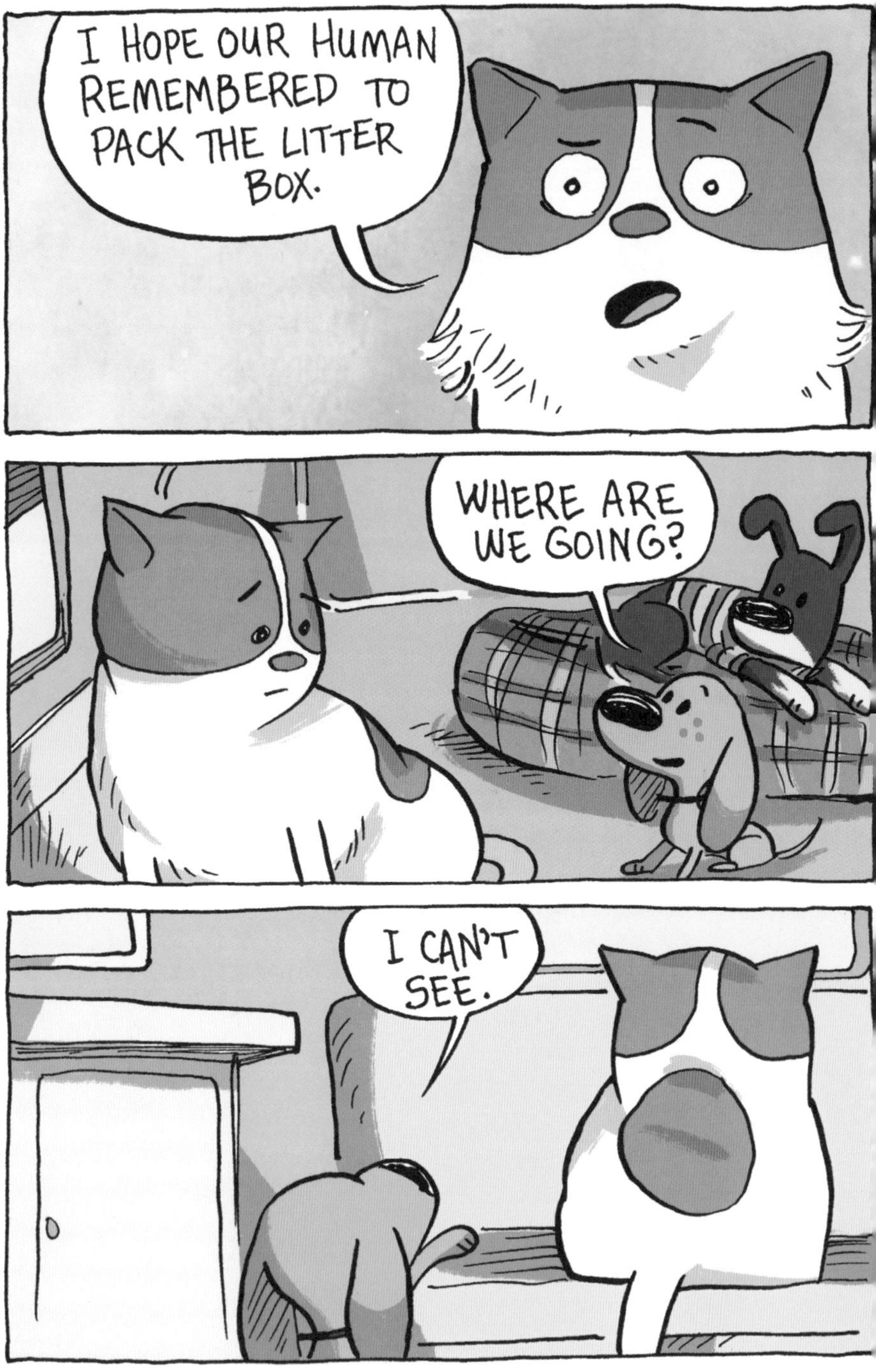
I HOPE OUR HUMAN REMEMBERED TO PACK THE LITTER BOX.
WHERE ARE WE GOING?
I CAN'T SEE.

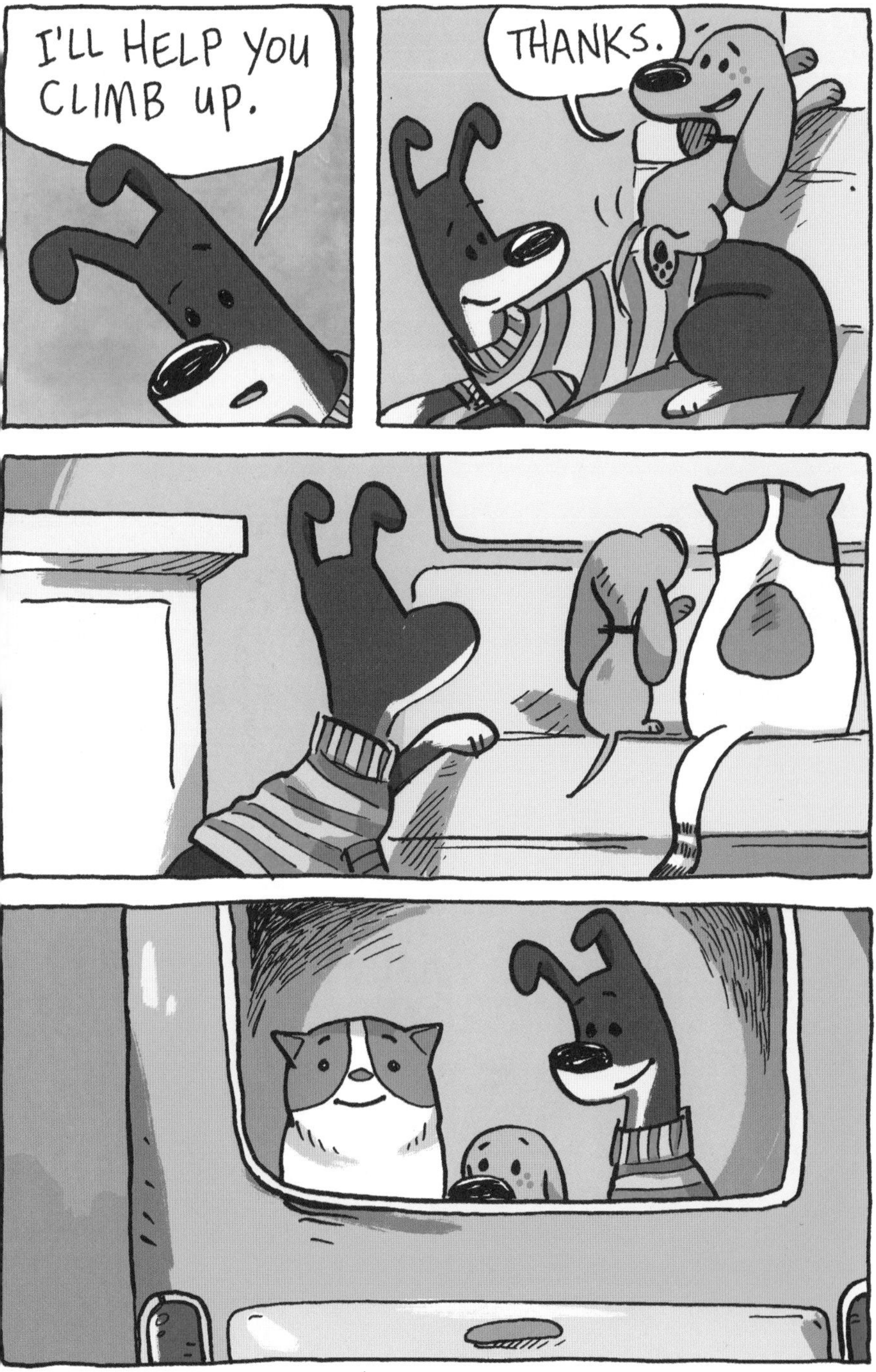
I'LL HELP YOU CLIMB UP.
THANKS.

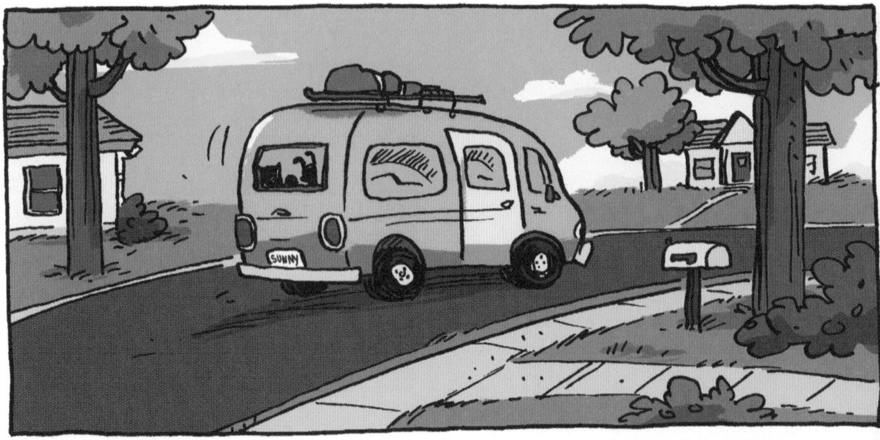
SUNNY

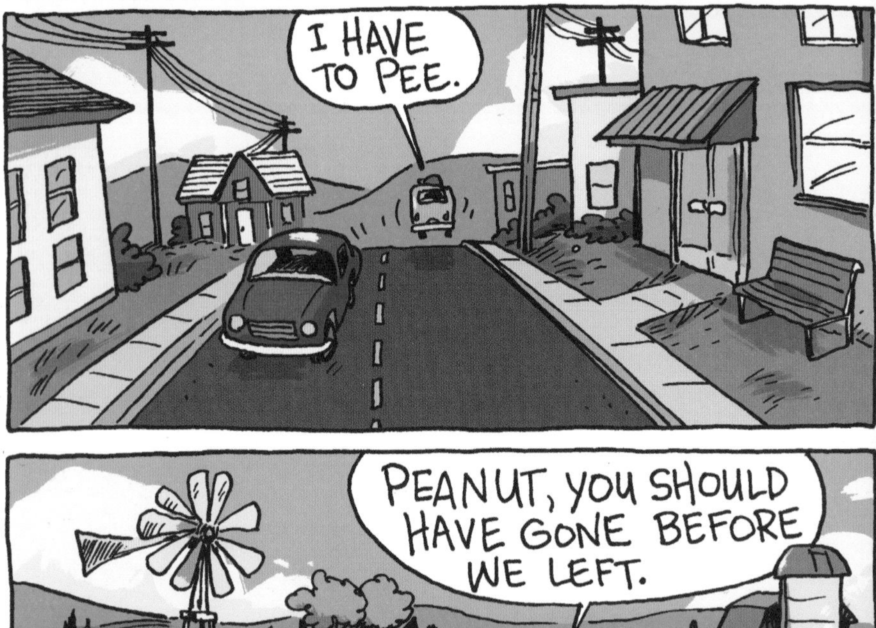
I HAVE TO PEE.

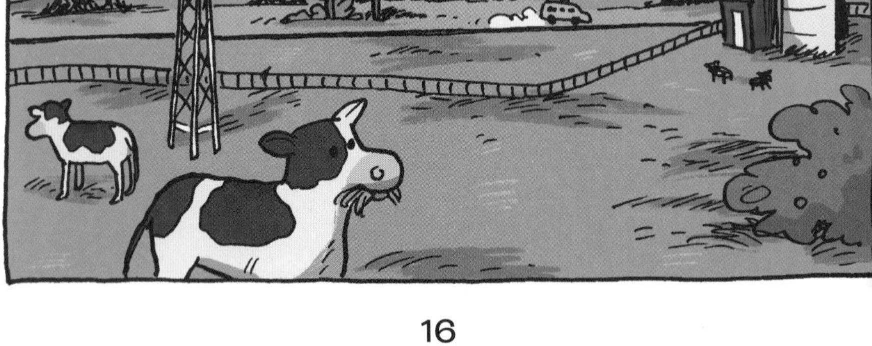
PEANUT, YOU SHOULD HAVE GONE BEFORE WE LEFT.

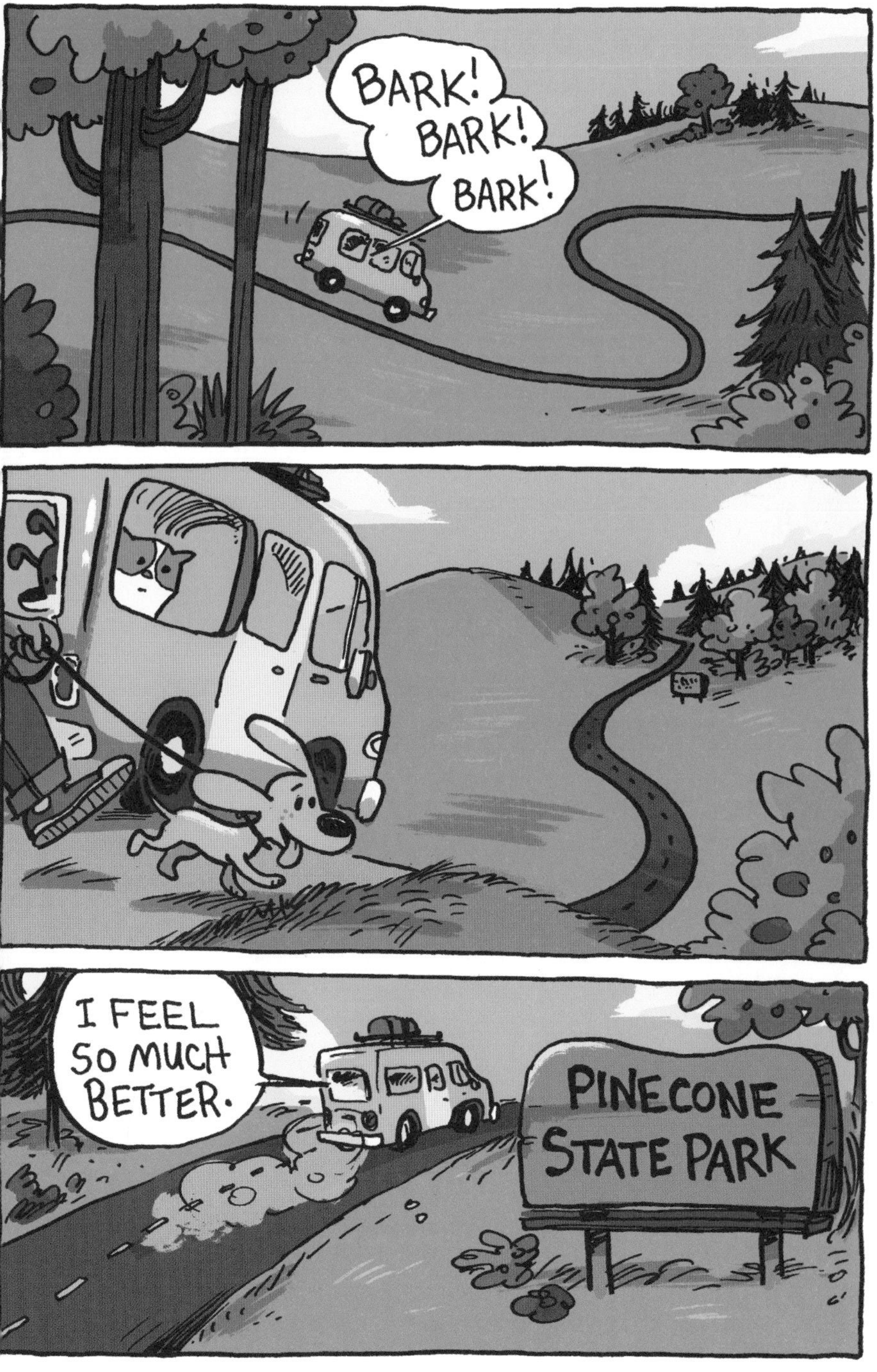
BARK!
BARK!
BARK!
I FEEL SO MUCH BETTER.
PINECONE STATE PARK

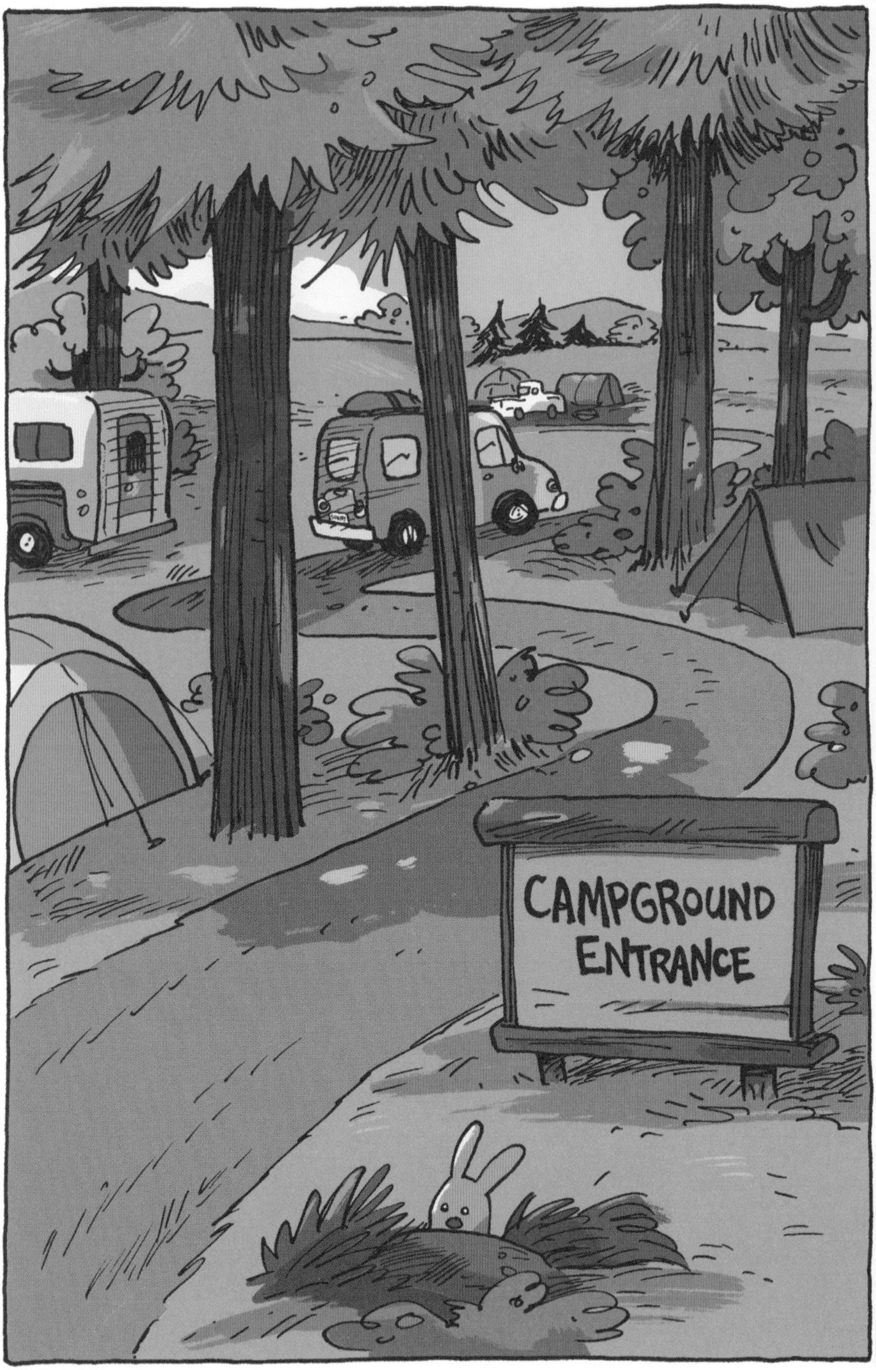
CAMPGROUND
ENTRANCE

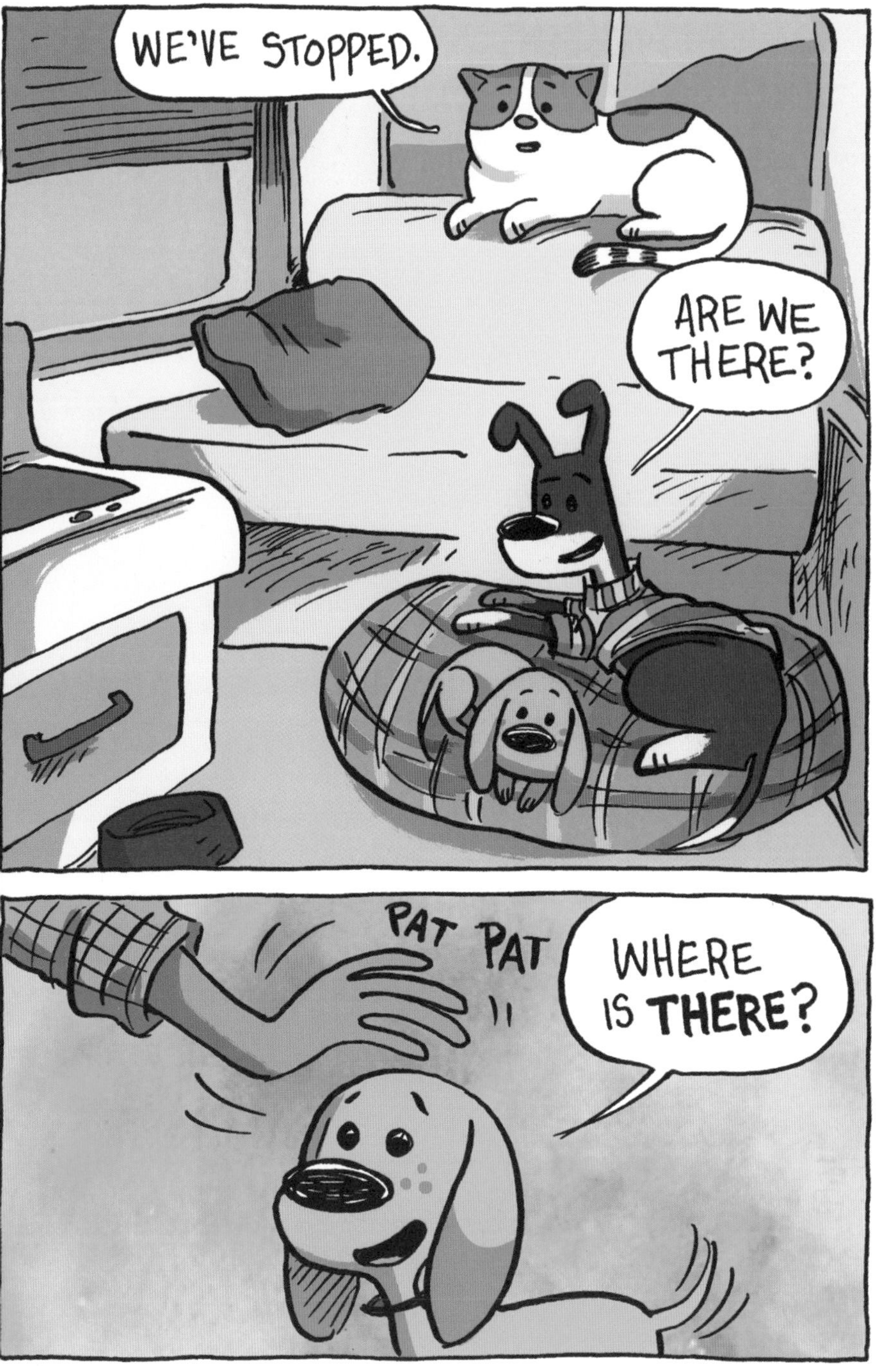
WE'VE STOPPED.
ARE WE THERE?
PAT PAT
WHERE IS THERE?

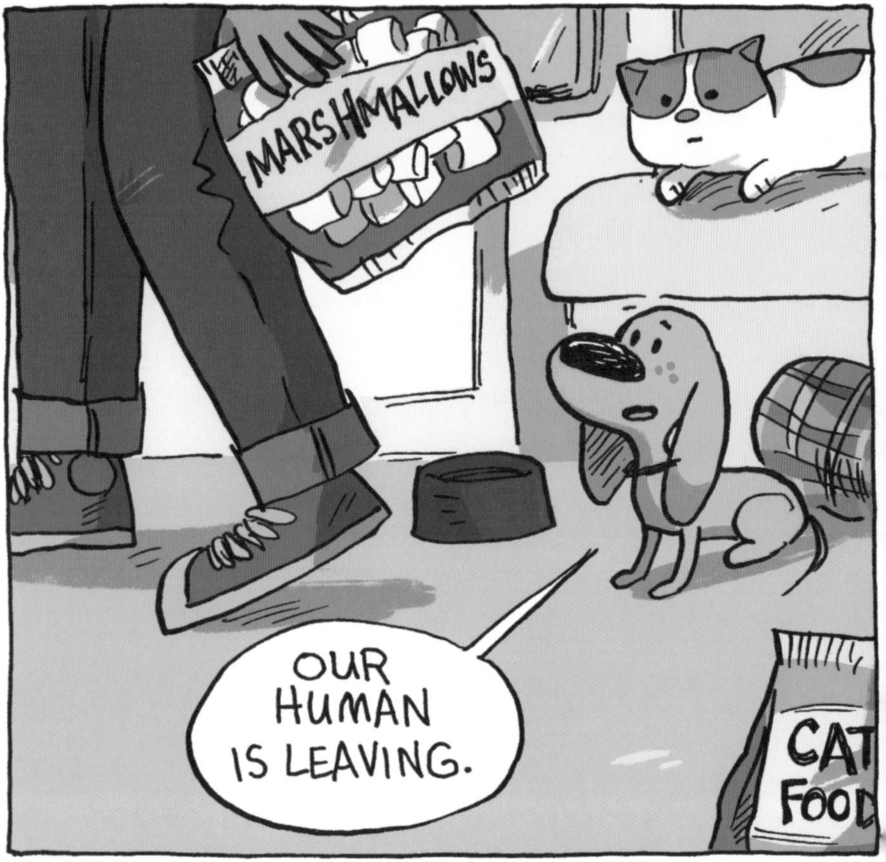
MARSHMALLOWS
OUR HUMAN IS LEAVING.
CAT FOOD

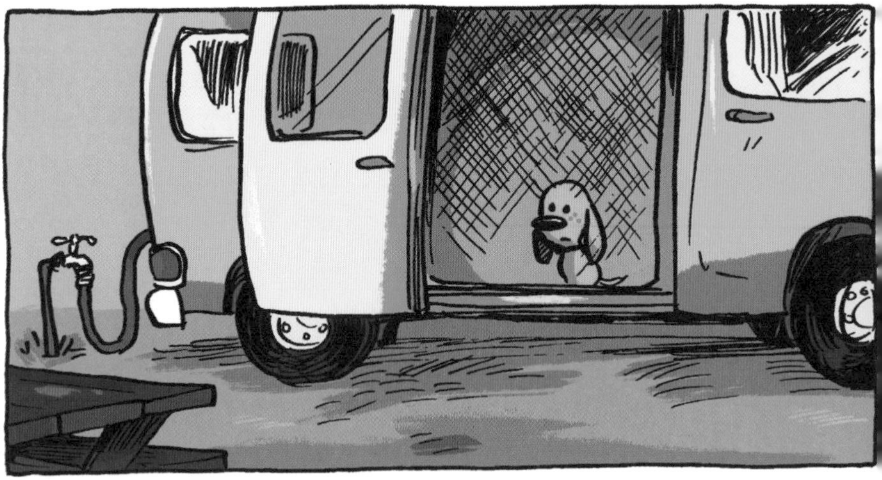

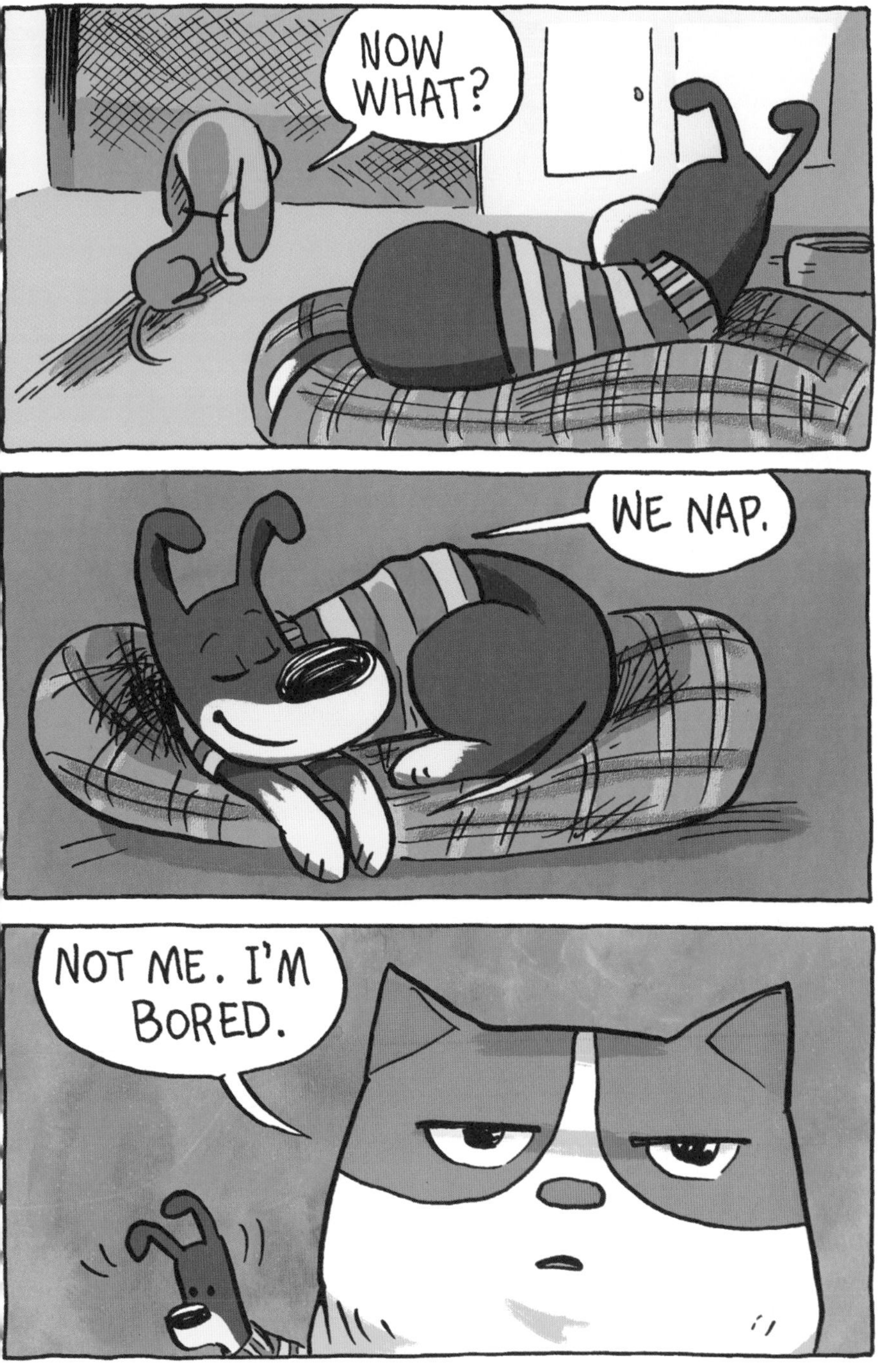
NOW WHAT?
WE NAP.
NOT ME. I'M BORED.

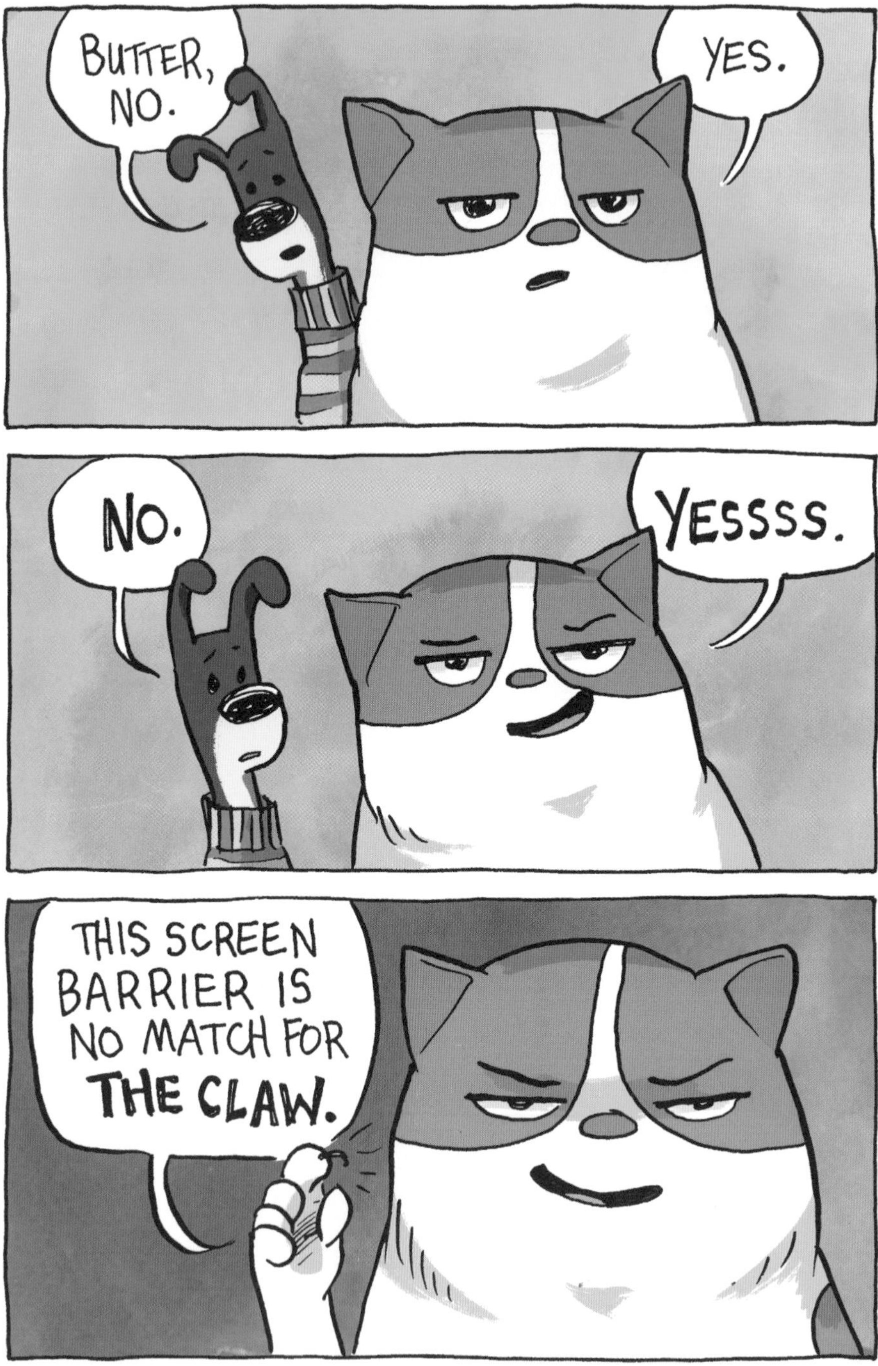
BUTTER, NO.
YES.
NO.
YESSSS.
THIS SCREEN BARRIER IS NO MATCH FOR **THE CLAW.**

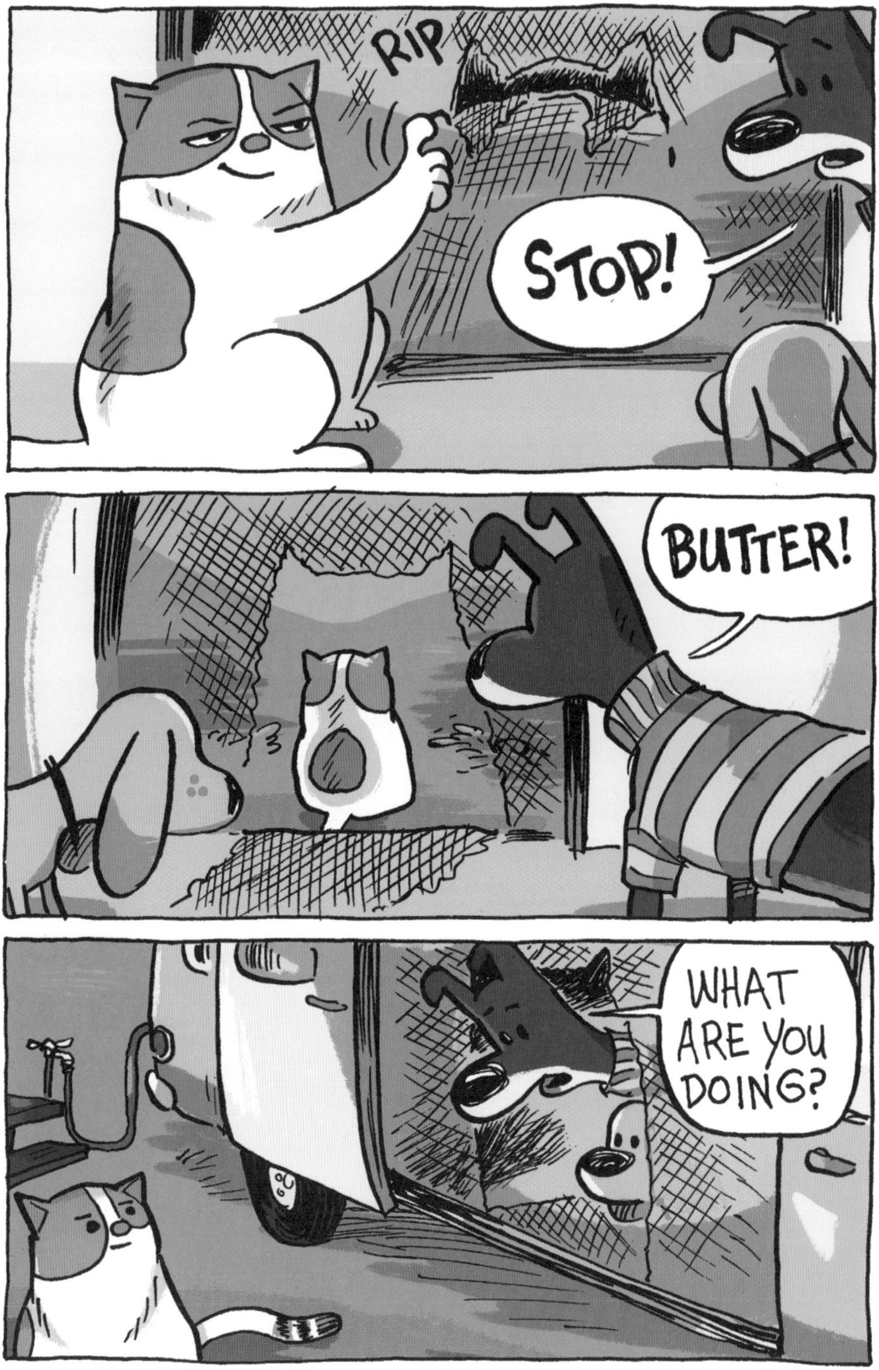
RIP
STOP!
BUTTER!
WHAT ARE YOU DOING?

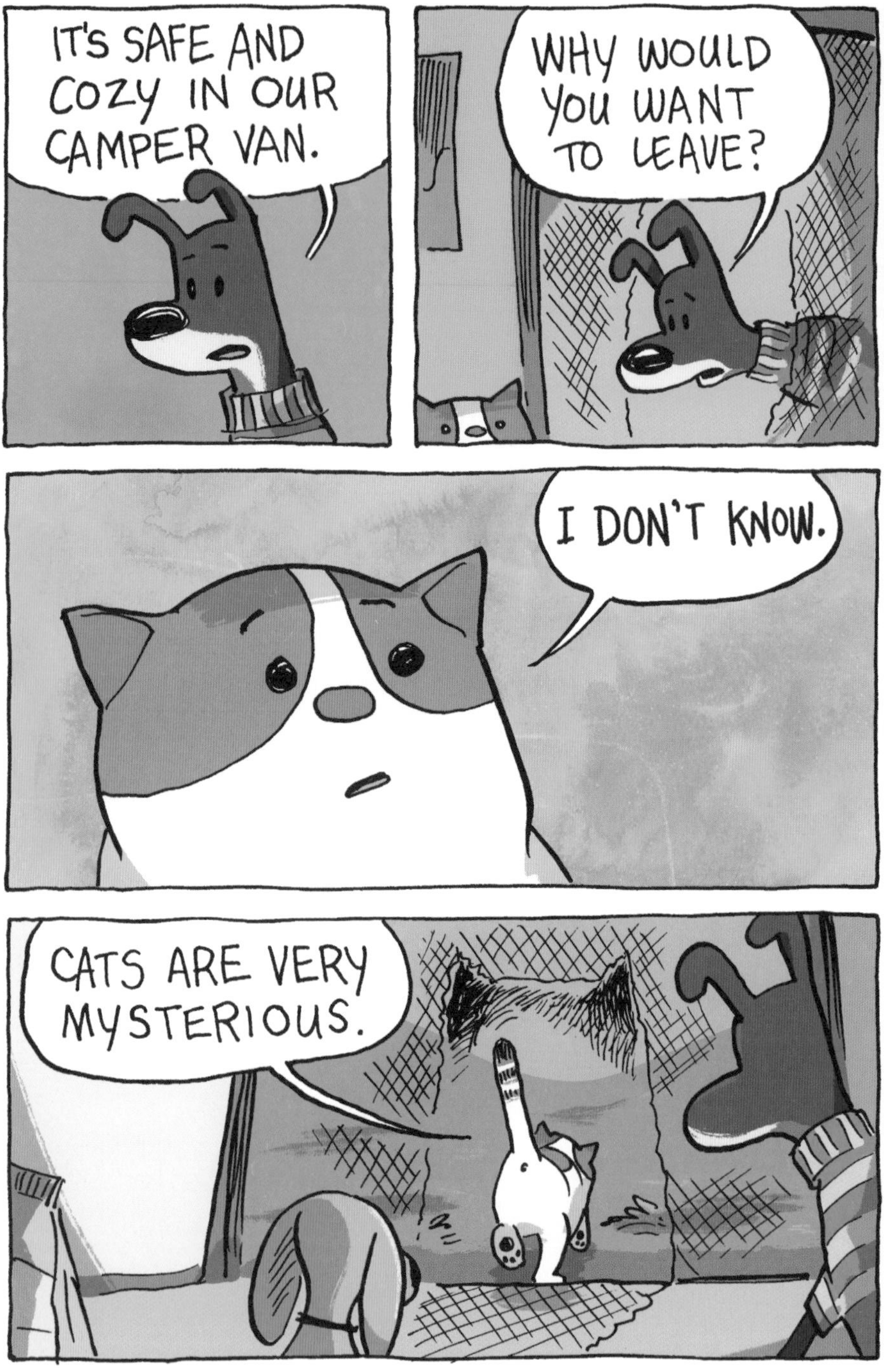
IT'S SAFE AND COZY IN OUR CAMPER VAN.
WHY WOULD YOU WANT TO LEAVE?
I DON'T KNOW.
CATS ARE VERY MYSTERIOUS.

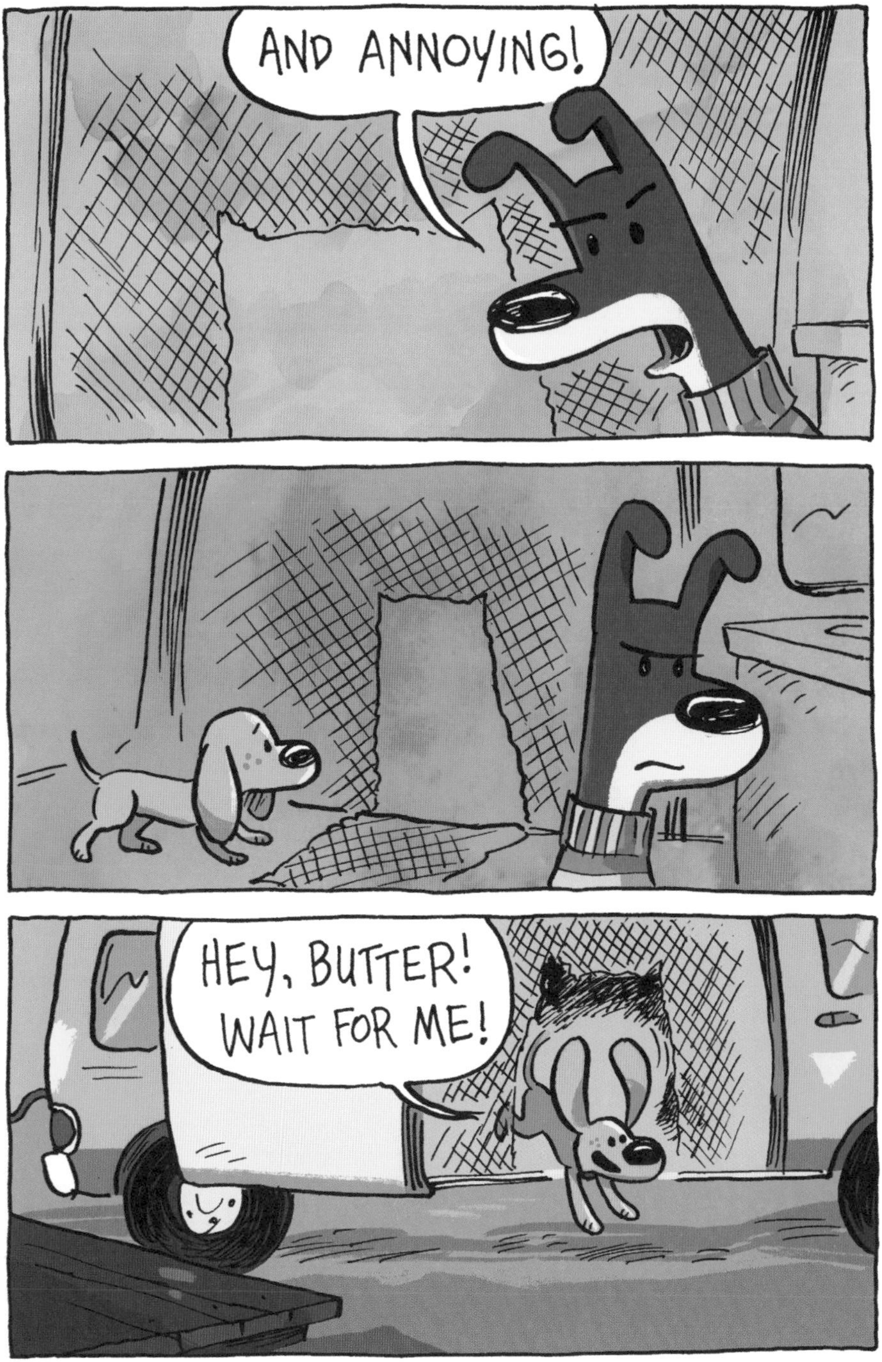
AND ANNOYING!
HEY, BUTTER! WAIT FOR ME!

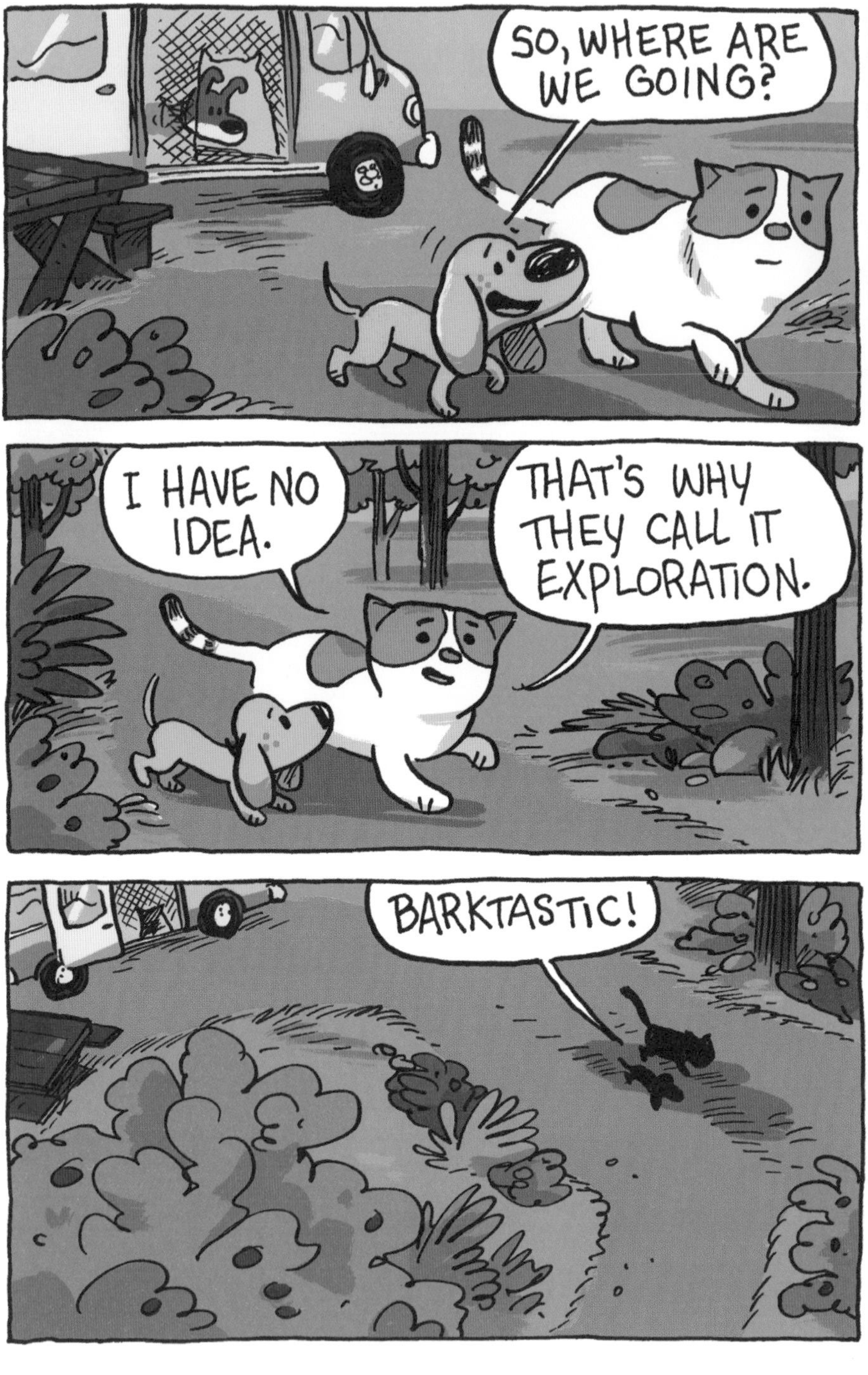
SO, WHERE ARE WE GOING?
I HAVE NO IDEA.
THAT'S WHY THEY CALL IT EXPLORATION.
BARKTASTIC!

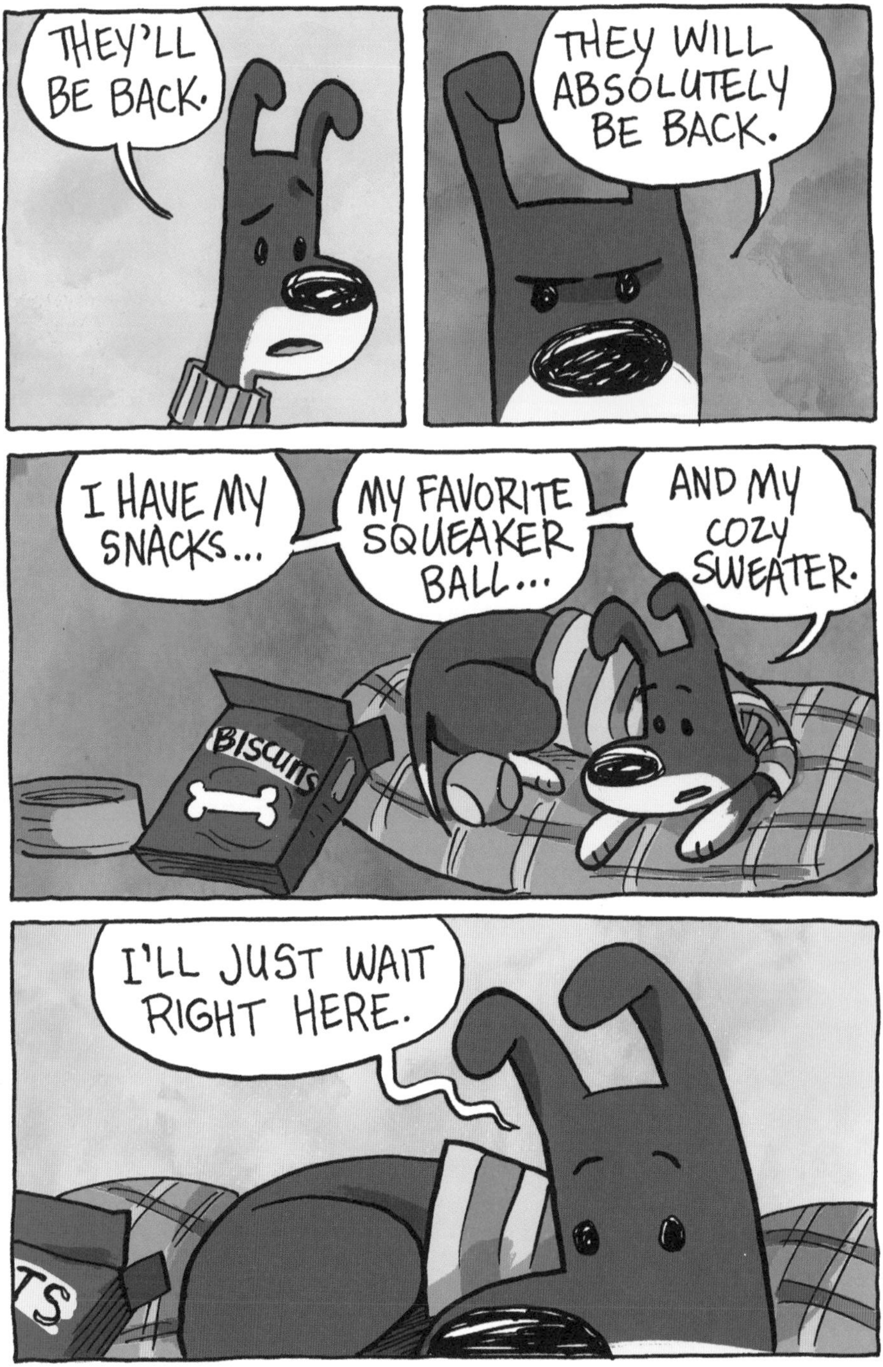
THEY'LL BE BACK.
THEY WILL ABSOLUTELY BE BACK.
I HAVE MY SNACKS...
MY FAVORITE SQUEAKER BALL...
AND MY COZY SWEATER.
BISCUITS
I'LL JUST WAIT RIGHT HERE.
TS

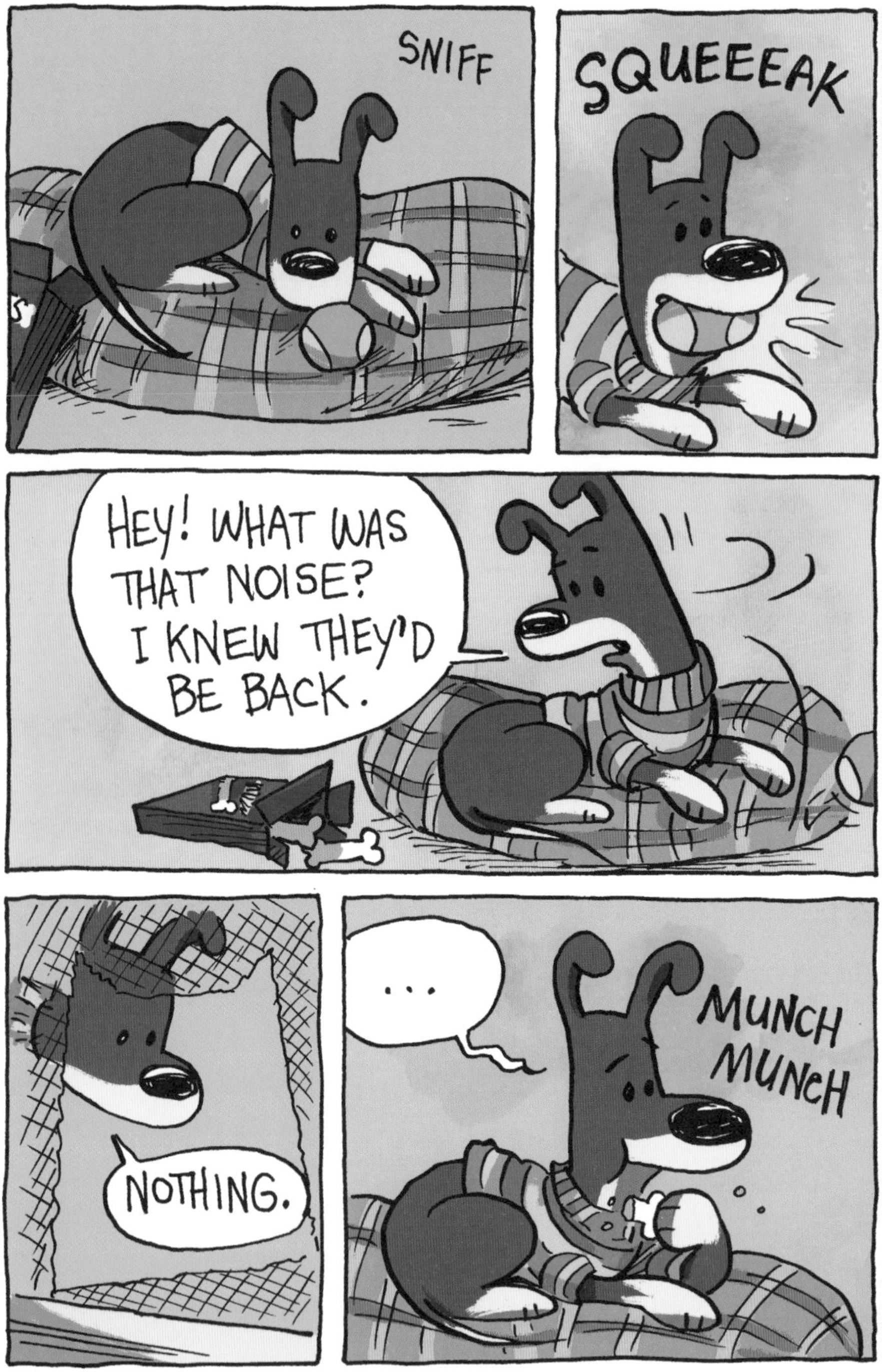
SNIFF
SQUEEEEAK
HEY! WHAT WAS THAT NOISE? I KNEW THEY'D BE BACK.
NOTHING.
. . .
MUNCH MUNCH

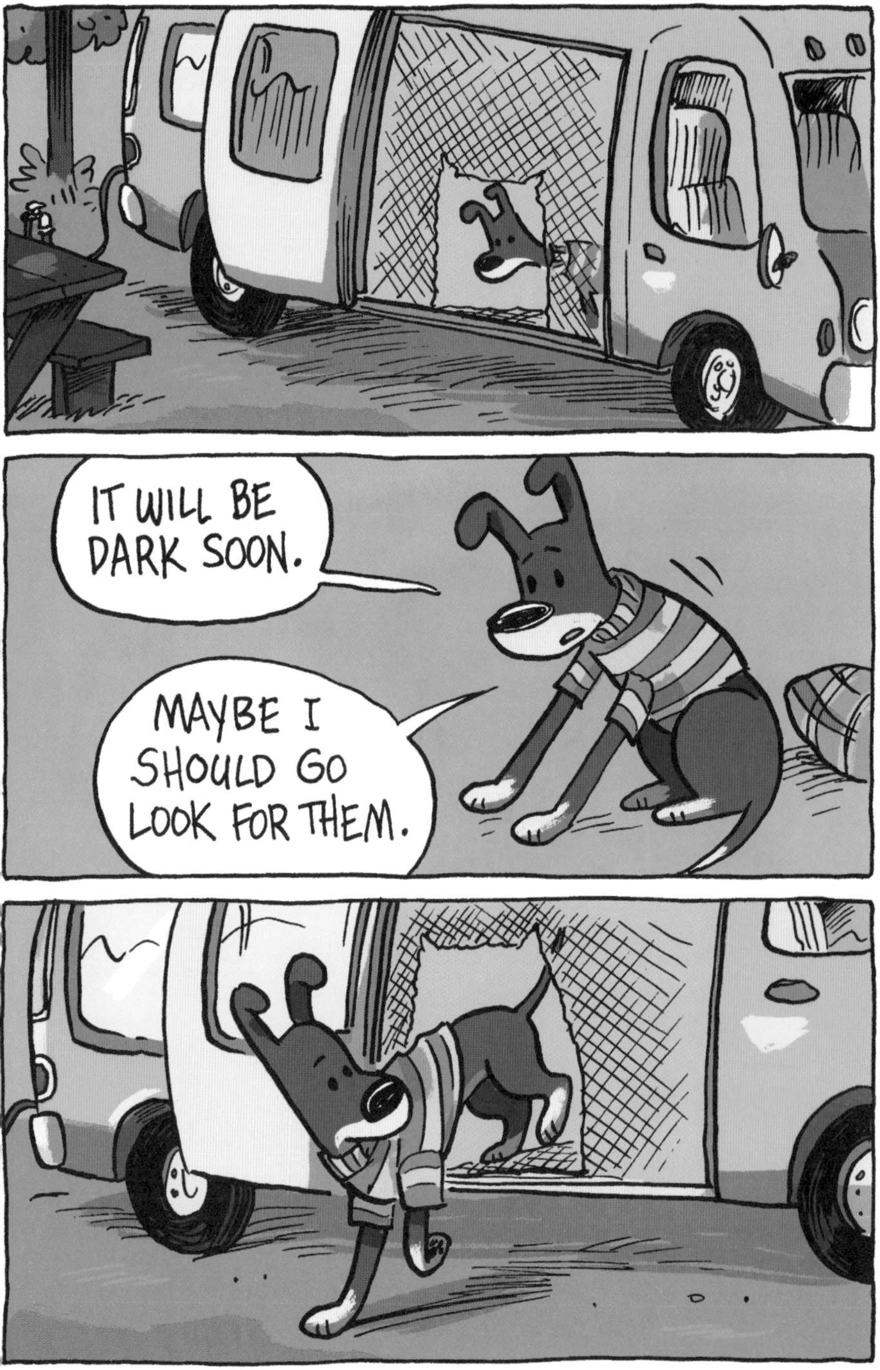

IT WILL BE DARK SOON.
MAYBE I SHOULD GO LOOK FOR THEM.

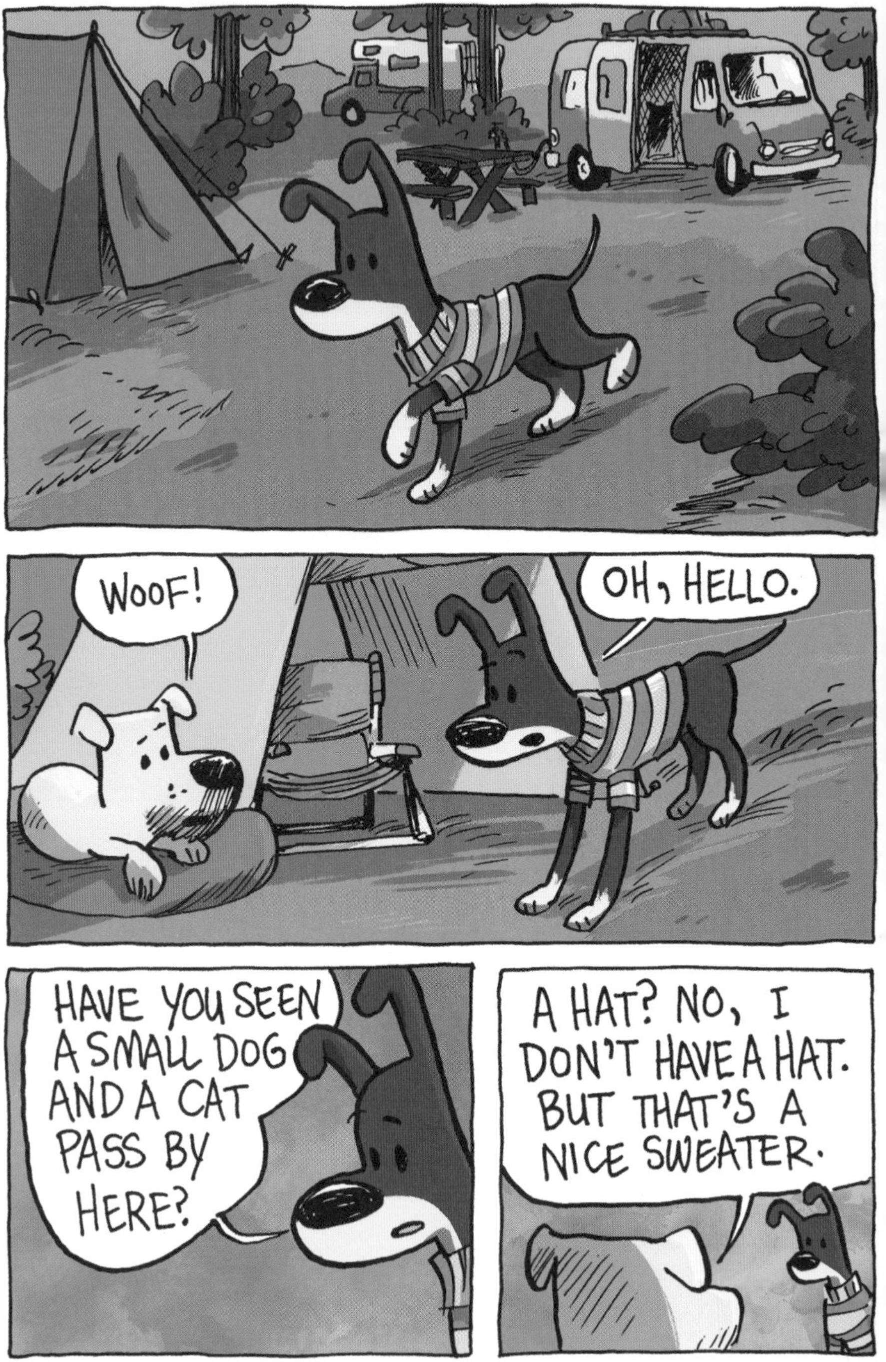
WOOF!
OH, HELLO.
HAVE YOU SEEN A SMALL DOG AND A CAT PASS BY HERE?
A HAT? NO, I DON'T HAVE A HAT. BUT THAT'S A NICE SWEATER.

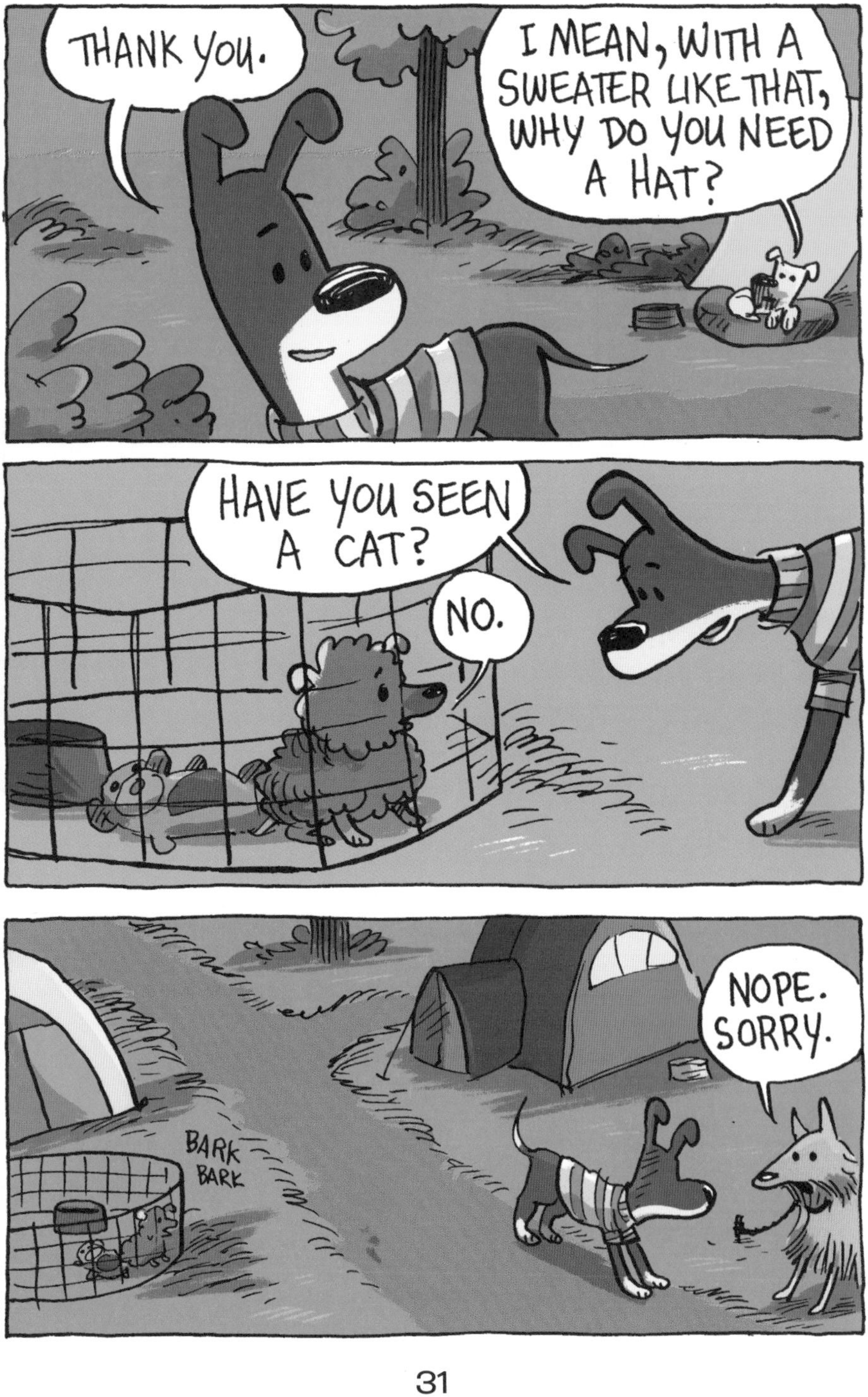
THANK YOU.
I MEAN, WITH A SWEATER LIKE THAT, WHY DO YOU NEED A HAT?
HAVE YOU SEEN A CAT?
NO.
NOPE. SORRY.
BARK BARK

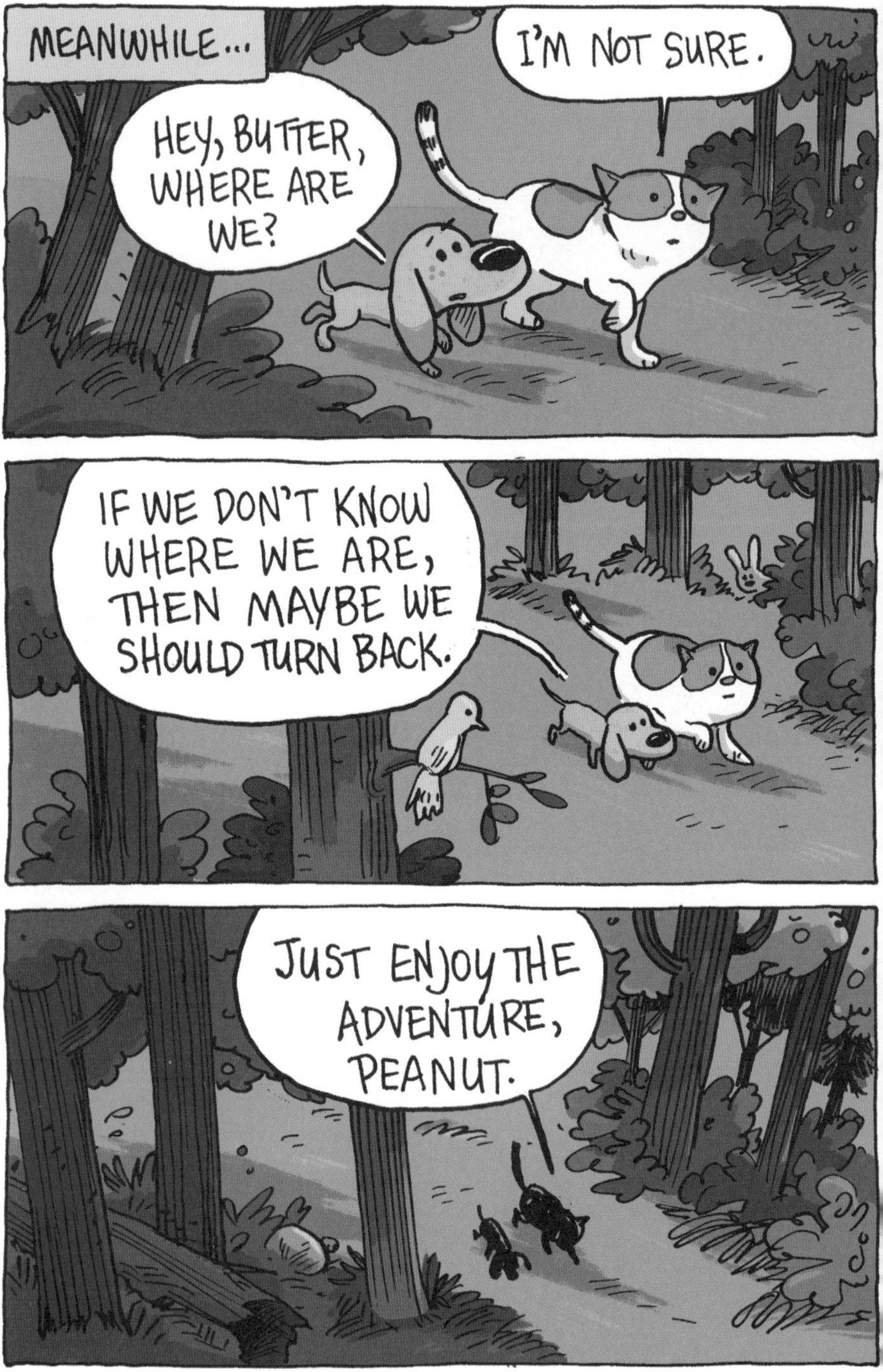
MEANWHILE...
HEY, BUTTER, WHERE ARE WE?
I'M NOT SURE.
IF WE DON'T KNOW WHERE WE ARE, THEN MAYBE WE SHOULD TURN BACK.
JUST ENJOY THE ADVENTURE, PEANUT.

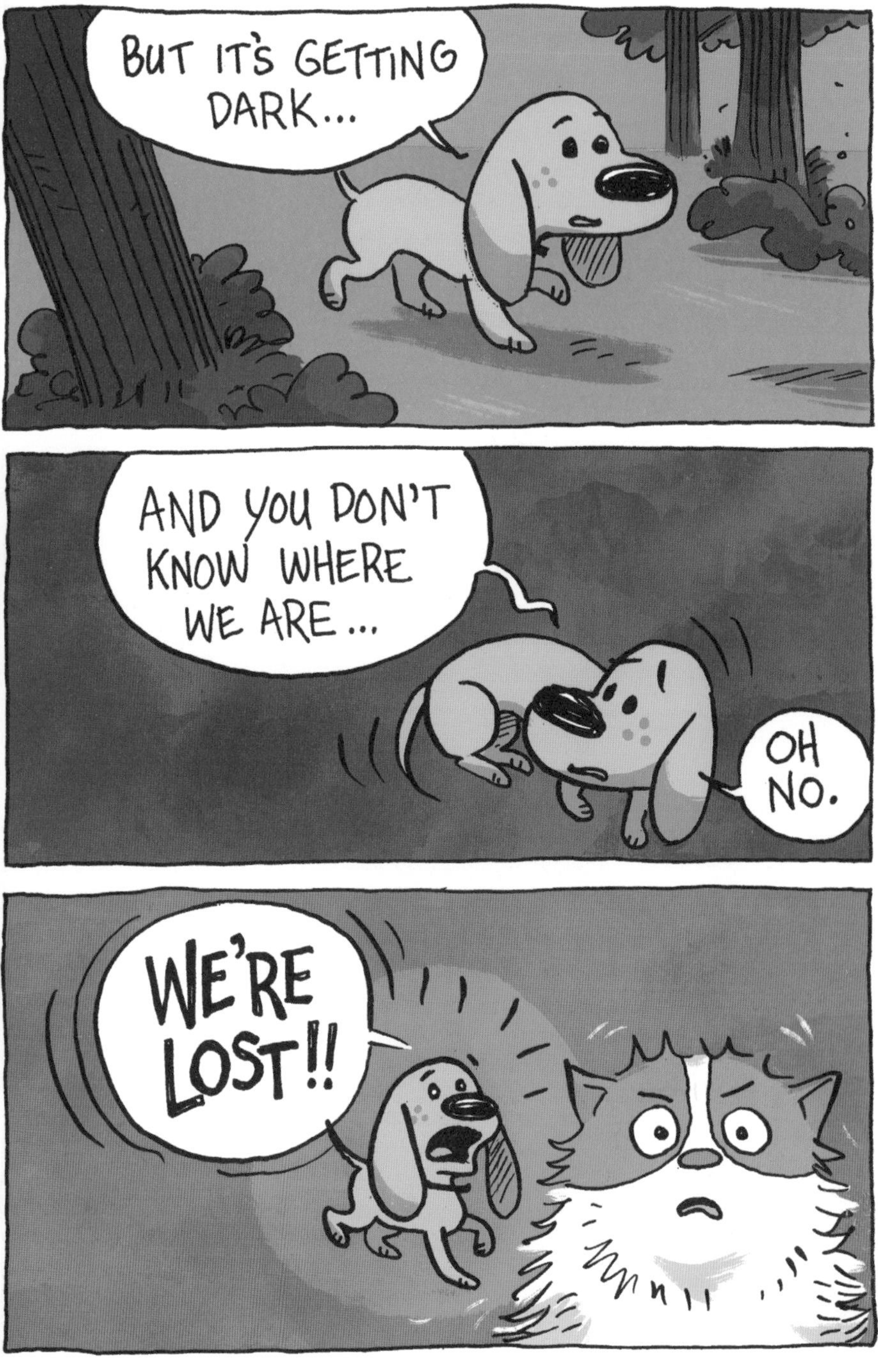
BUT IT'S GETTING DARK...
AND YOU DON'T KNOW WHERE WE ARE...
OH NO.
WE'RE LOST!!

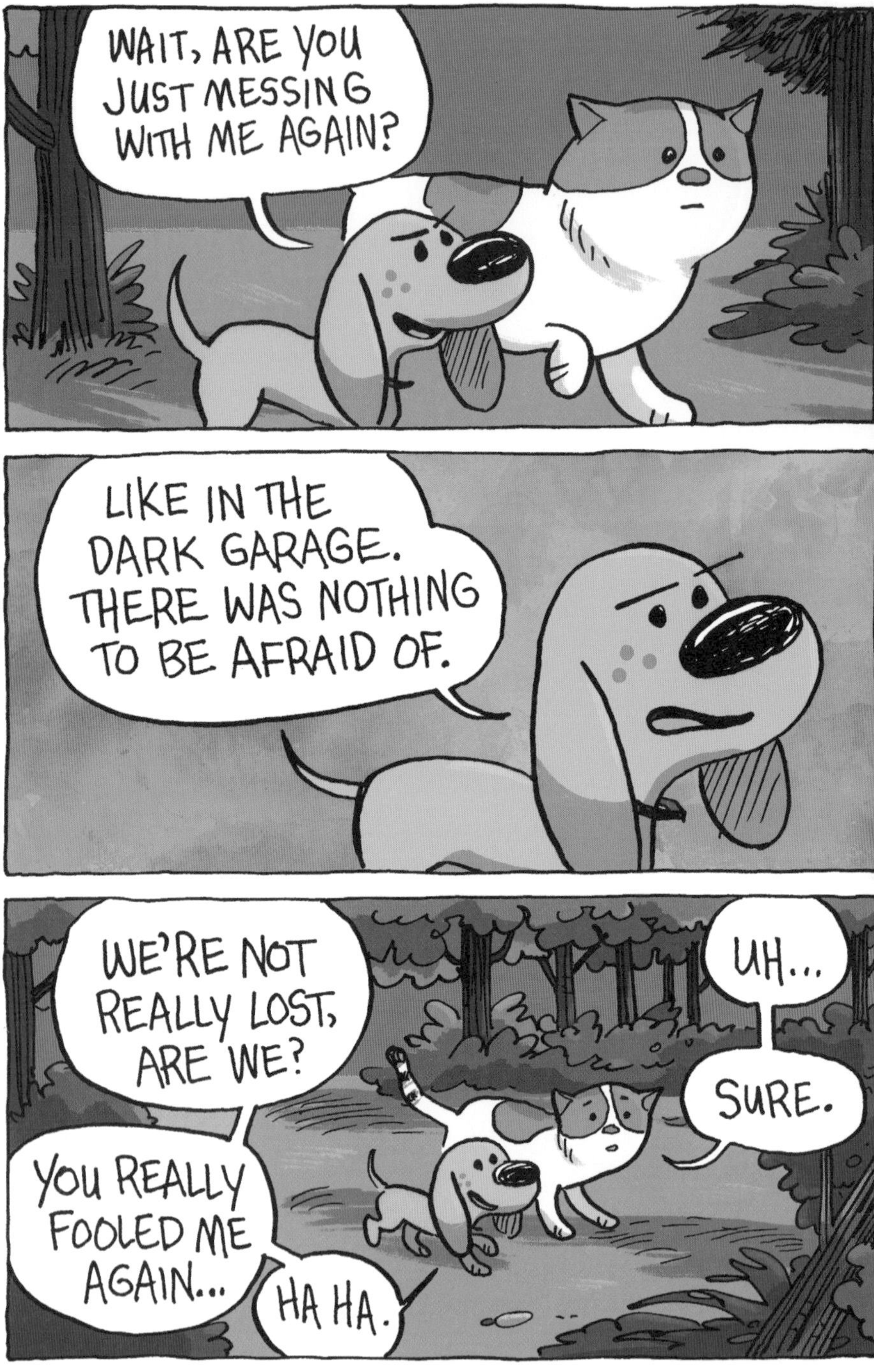
WAIT, ARE YOU JUST MESSING WITH ME AGAIN?
LIKE IN THE DARK GARAGE. THERE WAS NOTHING TO BE AFRAID OF.
WE'RE NOT REALLY LOST, ARE WE?
UH...
SURE.
YOU REALLY FOOLED ME AGAIN...
HA HA.

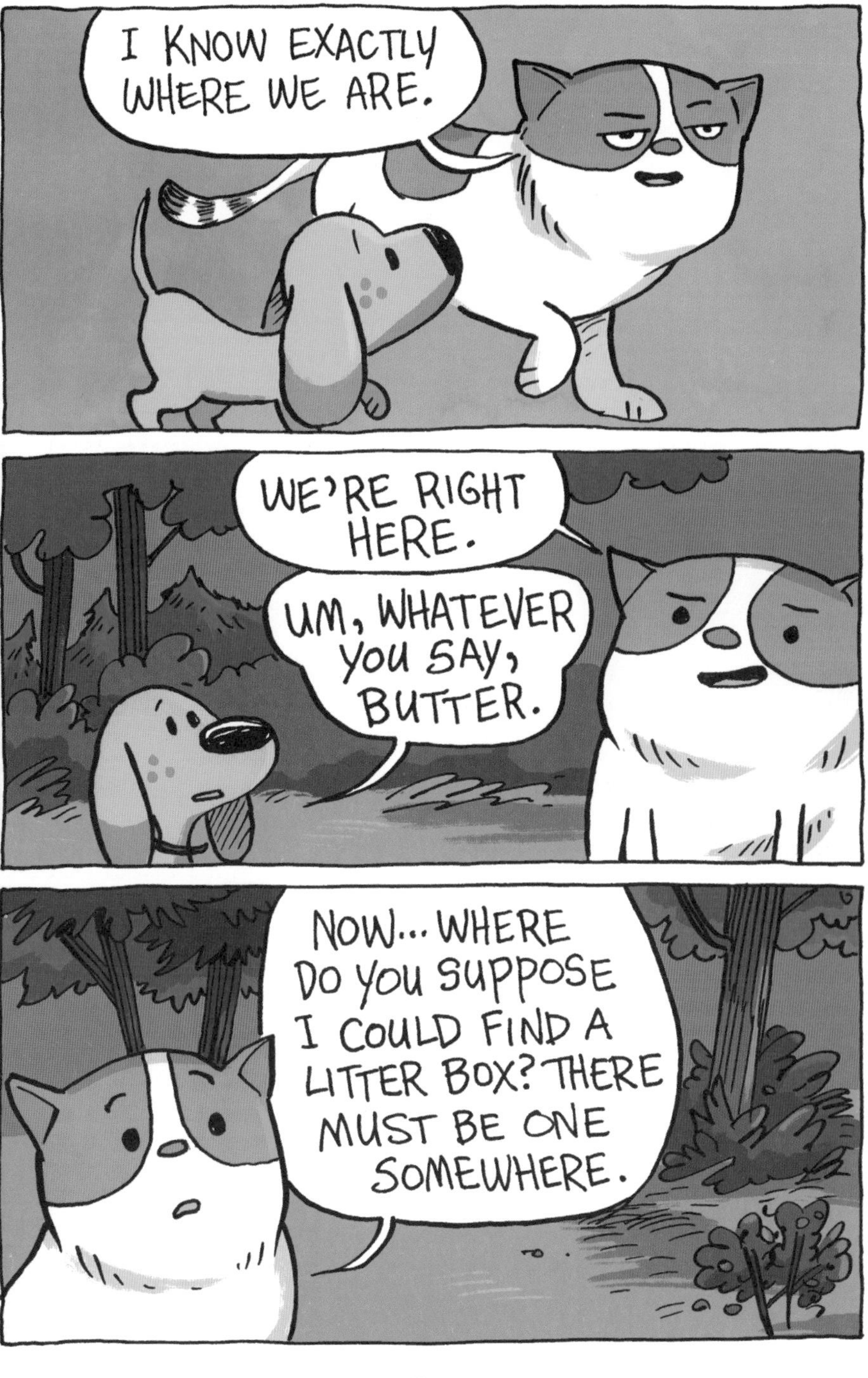
I KNOW EXACTLY WHERE WE ARE.
WE'RE RIGHT HERE.
UM, WHATEVER YOU SAY, BUTTER.
NOW... WHERE DO YOU SUPPOSE I COULD FIND A LITTER BOX? THERE MUST BE ONE SOMEWHERE.

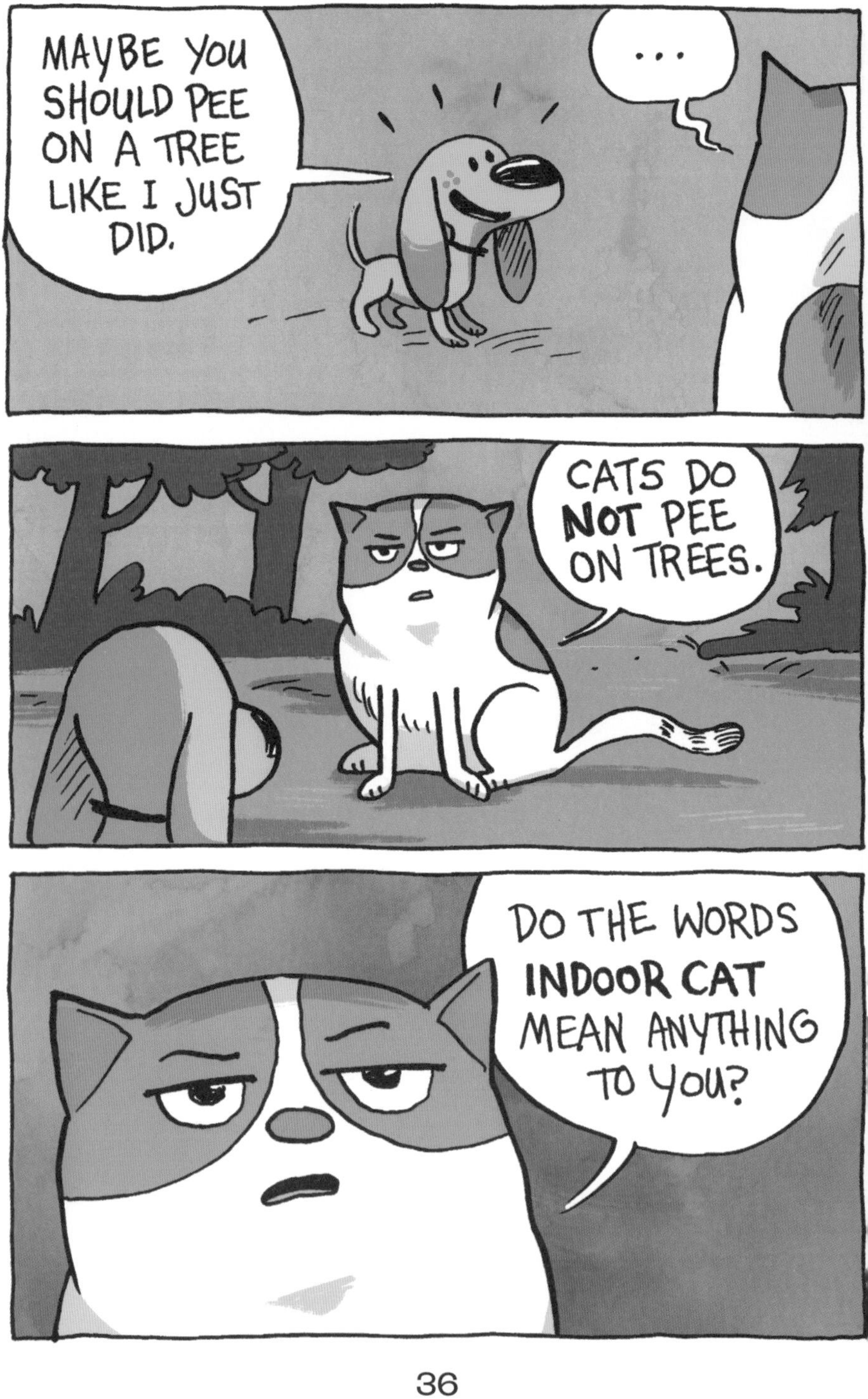
MAYBE YOU SHOULD PEE ON A TREE LIKE I JUST DID.
...
CATS DO **NOT** PEE ON TREES.
DO THE WORDS **INDOOR CAT** MEAN ANYTHING TO YOU?

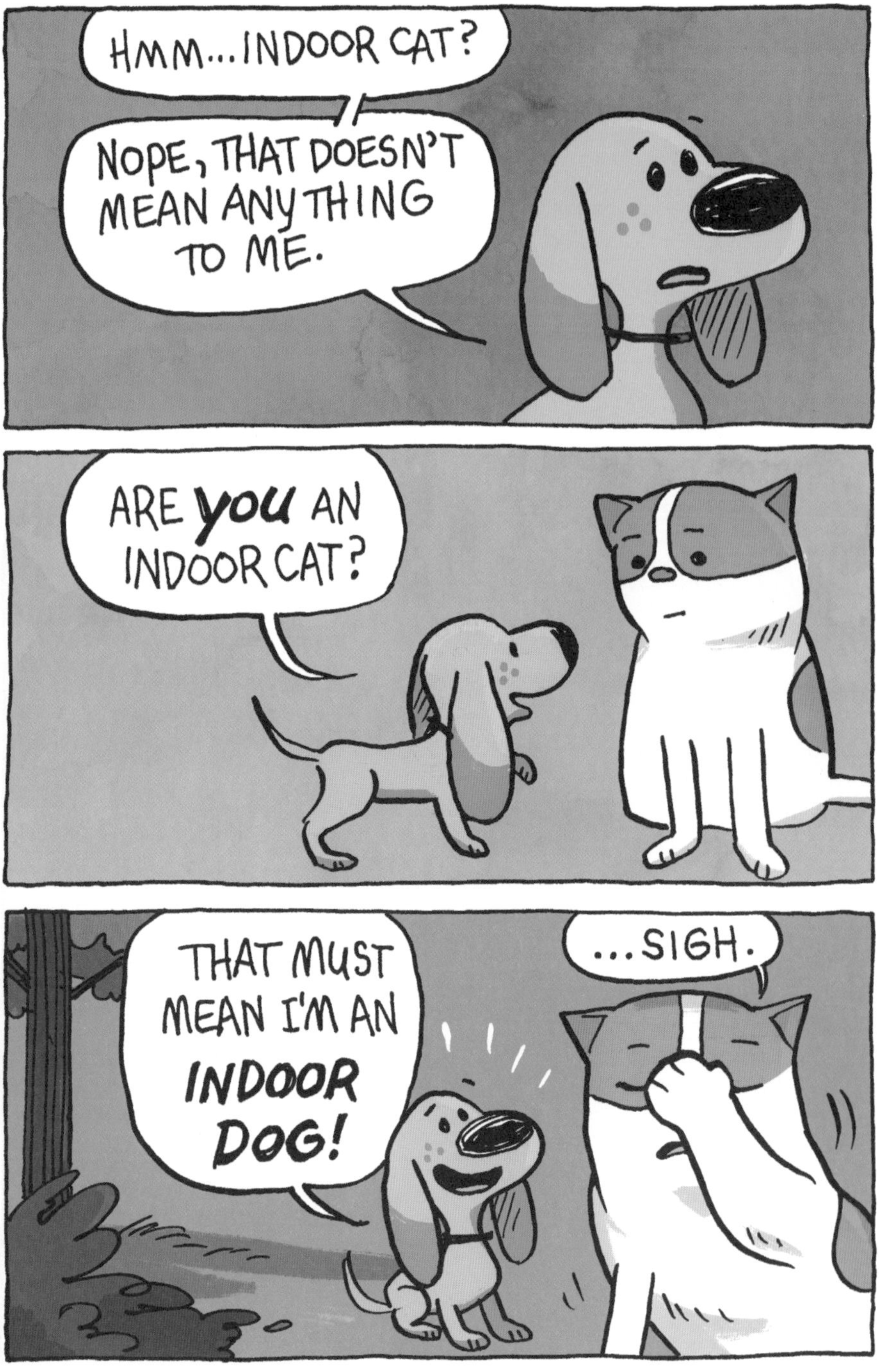
HMM...INDOOR CAT?
NOPE, THAT DOESN'T MEAN ANYTHING TO ME.
ARE **YOU** AN INDOOR CAT?
THAT MUST MEAN I'M AN **INDOOR DOG!**
...SIGH.

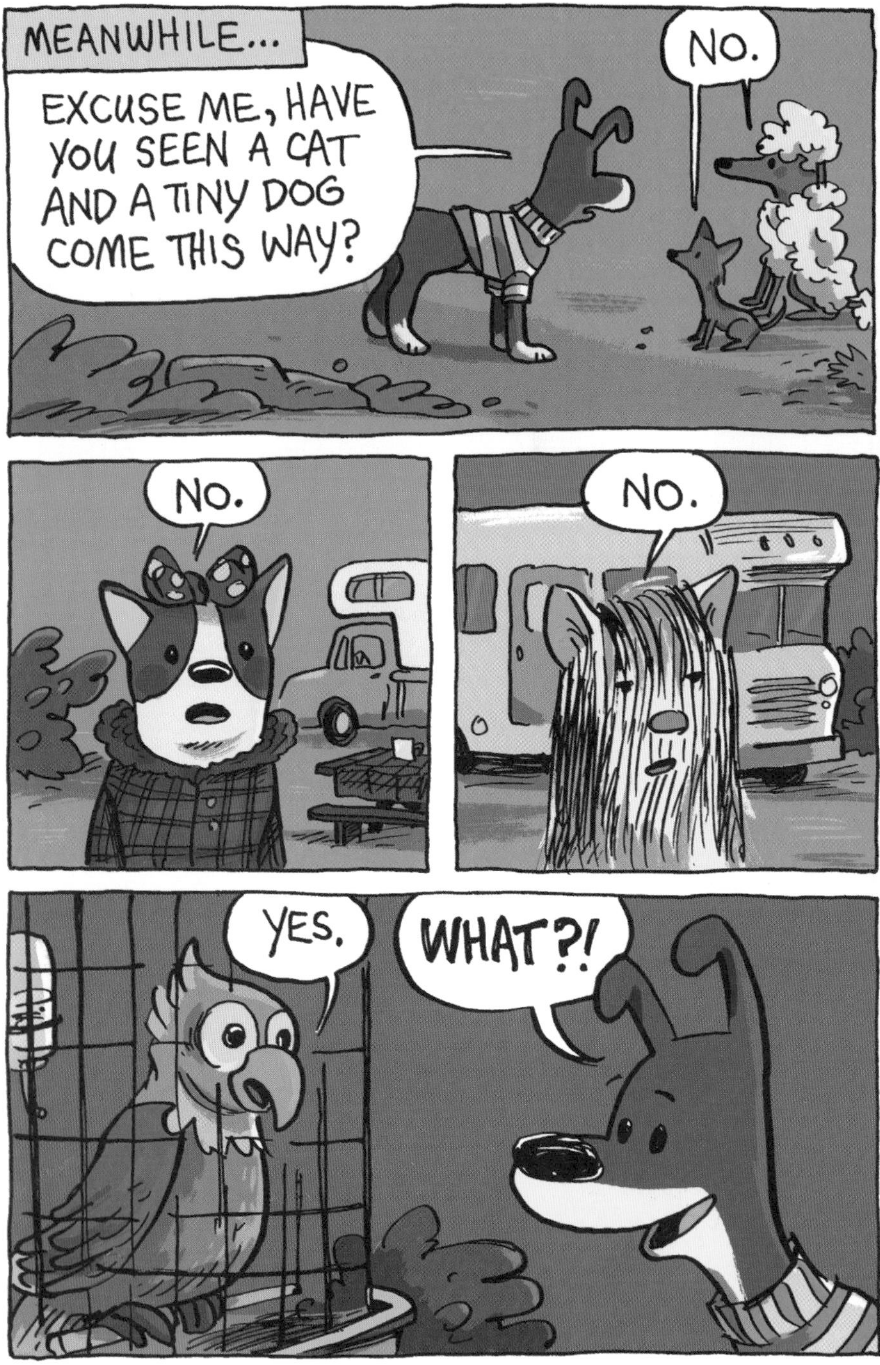
MEANWHILE...
EXCUSE ME, HAVE YOU SEEN A CAT AND A TINY DOG COME THIS WAY?
NO.
NO.
NO.
YES.
WHAT?!

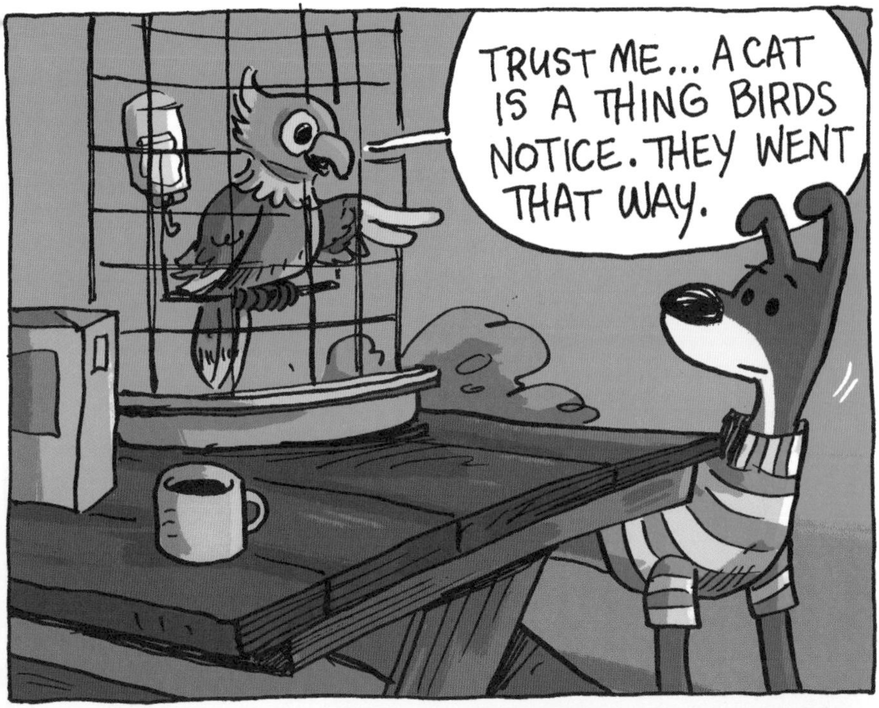
TRUST ME... A CAT IS A THING BIRDS NOTICE. THEY WENT THAT WAY.

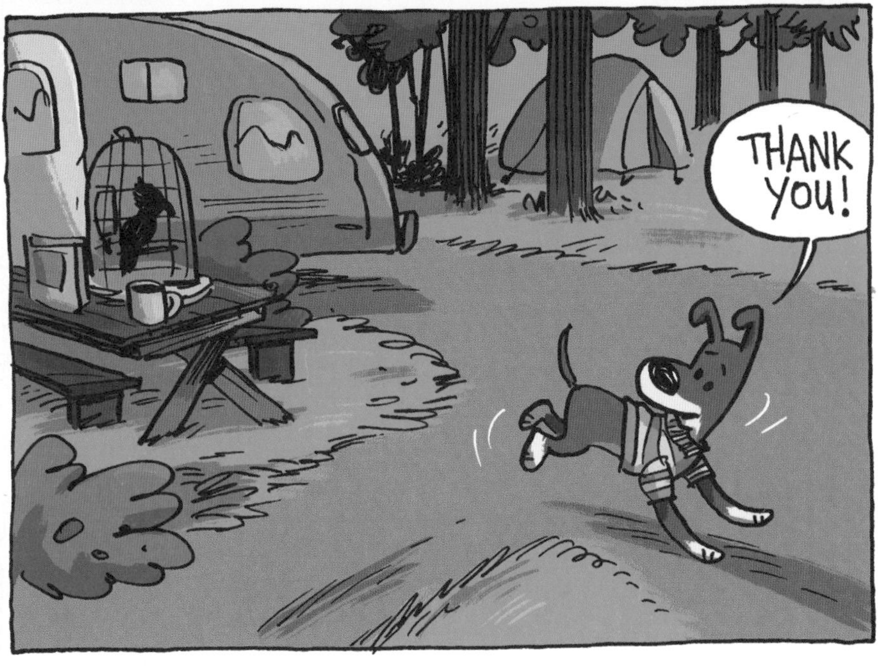
THANK YOU!

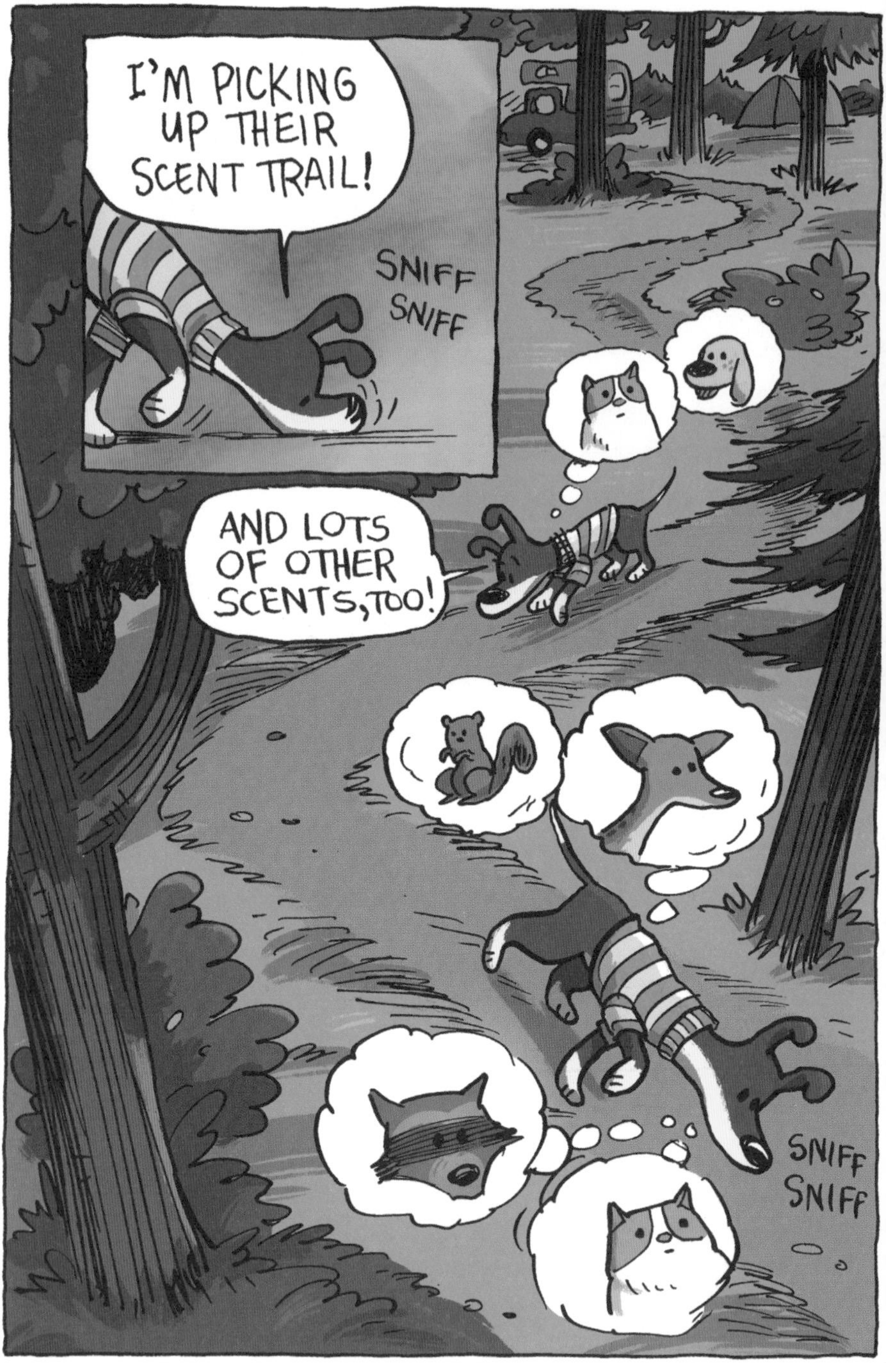
I'M PICKING UP THEIR SCENT TRAIL!
SNIFF SNIFF
AND LOTS OF OTHER SCENTS, TOO!
SNIFF SNIFF

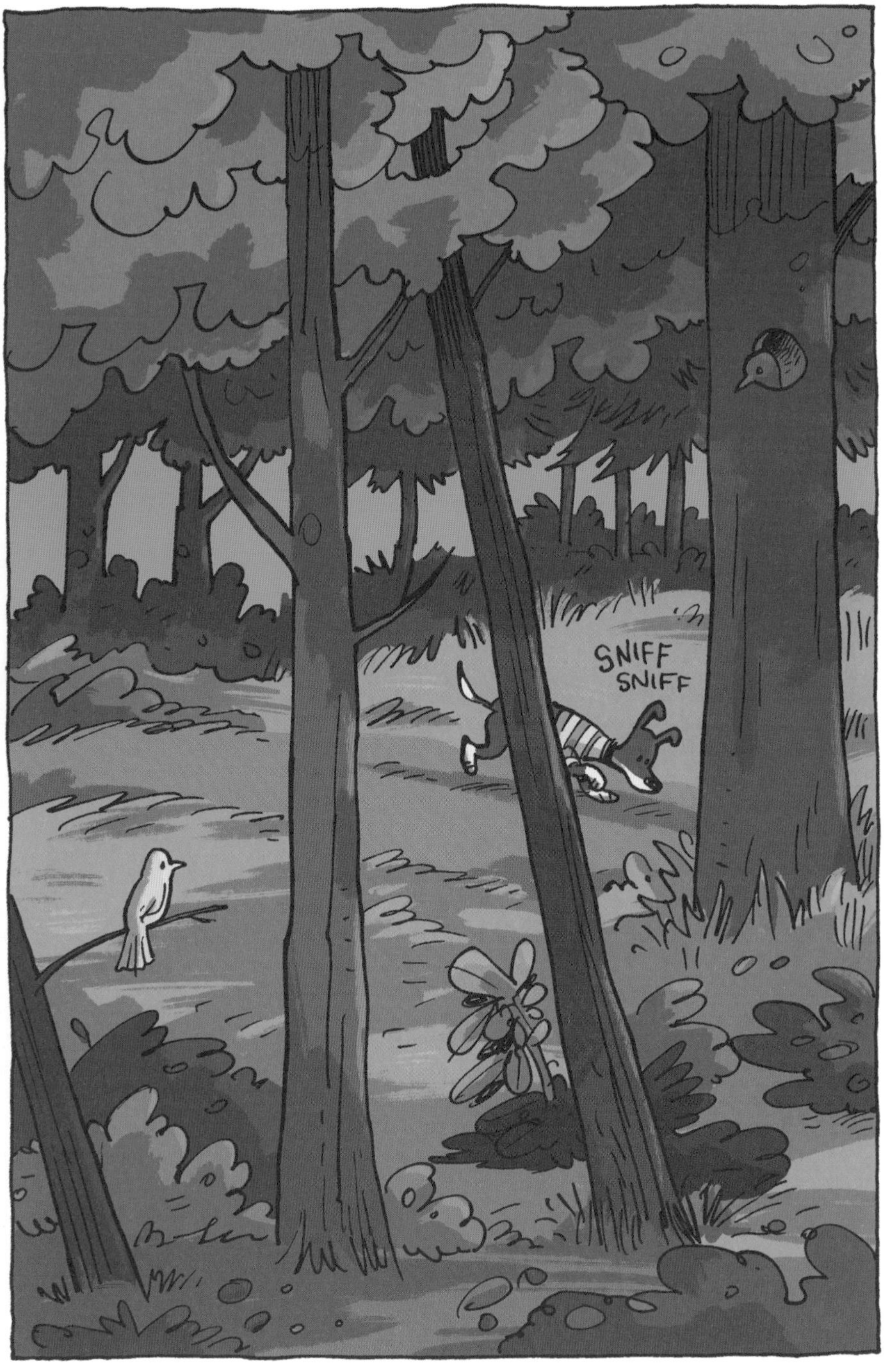
SNIFF
SNIFF

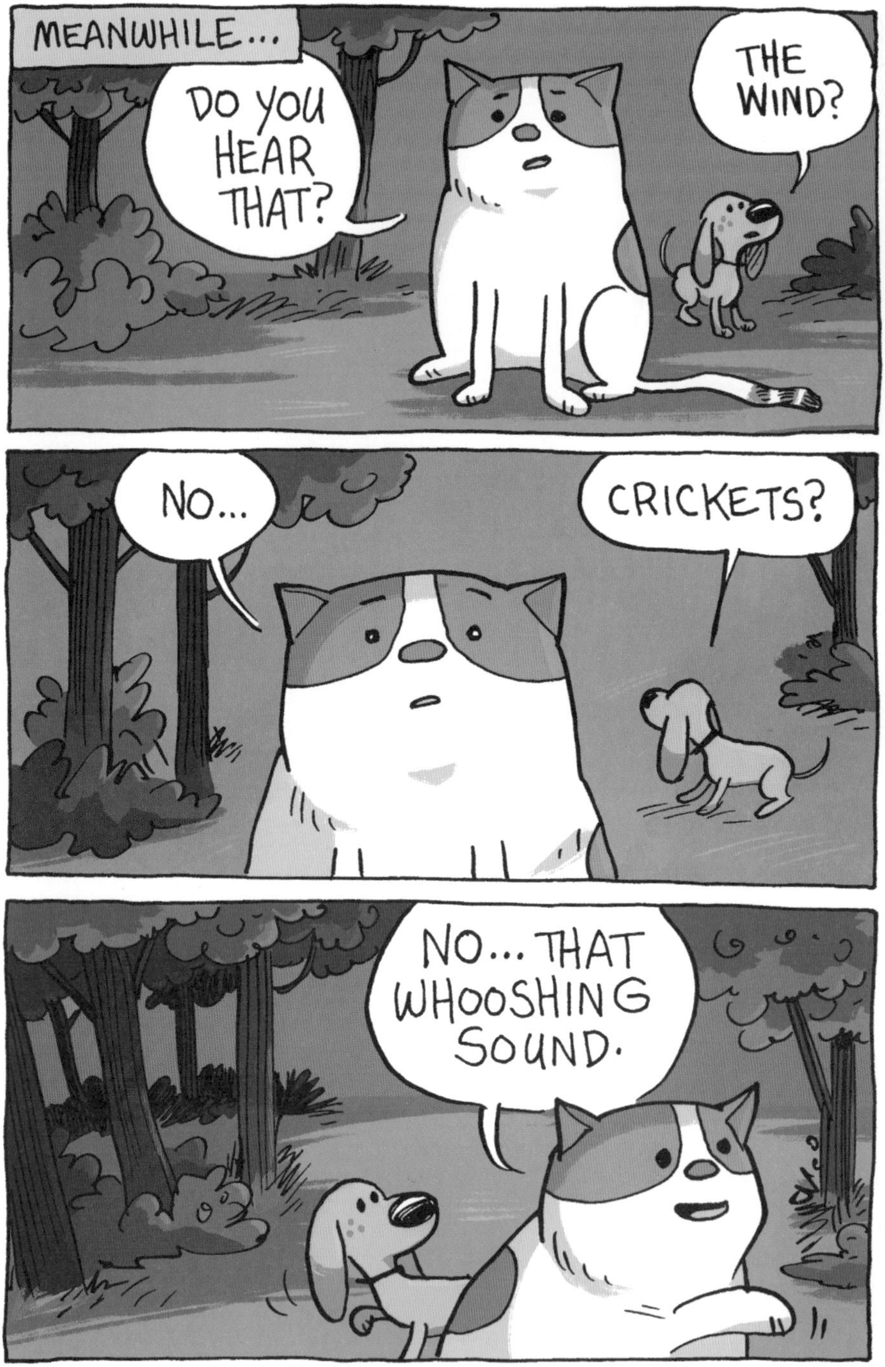
MEANWHILE...
DO YOU HEAR THAT?
THE WIND?
NO...
CRICKETS?
NO... THAT WHOOSHING SOUND.

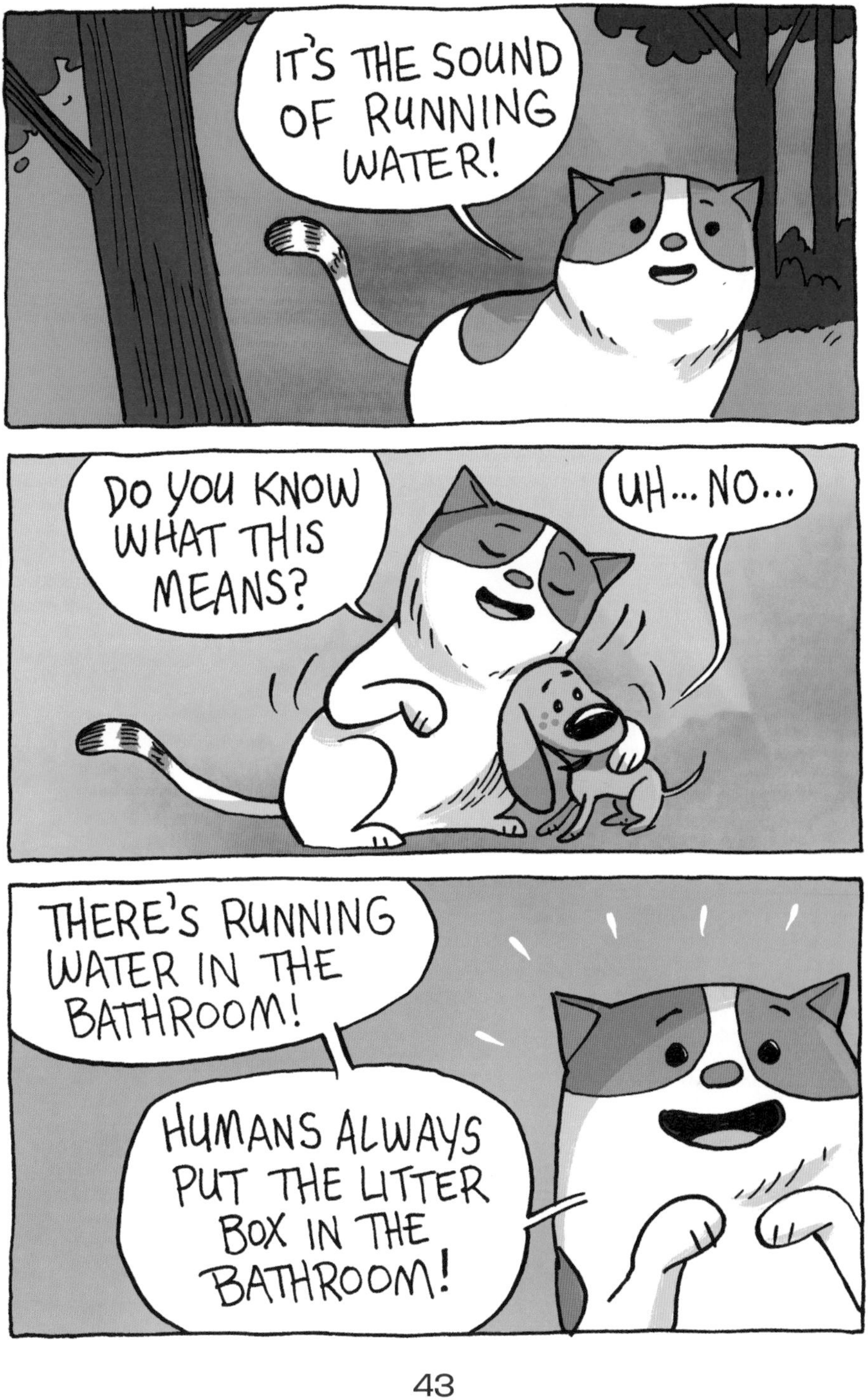
IT'S THE SOUND OF RUNNING WATER!
DO YOU KNOW WHAT THIS MEANS?
UH... NO...
THERE'S RUNNING WATER IN THE BATHROOM!
HUMANS ALWAYS PUT THE LITTER BOX IN THE BATHROOM!

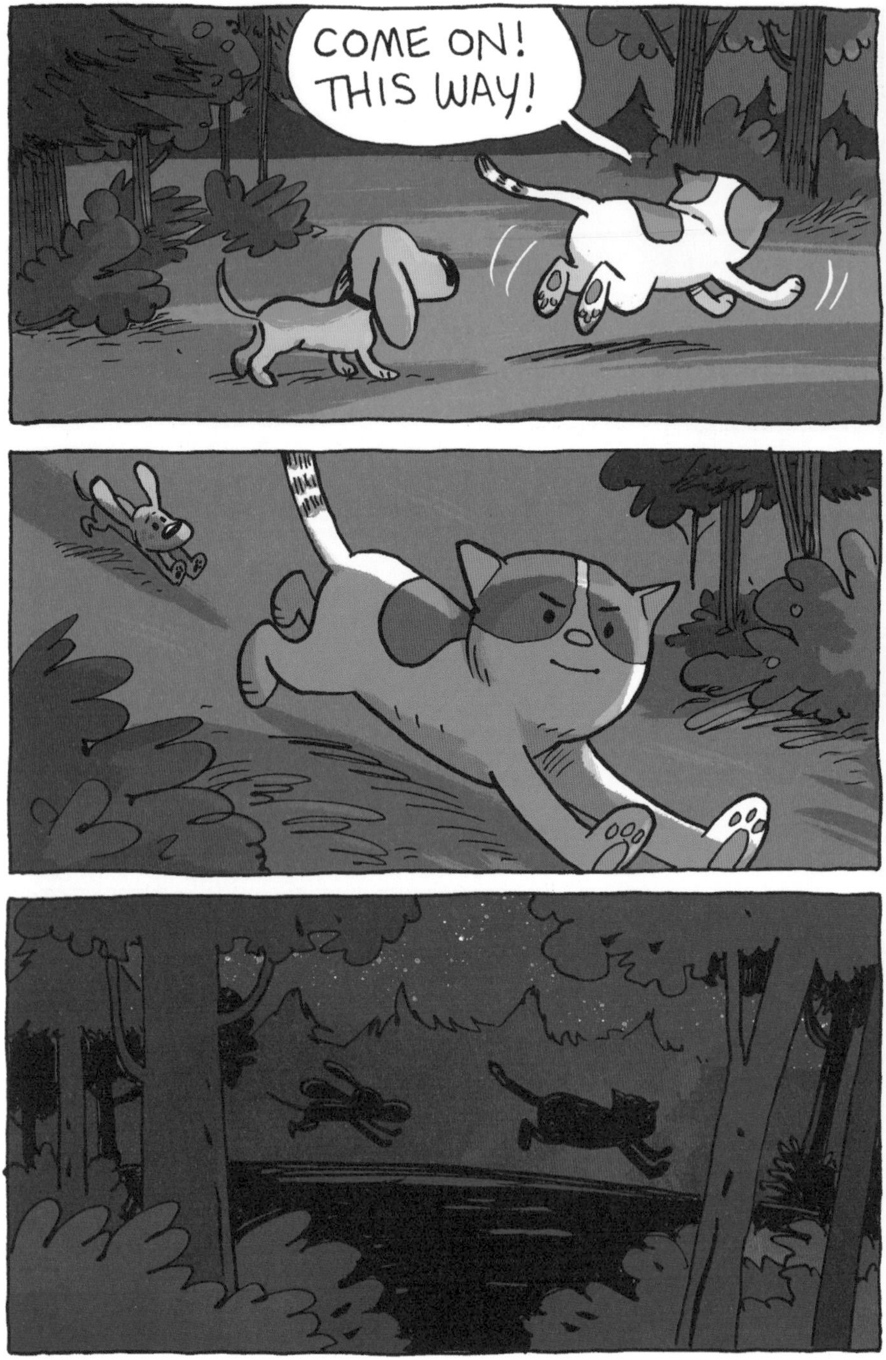
COME ON! THIS WAY!

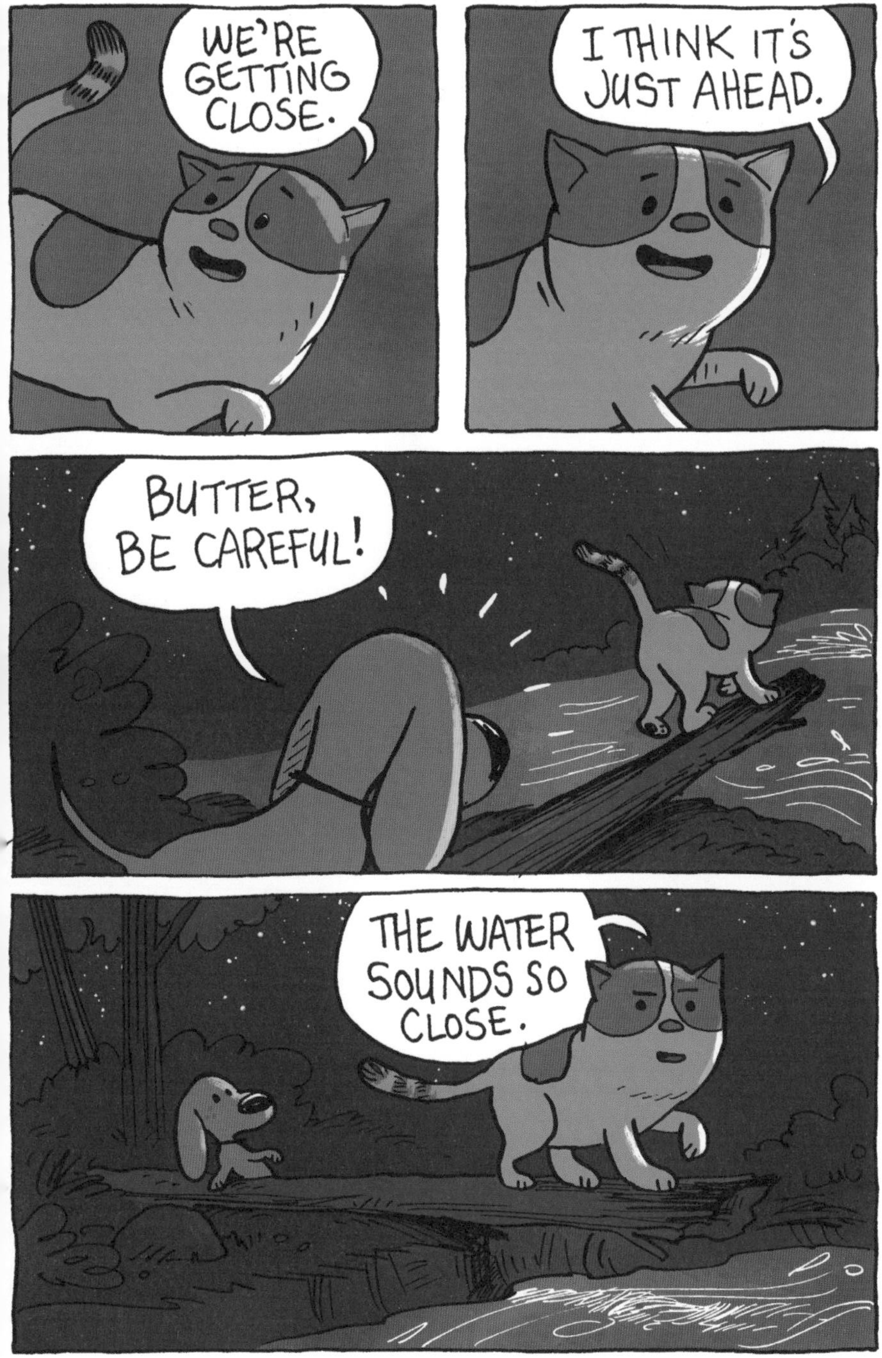
WE'RE GETTING CLOSE.
I THINK IT'S JUST AHEAD.
BUTTER, BE CAREFUL!
THE WATER SOUNDS SO CLOSE.

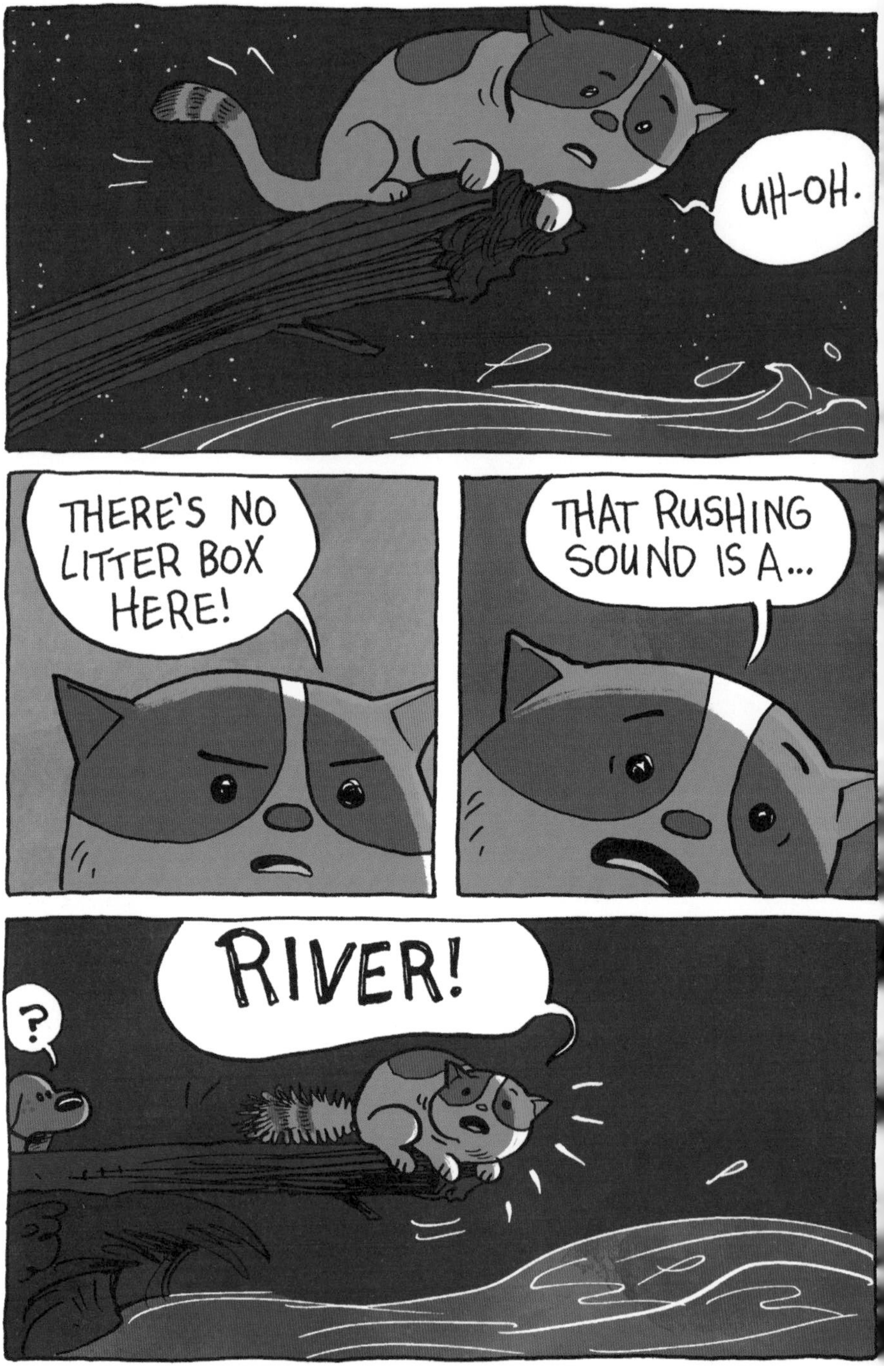
UH-OH.
THERE'S NO LITTER BOX HERE!
THAT RUSHING SOUND IS A...
?
RIVER!

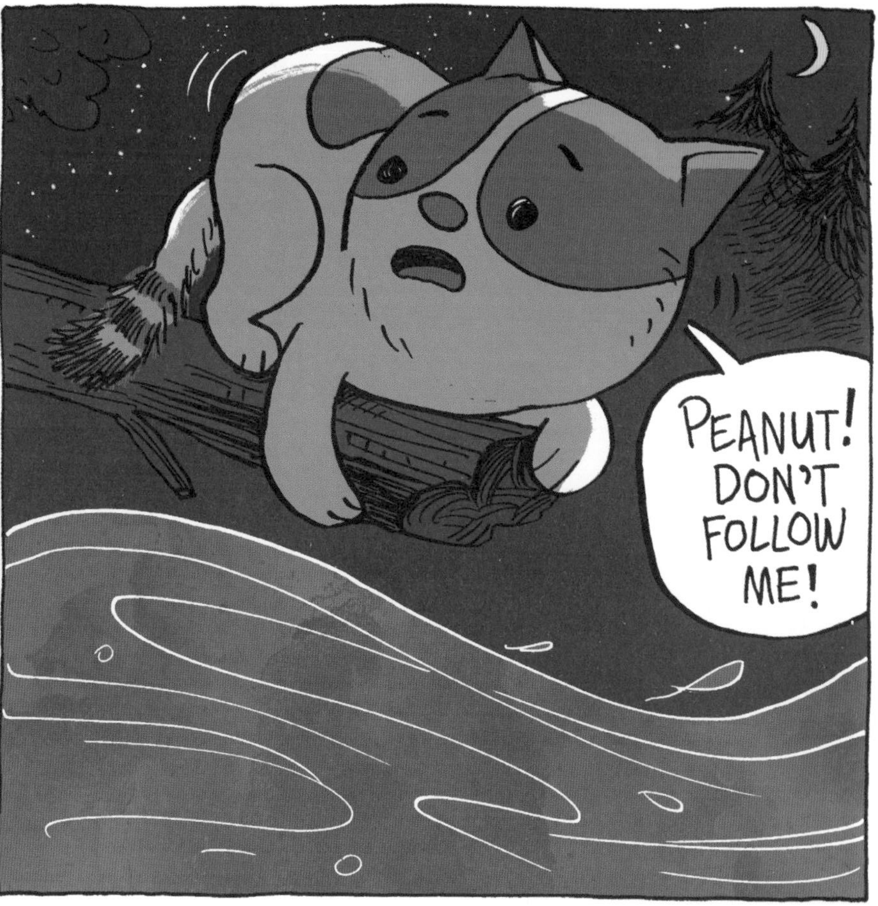
PEANUT! DON'T FOLLOW ME!

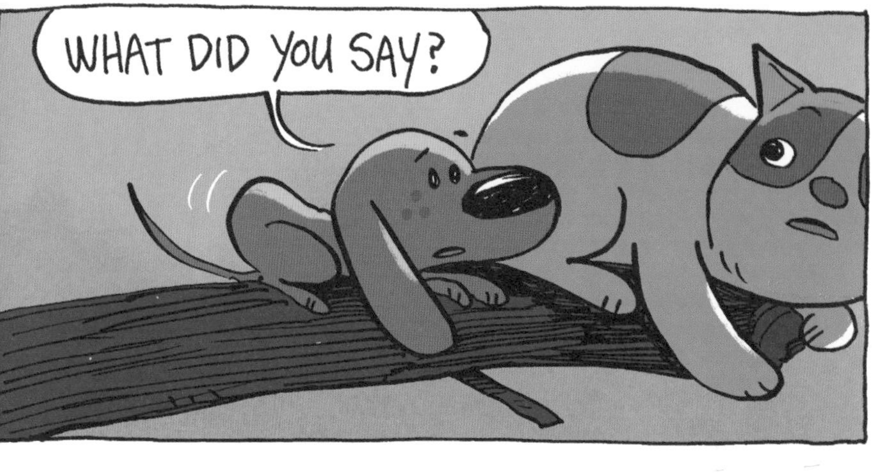
WHAT DID YOU SAY?

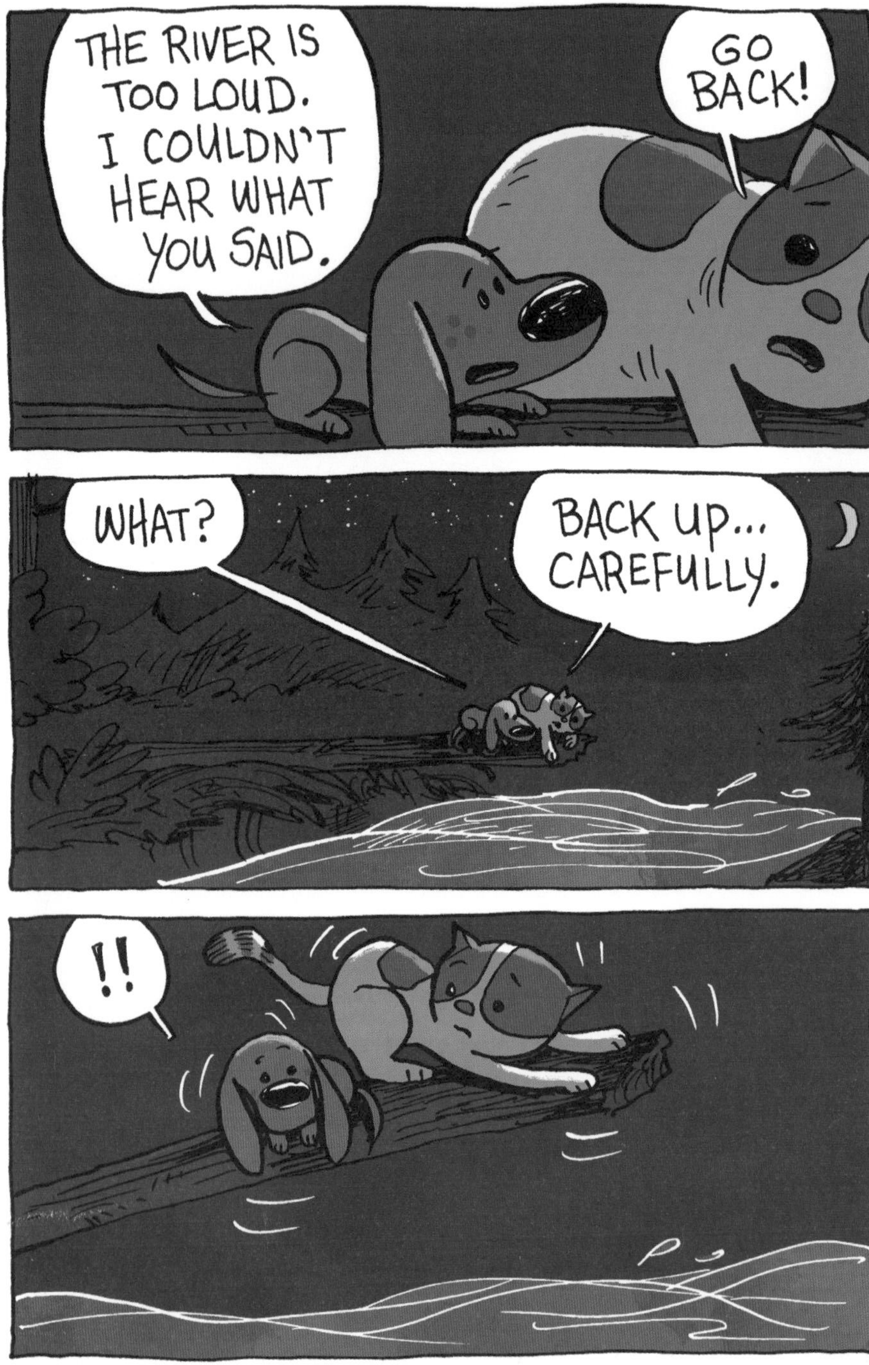
THE RIVER IS TOO LOUD. I COULDN'T HEAR WHAT YOU SAID.
GO BACK!
WHAT?
BACK UP... CAREFULLY.
!!

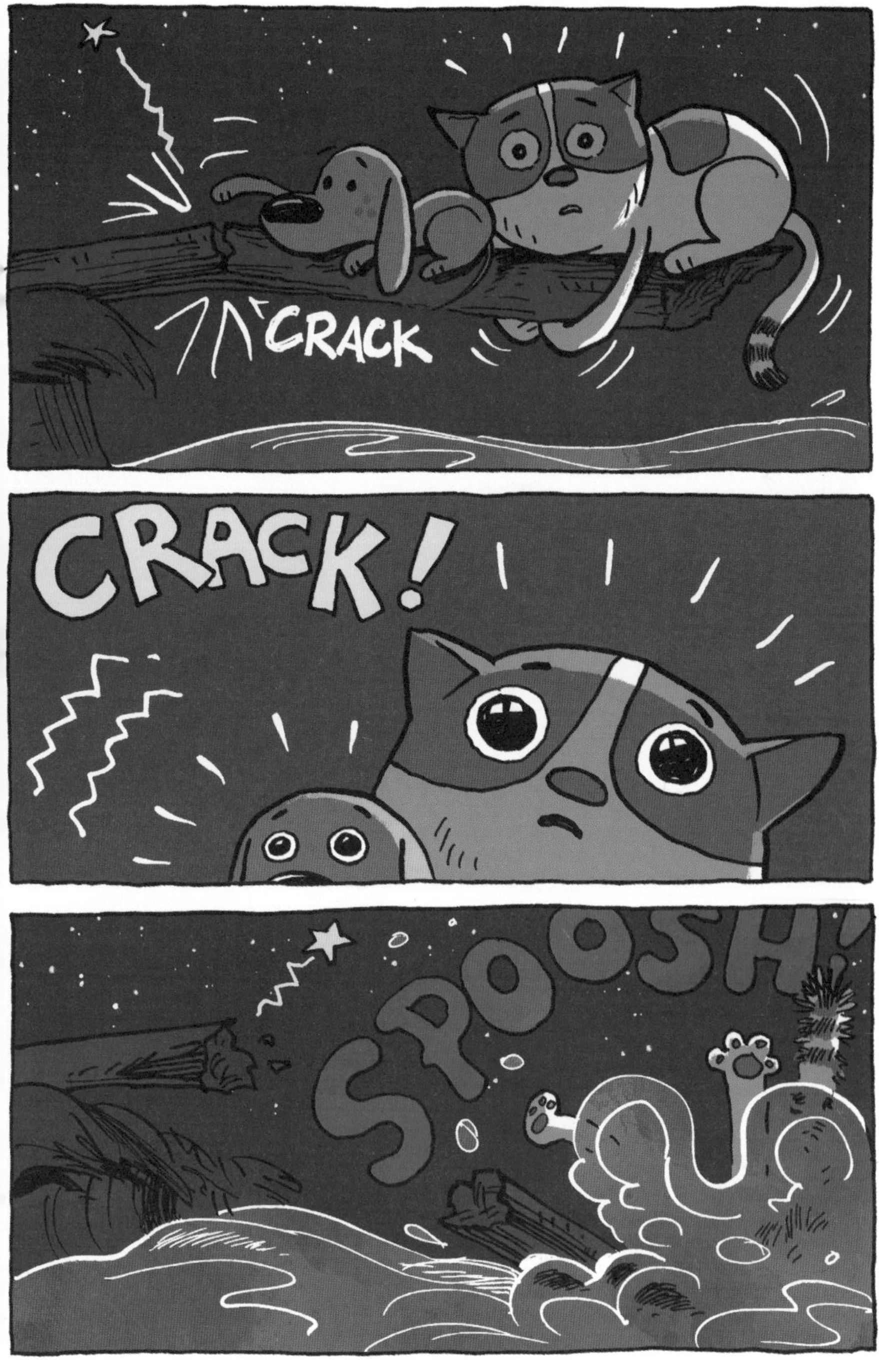
CRACK
CRACK!
SPOOSH!

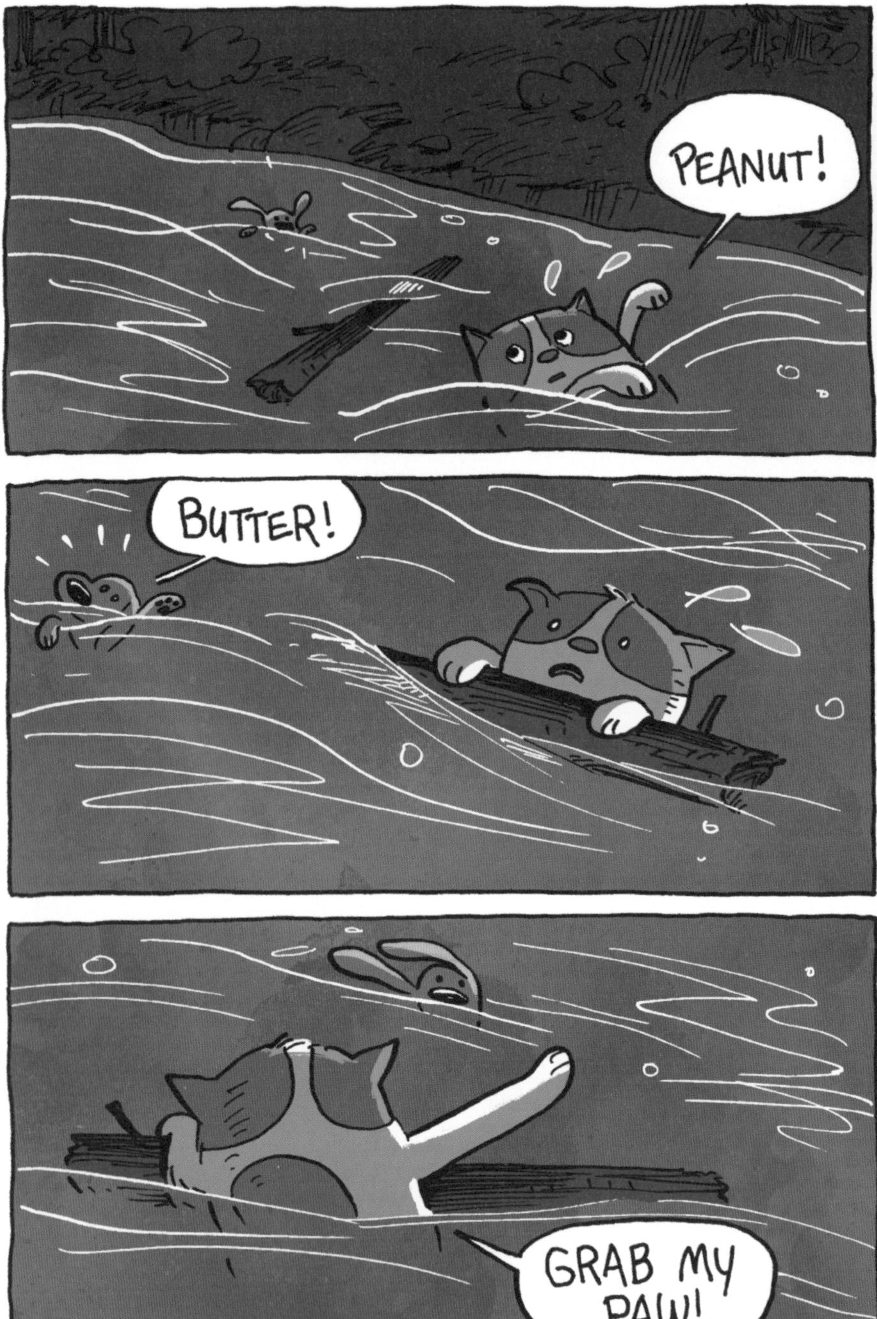
PEANUT!
BUTTER!
GRAB MY PAW!

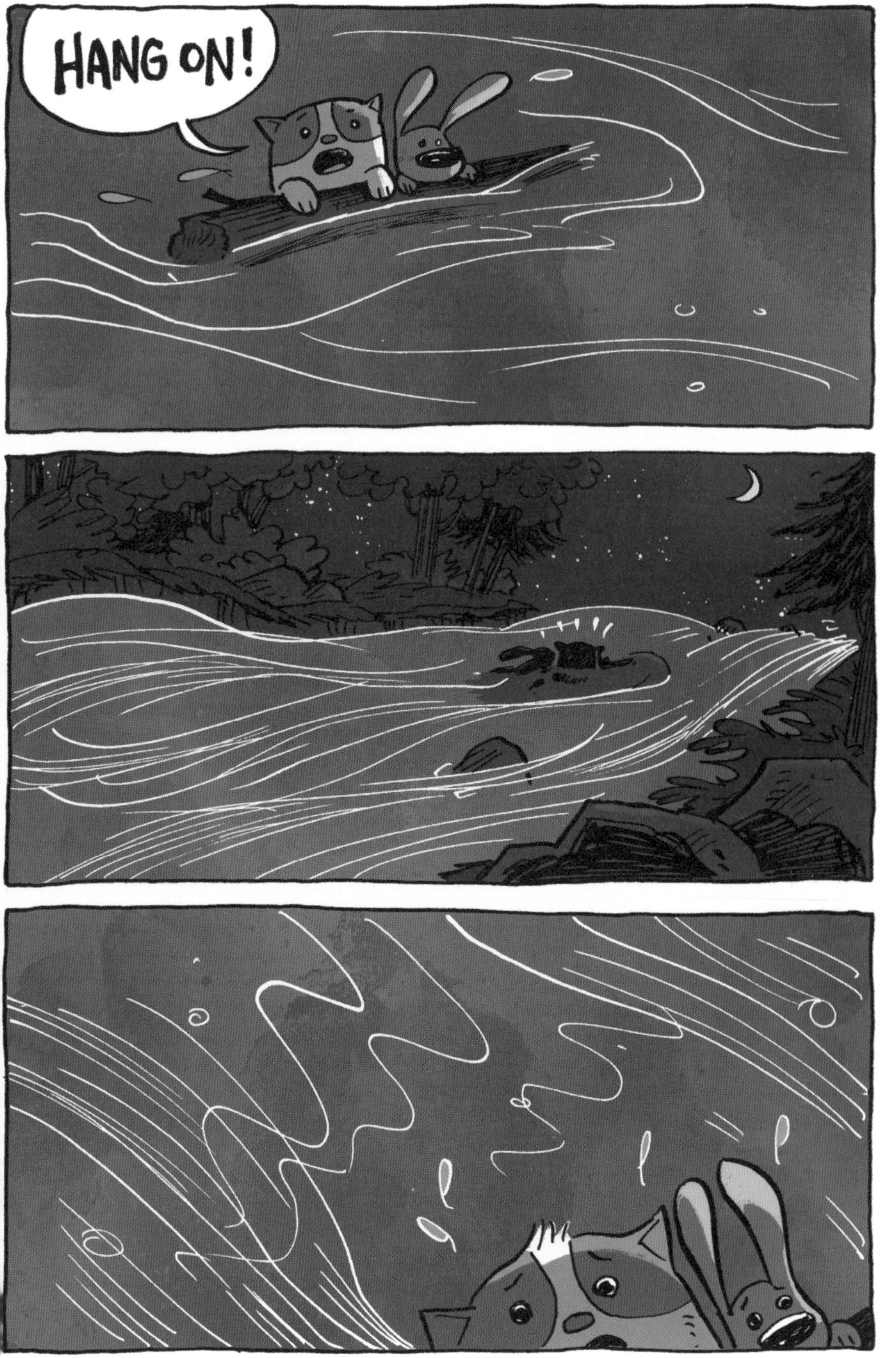
HANG ON!

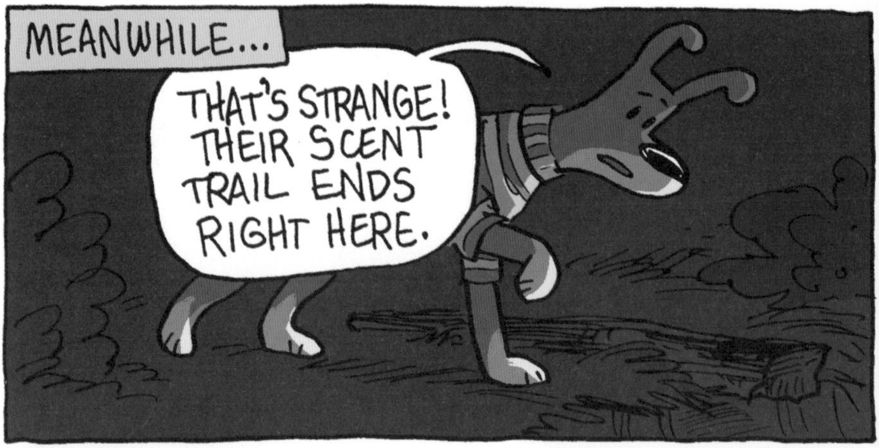
MEANWHILE...
THAT'S STRANGE! THEIR SCENT TRAIL ENDS RIGHT HERE.

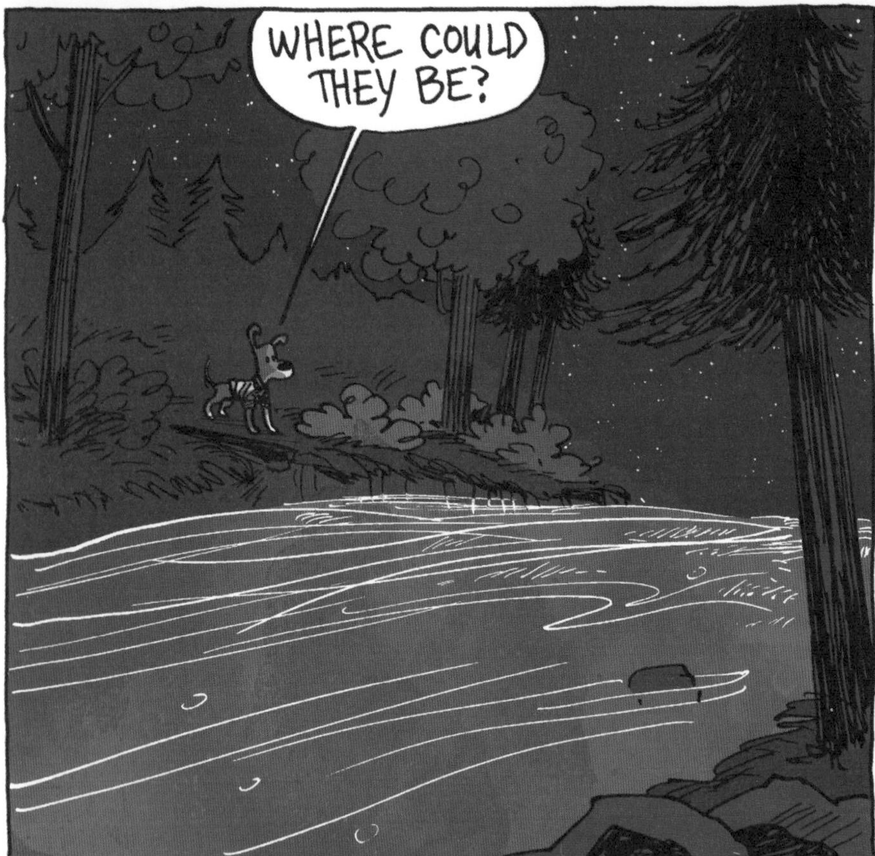
WHERE COULD THEY BE?

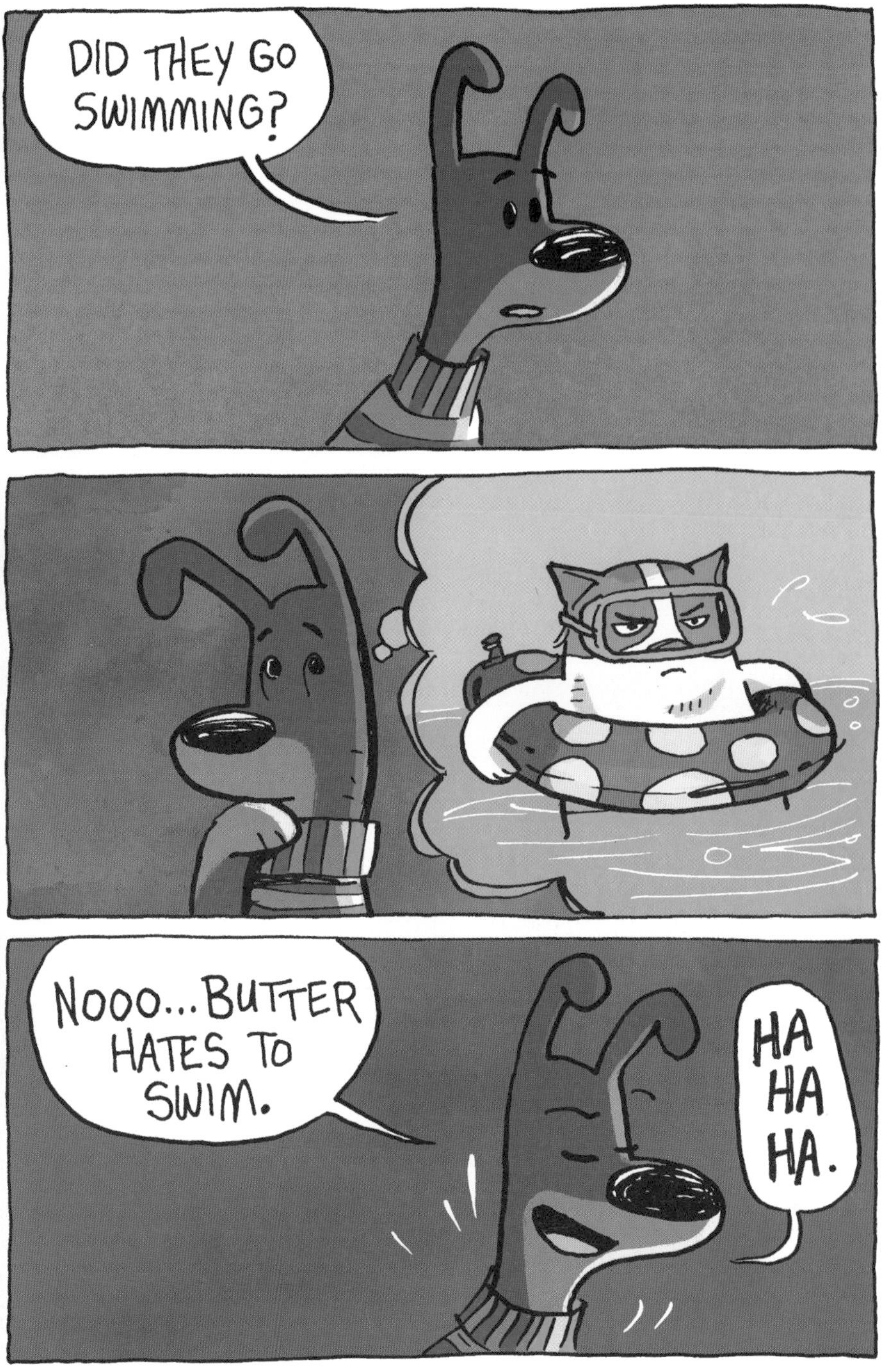
DID THEY GO SWIMMING?
NOOO...BUTTER HATES TO SWIM.
HA HA HA.

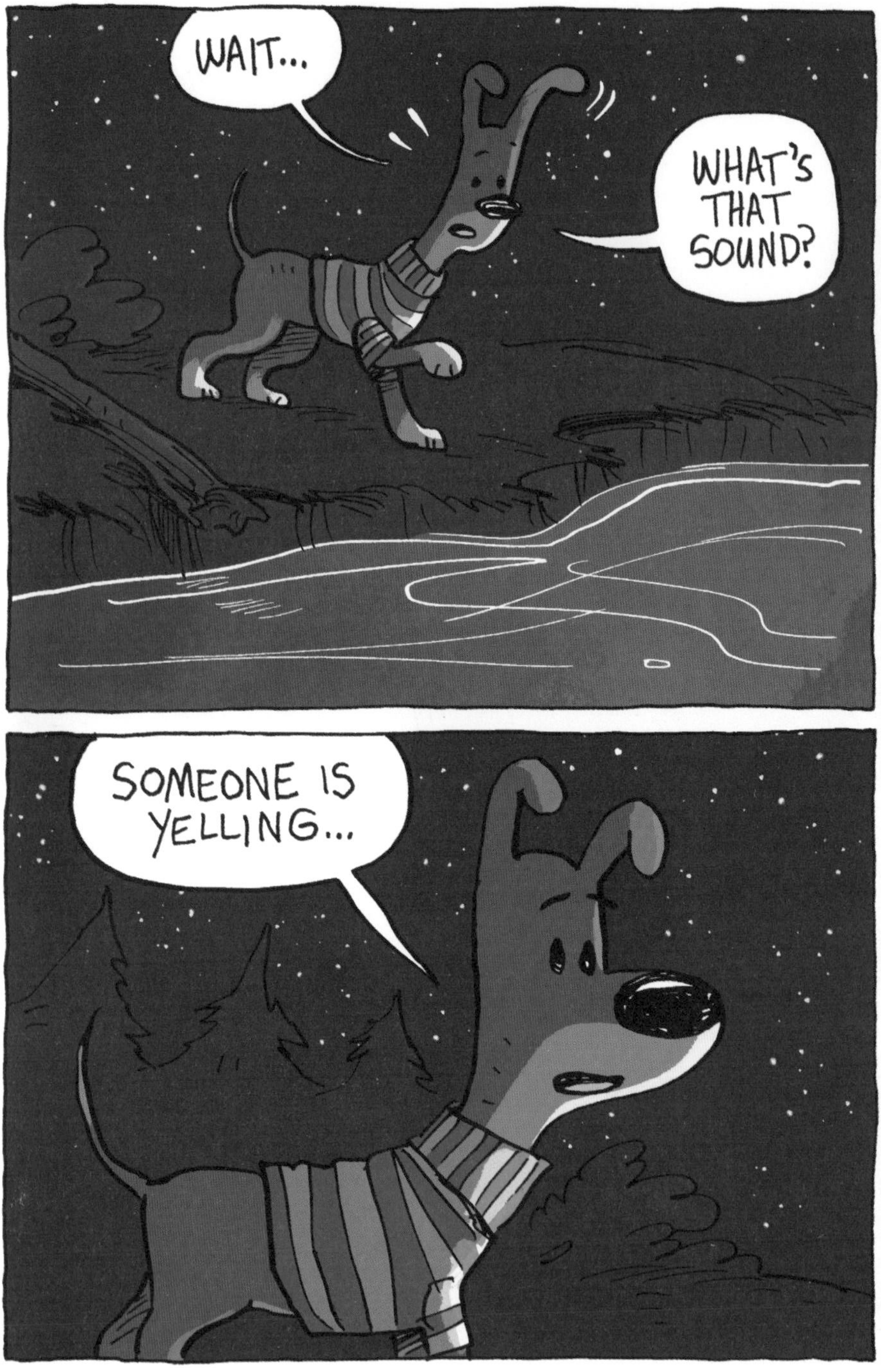
WAIT...
WHAT'S THAT SOUND?
SOMEONE IS YELLING...

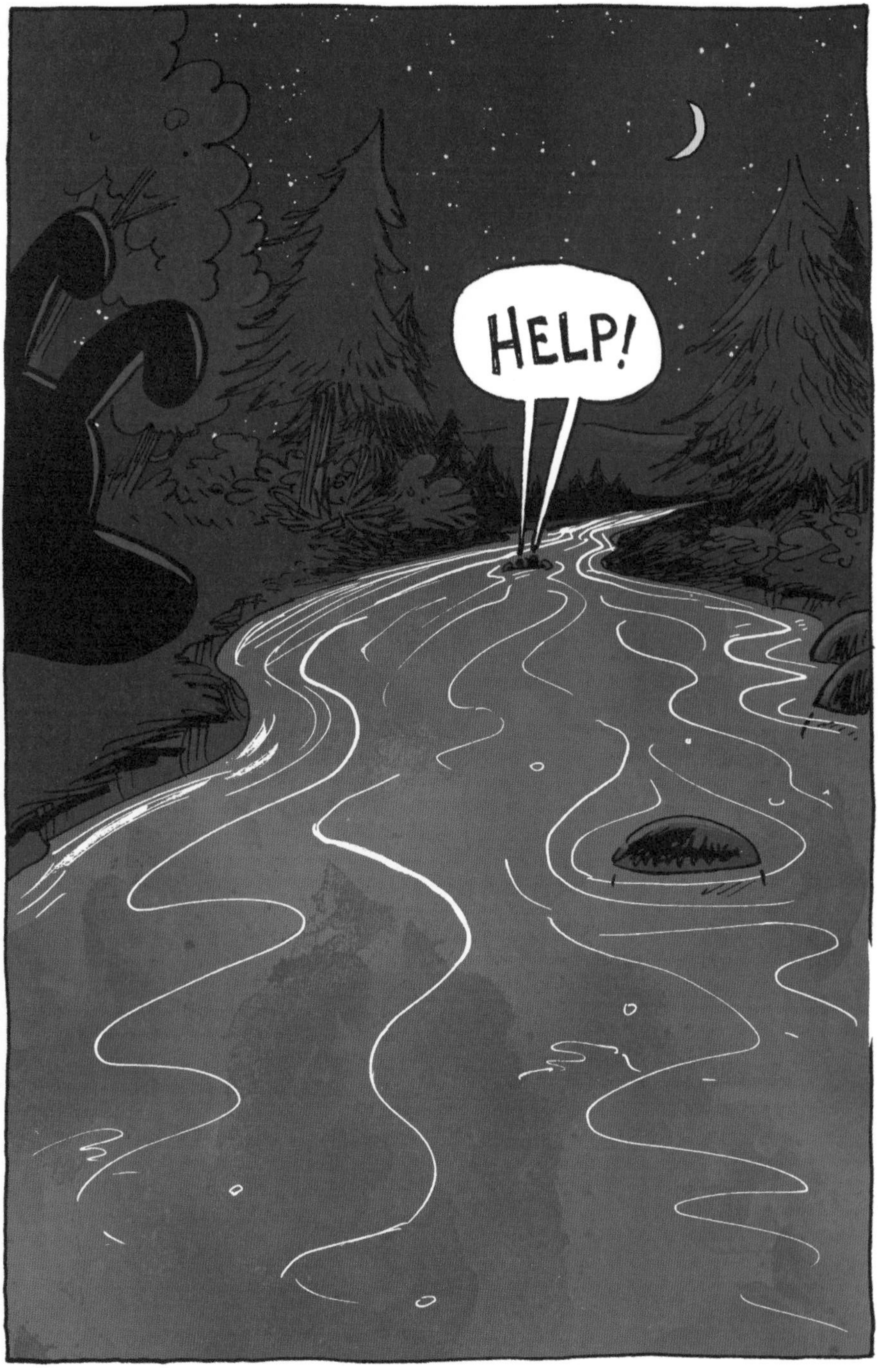
HELP!

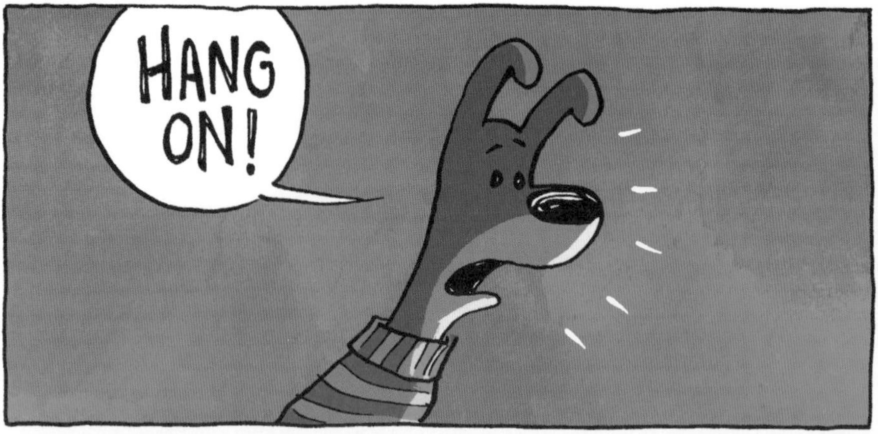
HANG ON!

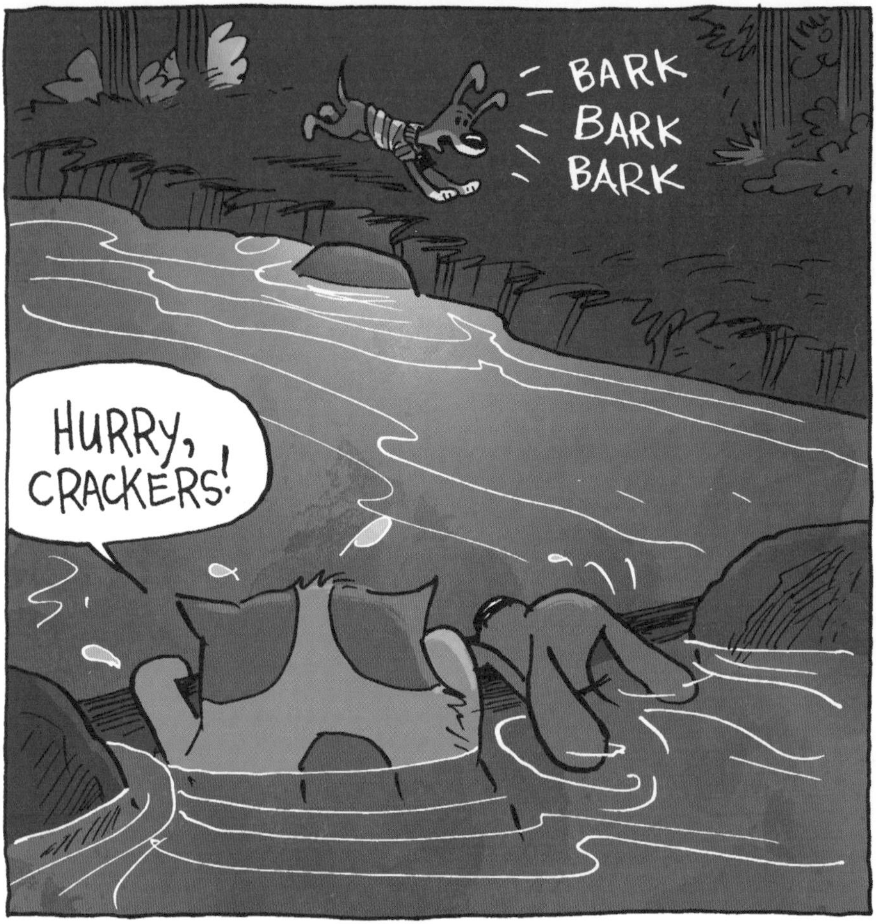
BARK
BARK
BARK
HURRY, CRACKERS!

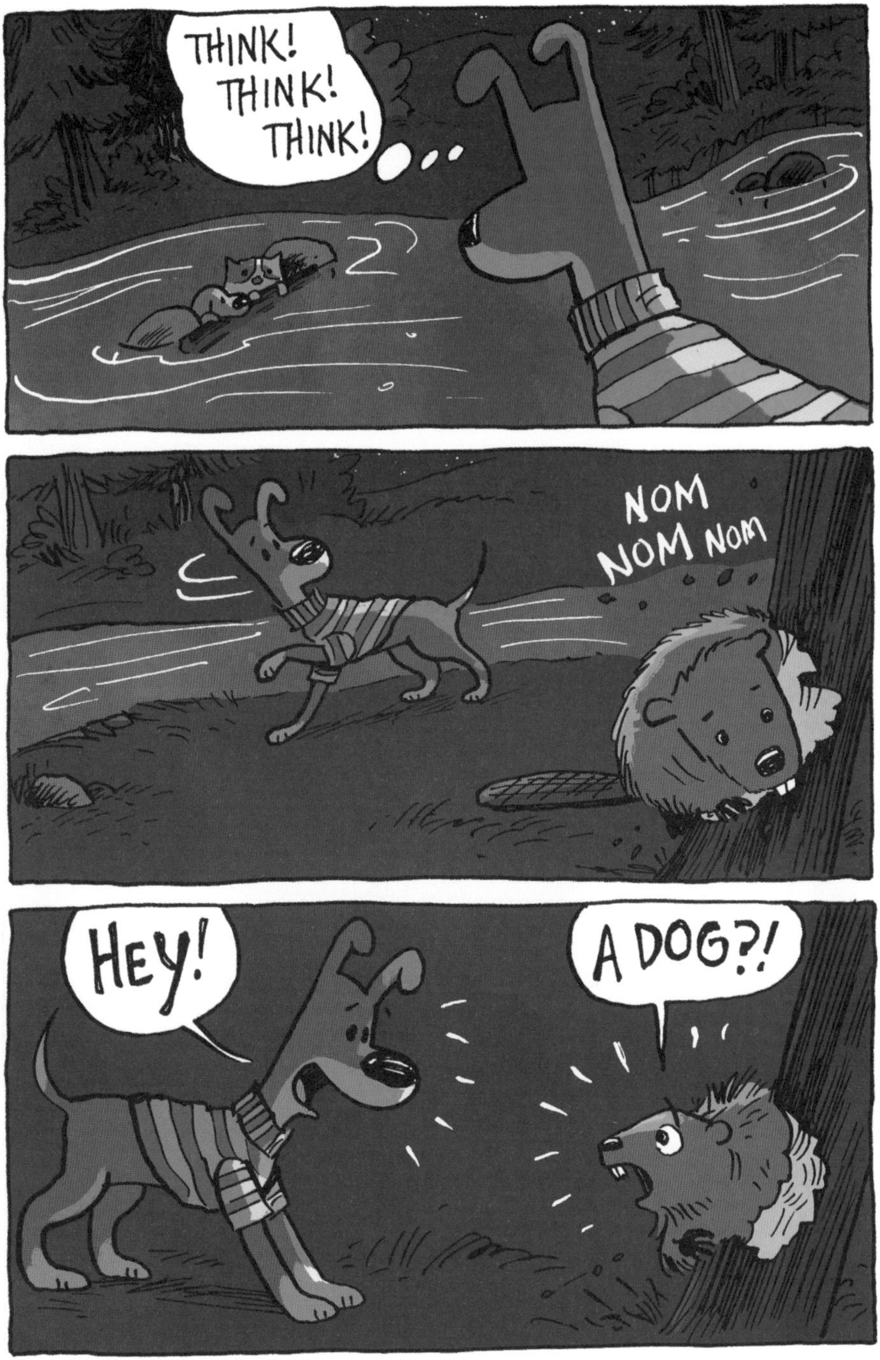
THINK!
THINK!
THINK!
NOM
NOM NOM
HEY!
A DOG?!

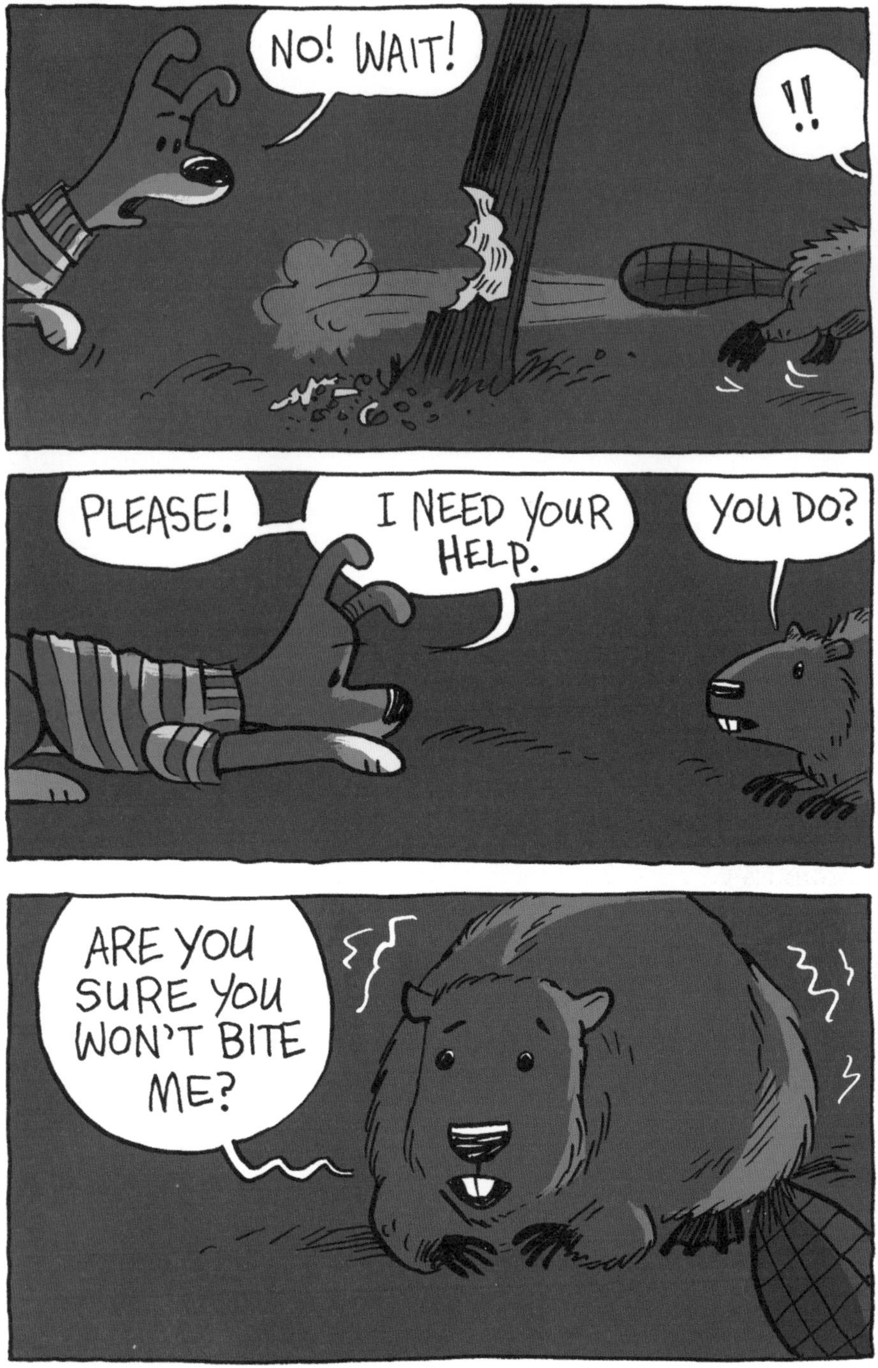
NO! WAIT!
!!
PLEASE!
I NEED YOUR HELP.
YOU DO?
ARE YOU SURE YOU WON'T BITE ME?

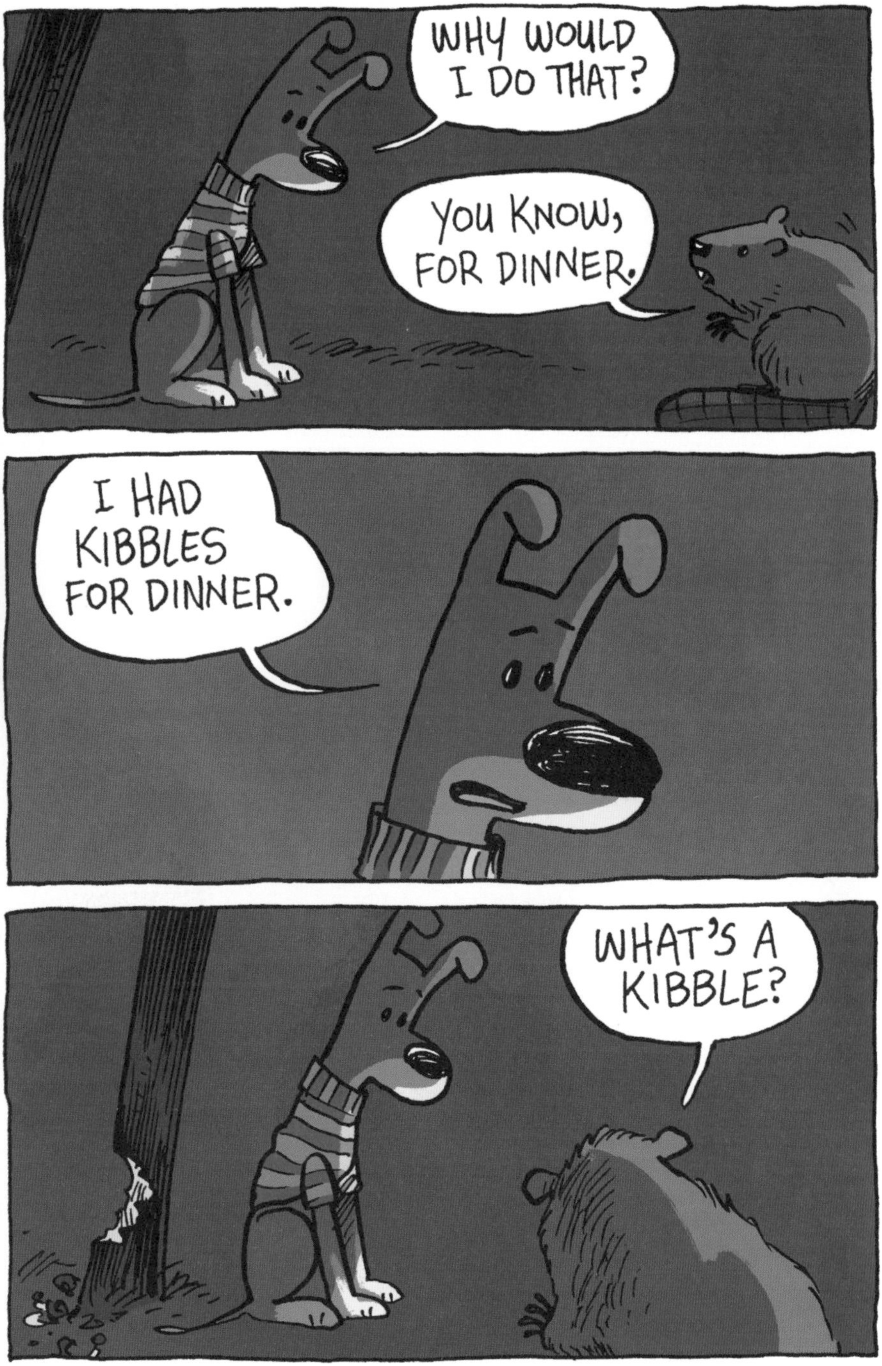
WHY WOULD I DO THAT?
YOU KNOW, FOR DINNER.
I HAD KIBBLES FOR DINNER.
WHAT'S A KIBBLE?

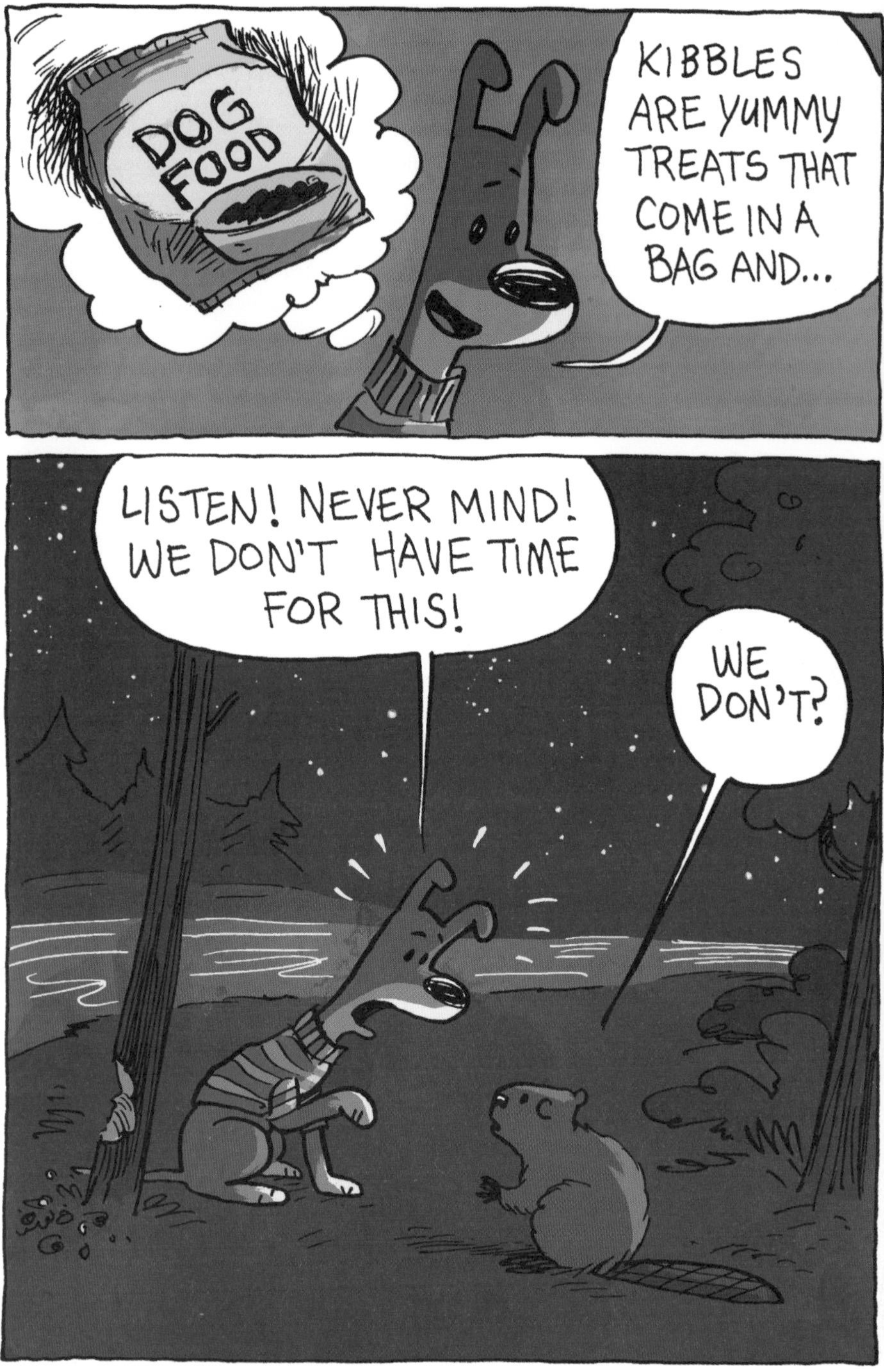
DOG FOOD
KIBBLES ARE YUMMY TREATS THAT COME IN A BAG AND...
LISTEN! NEVER MIND! WE DON'T HAVE TIME FOR THIS!
WE DON'T?

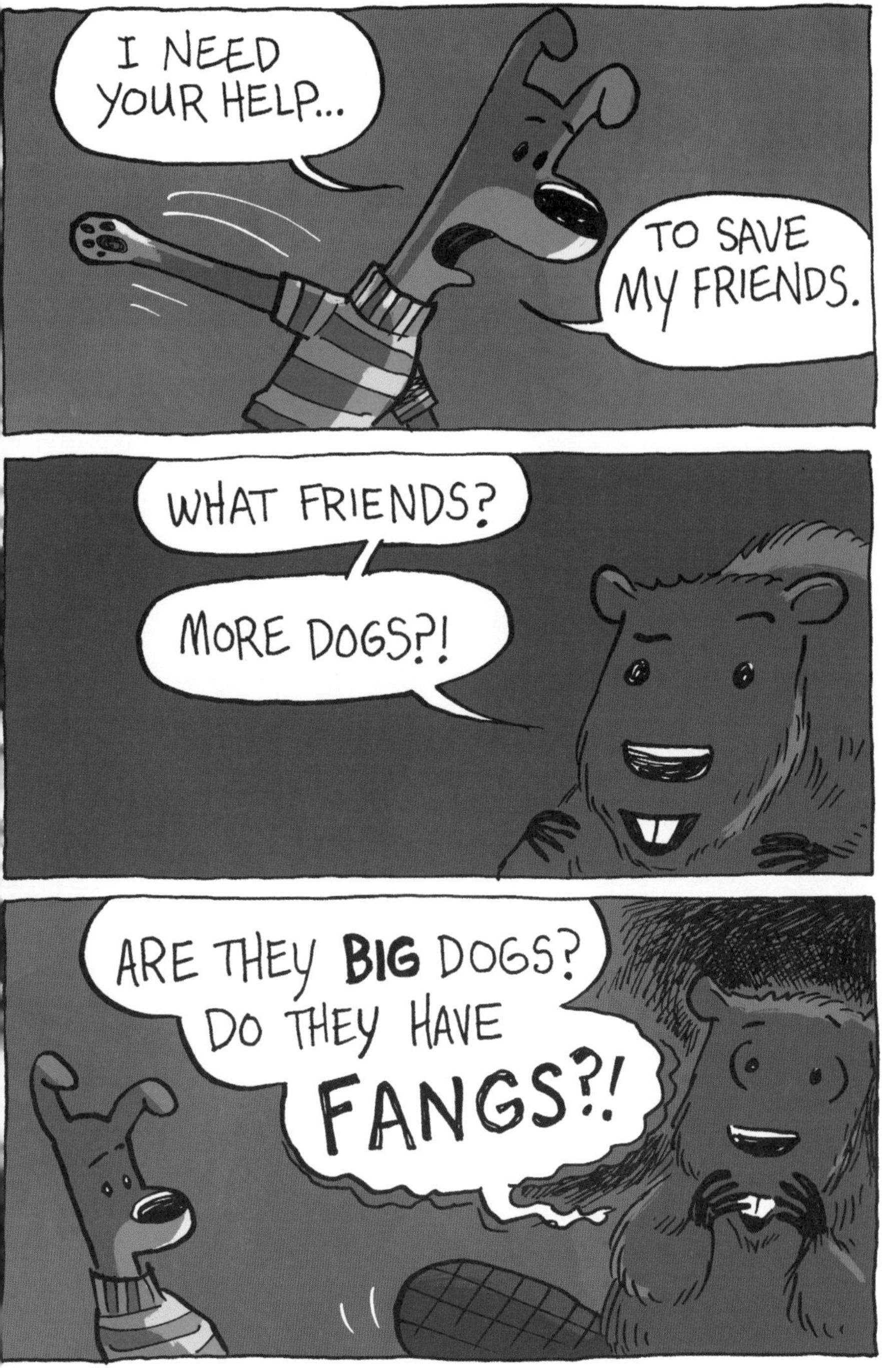
I NEED YOUR HELP...
TO SAVE MY FRIENDS.
WHAT FRIENDS?
MORE DOGS?!
ARE THEY **BIG** DOGS? DO THEY HAVE FANGS?!

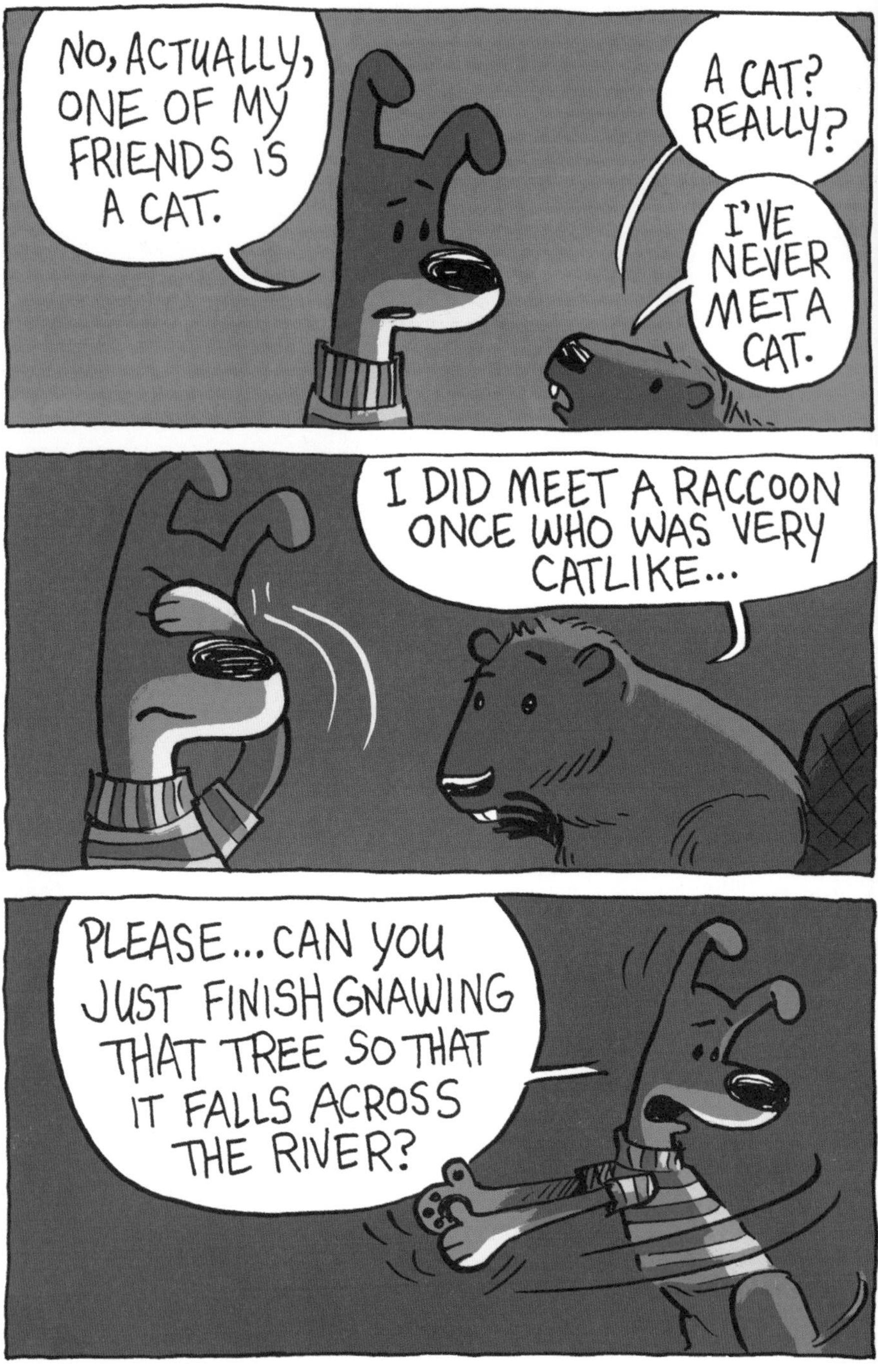
NO, ACTUALLY, ONE OF MY FRIENDS IS A CAT.
A CAT? REALLY?
I'VE NEVER MET A CAT.
I DID MEET A RACCOON ONCE WHO WAS VERY CATLIKE...
PLEASE... CAN YOU JUST FINISH GNAWING THAT TREE SO THAT IT FALLS ACROSS THE RIVER?

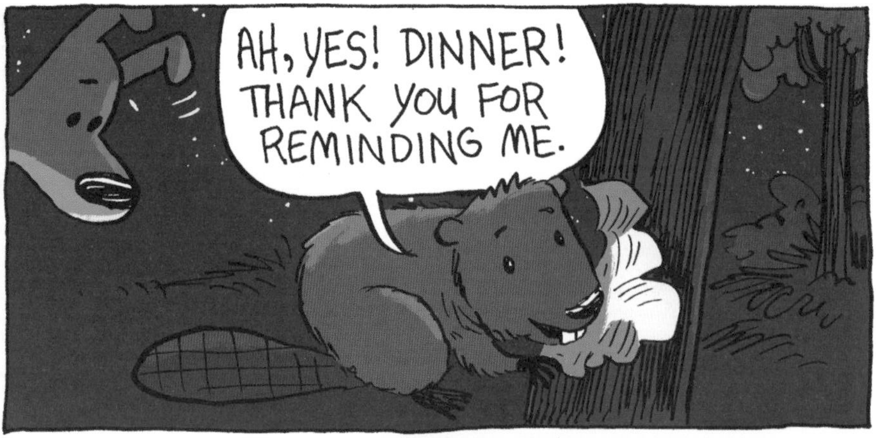
AH, YES! DINNER! THANK YOU FOR REMINDING ME.

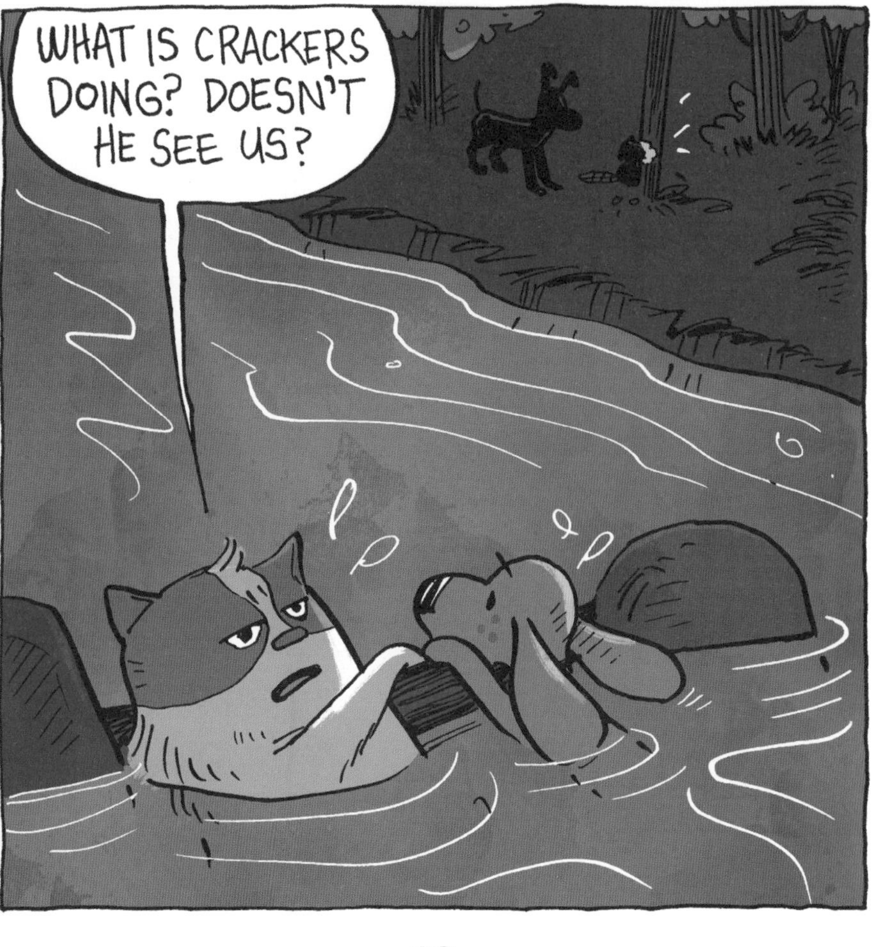
WHAT IS CRACKERS DOING? DOESN'T HE SEE US?

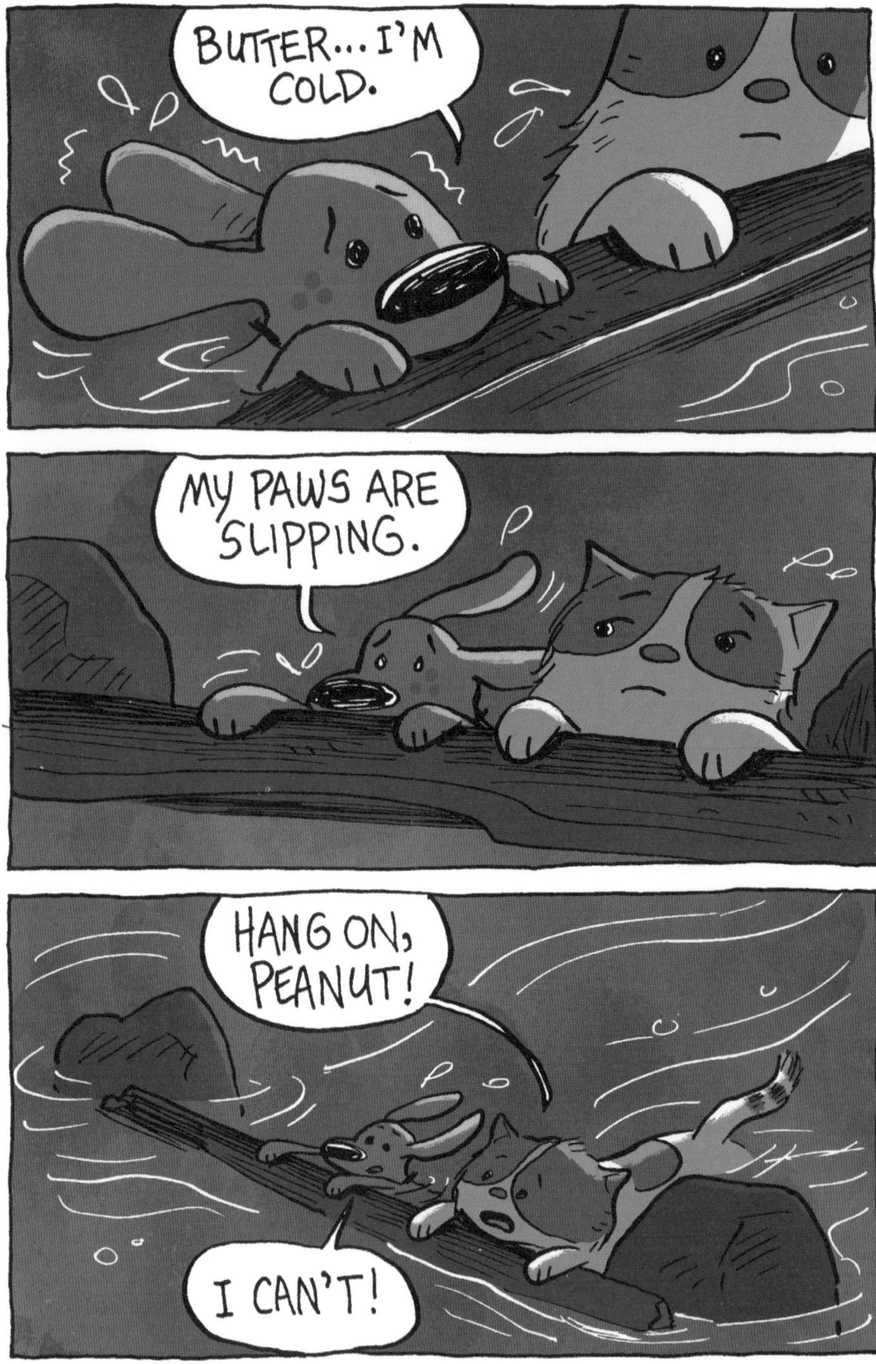
BUTTER... I'M COLD.
MY PAWS ARE SLIPPING.
HANG ON, PEANUT!
I CAN'T!

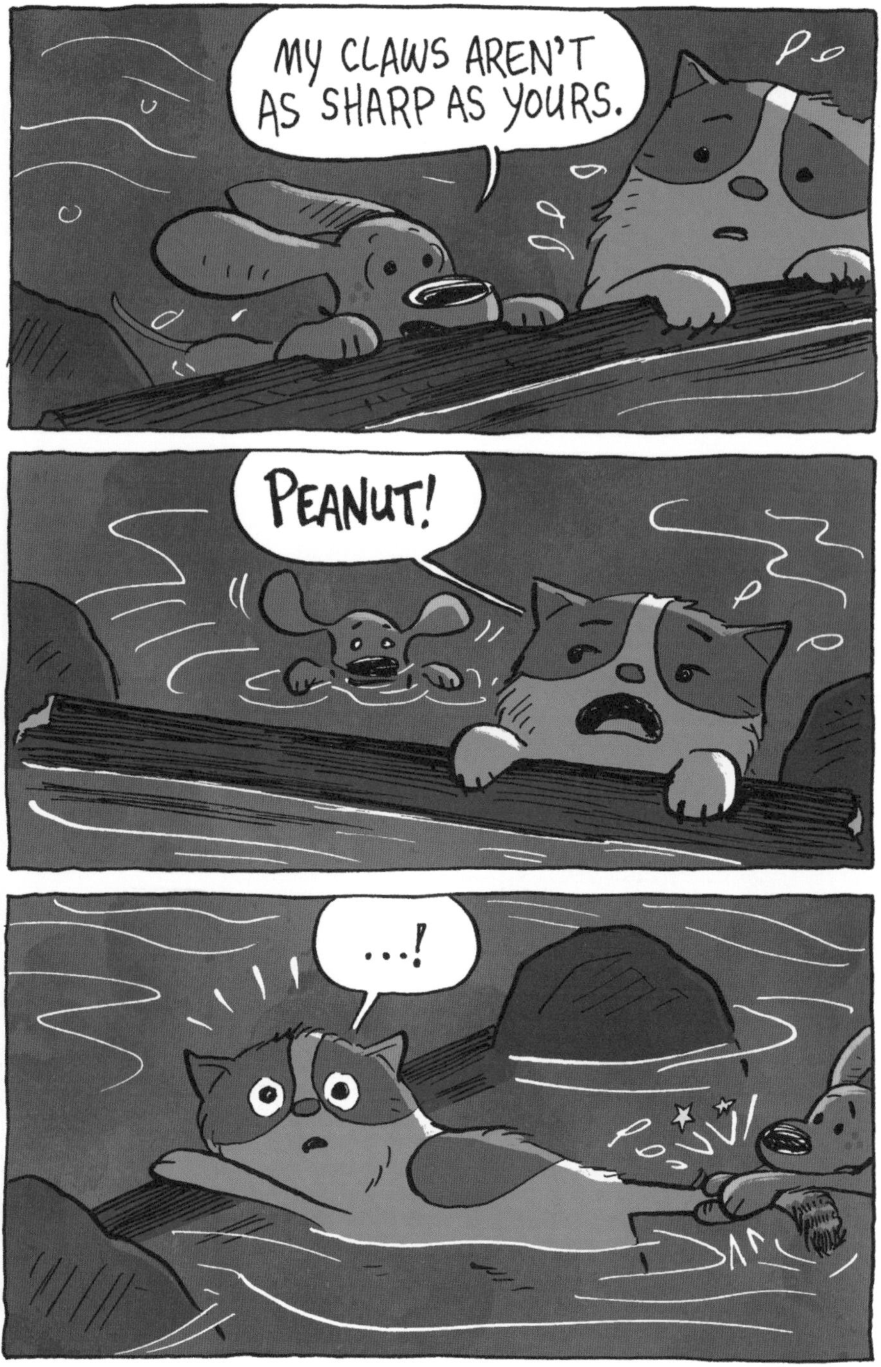
MY CLAWS AREN'T AS SHARP AS YOURS.
PEANUT!
...!

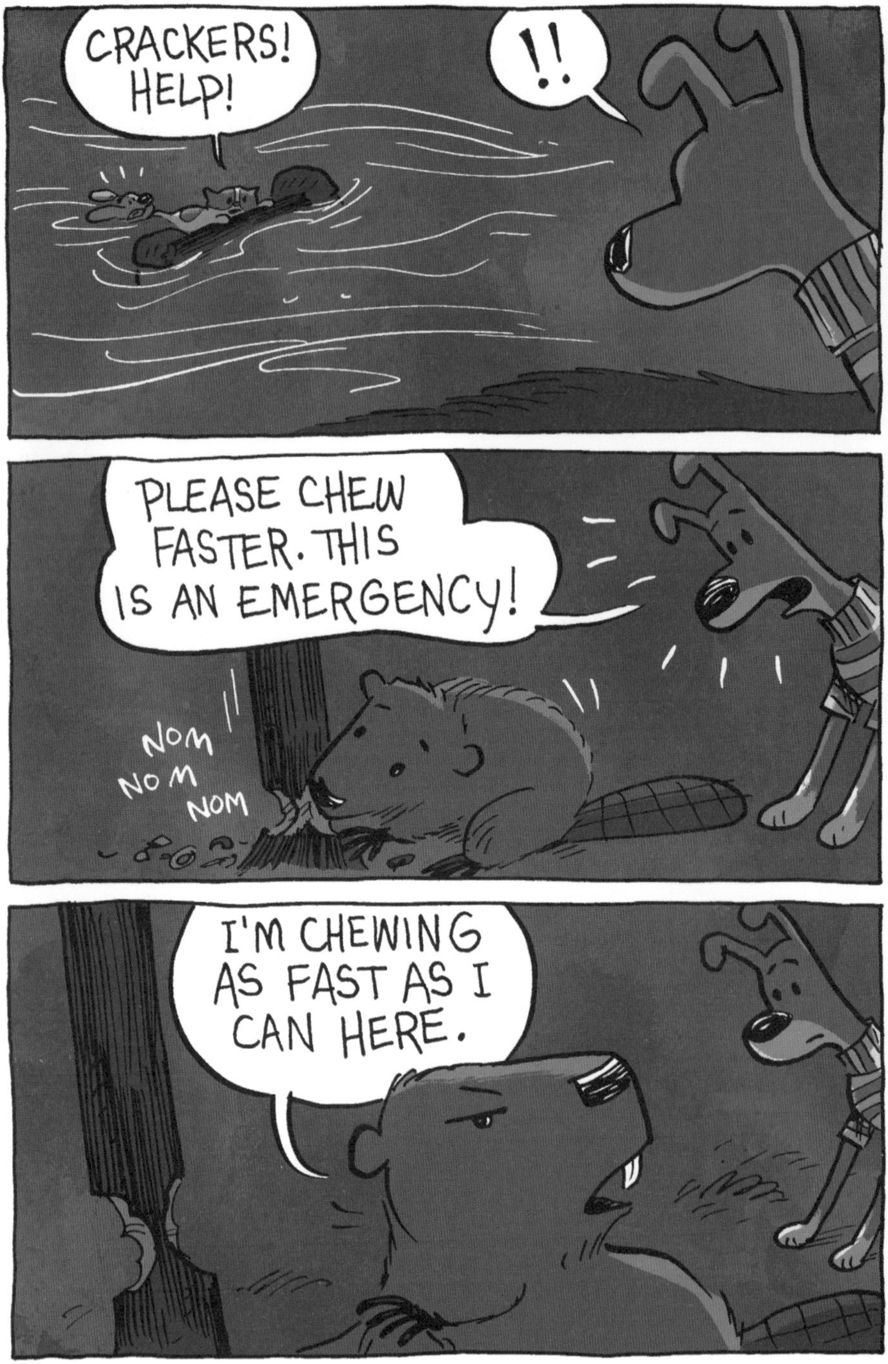
CRACKERS! HELP!
!!
PLEASE CHEW FASTER. THIS IS AN EMERGENCY!
NOM NOM NOM
I'M CHEWING AS FAST AS I CAN HERE.

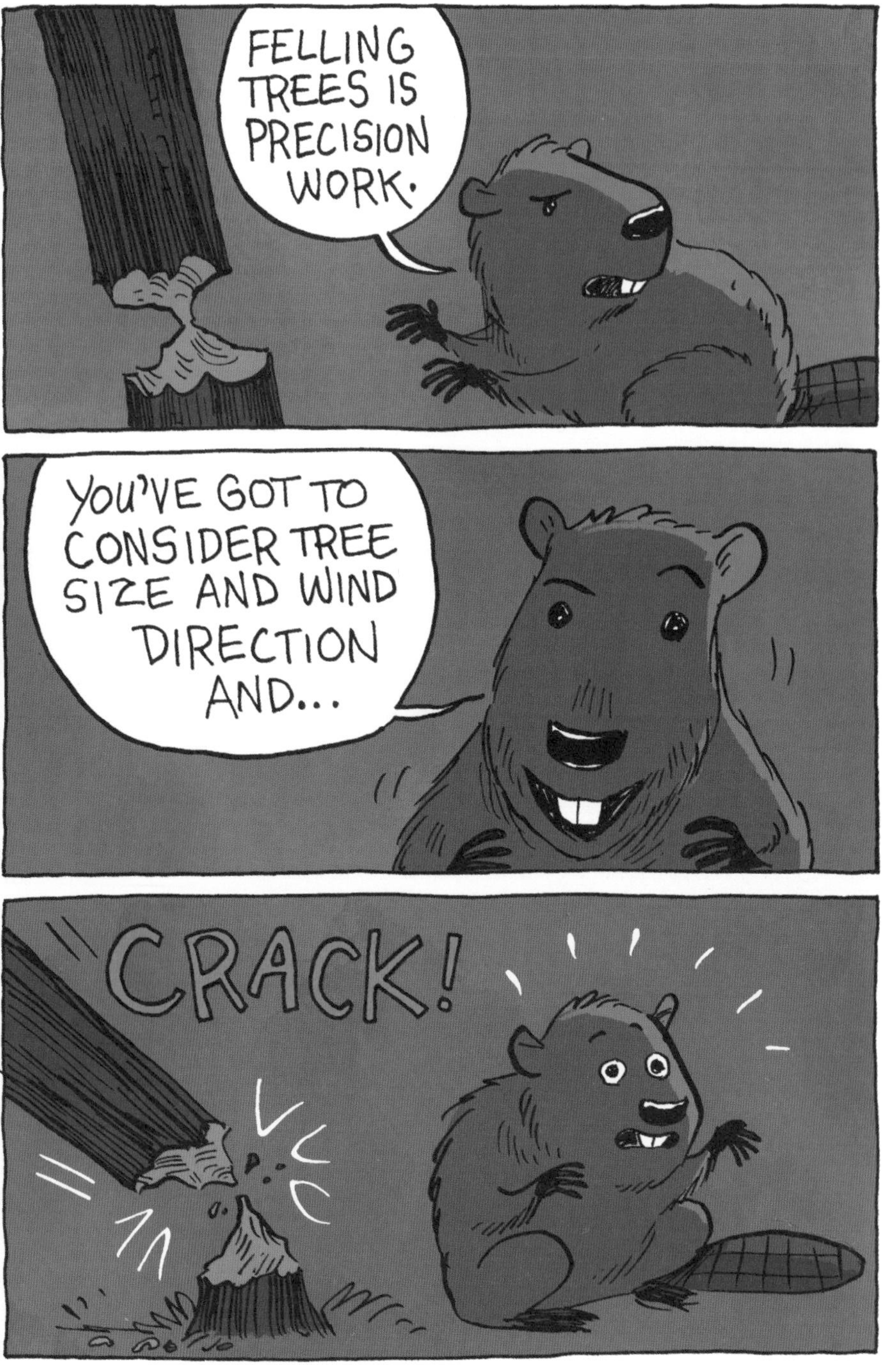
FELLING TREES IS PRECISION WORK.
YOU'VE GOT TO CONSIDER TREE SIZE AND WIND DIRECTION AND...
CRACK!

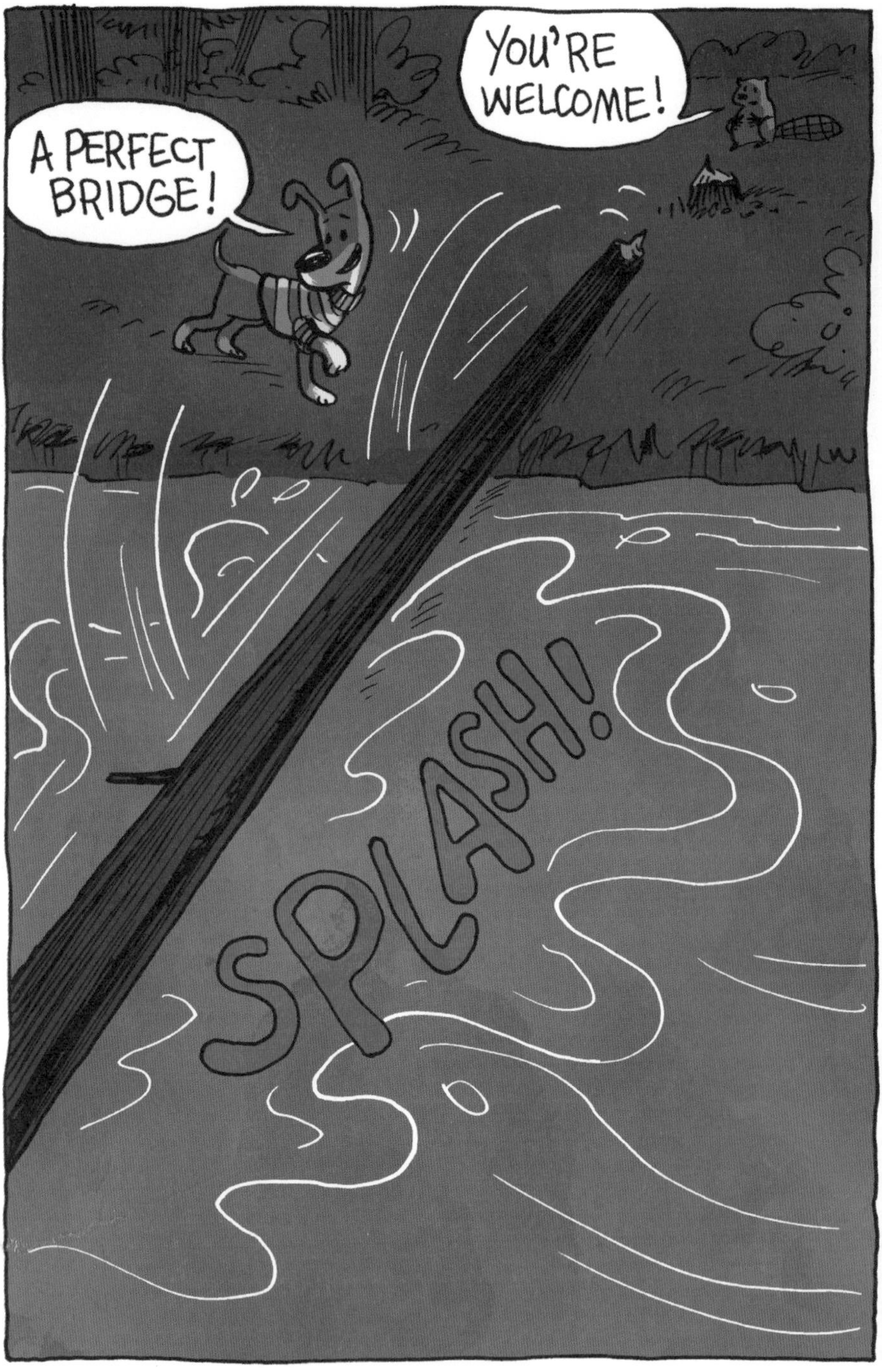
A PERFECT BRIDGE!
YOU'RE WELCOME!
SPLASH!

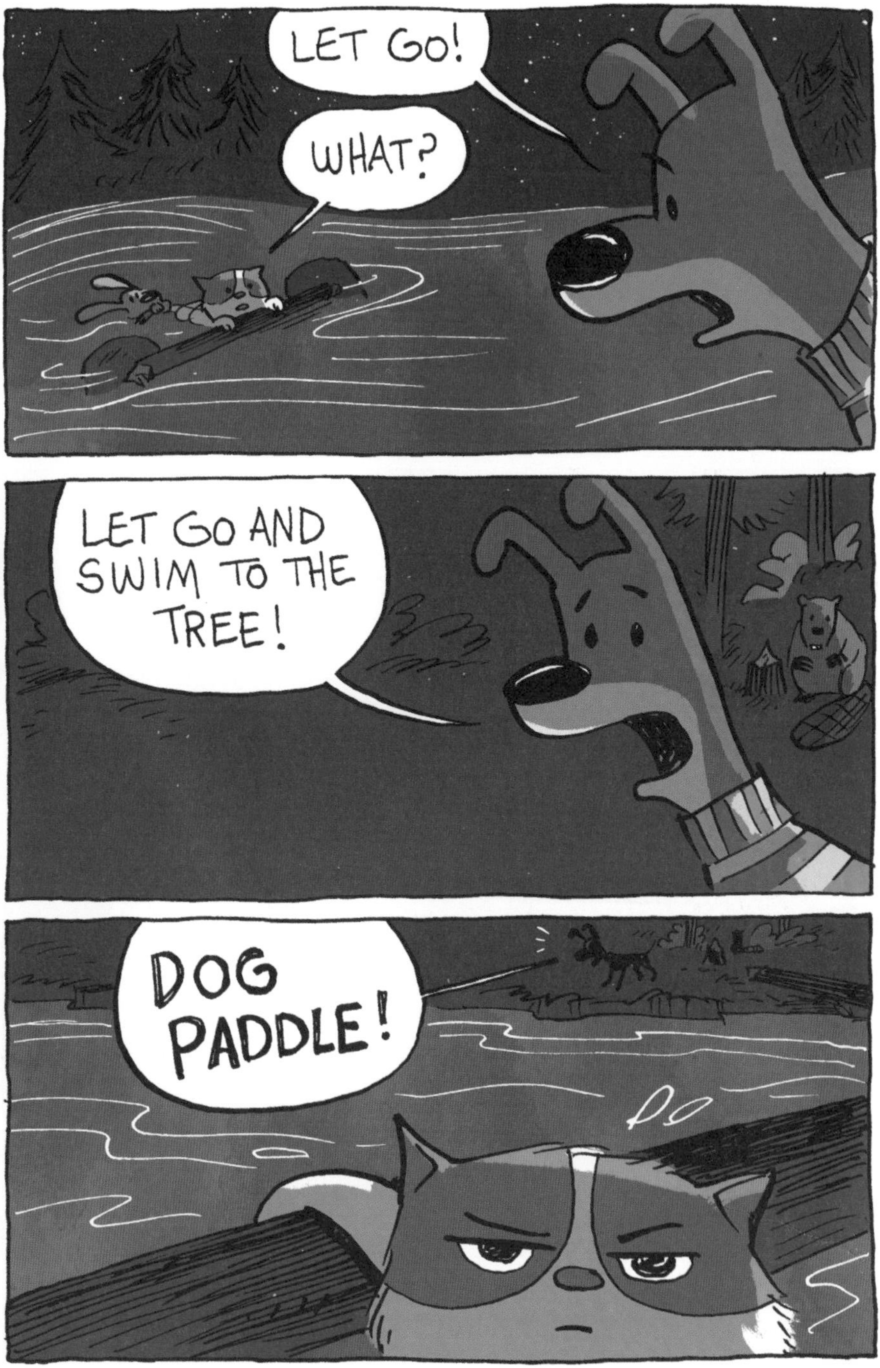
LET GO!
WHAT?
LET GO AND SWIM TO THE TREE!
DOG PADDLE!

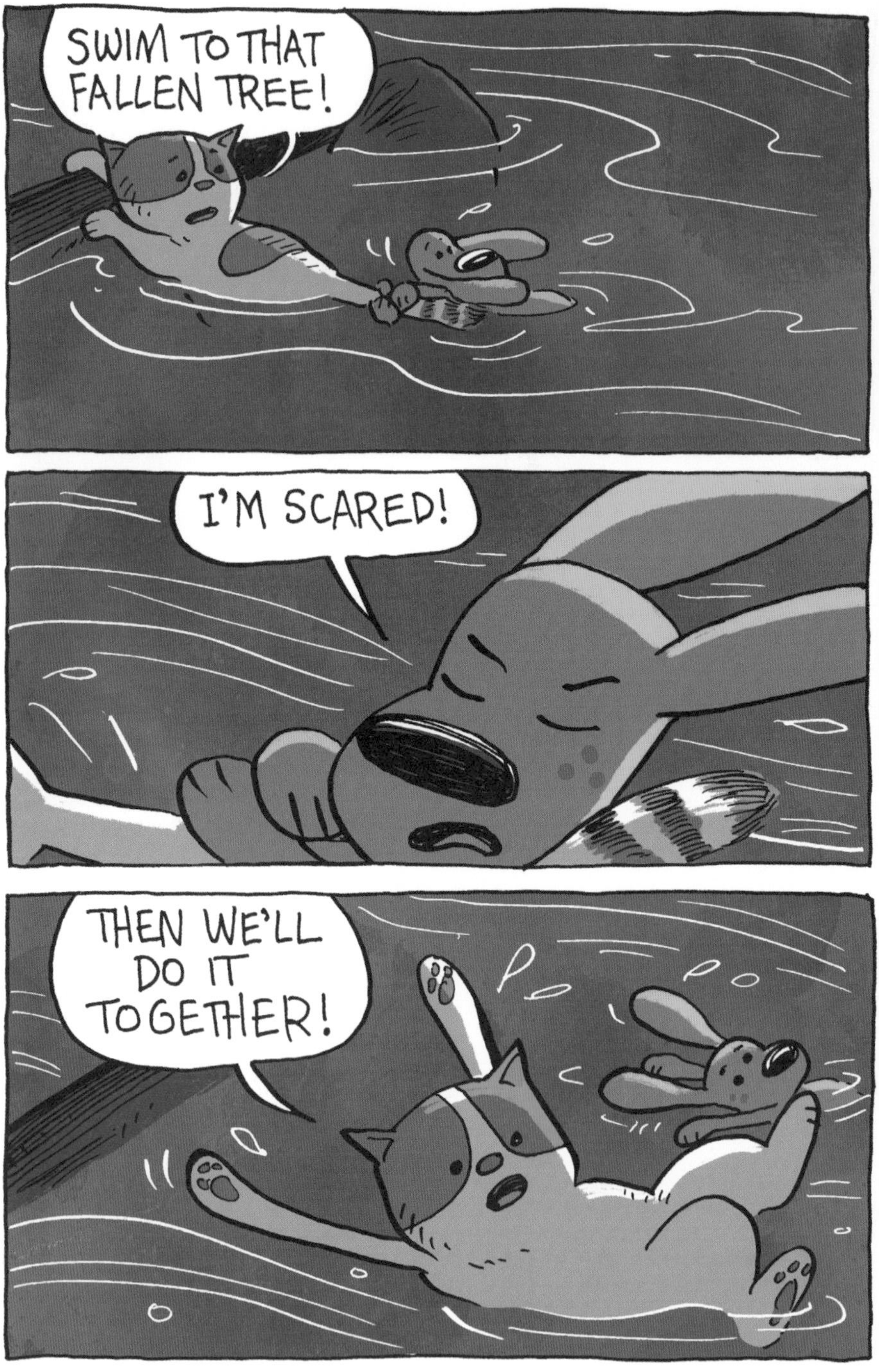
SWIM TO THAT FALLEN TREE!
I'M SCARED!
THEN WE'LL DO IT TOGETHER!

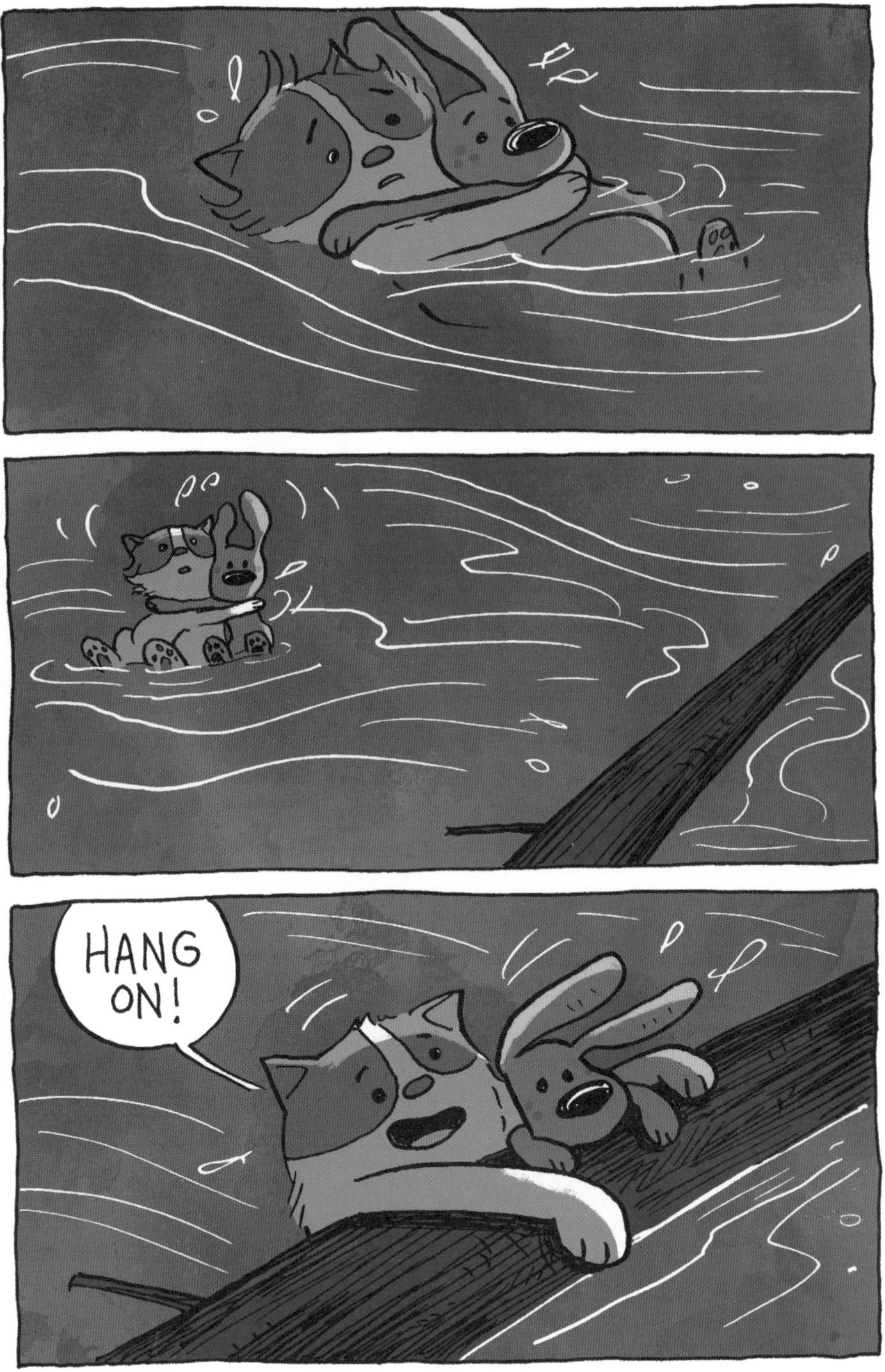
HANG ON!

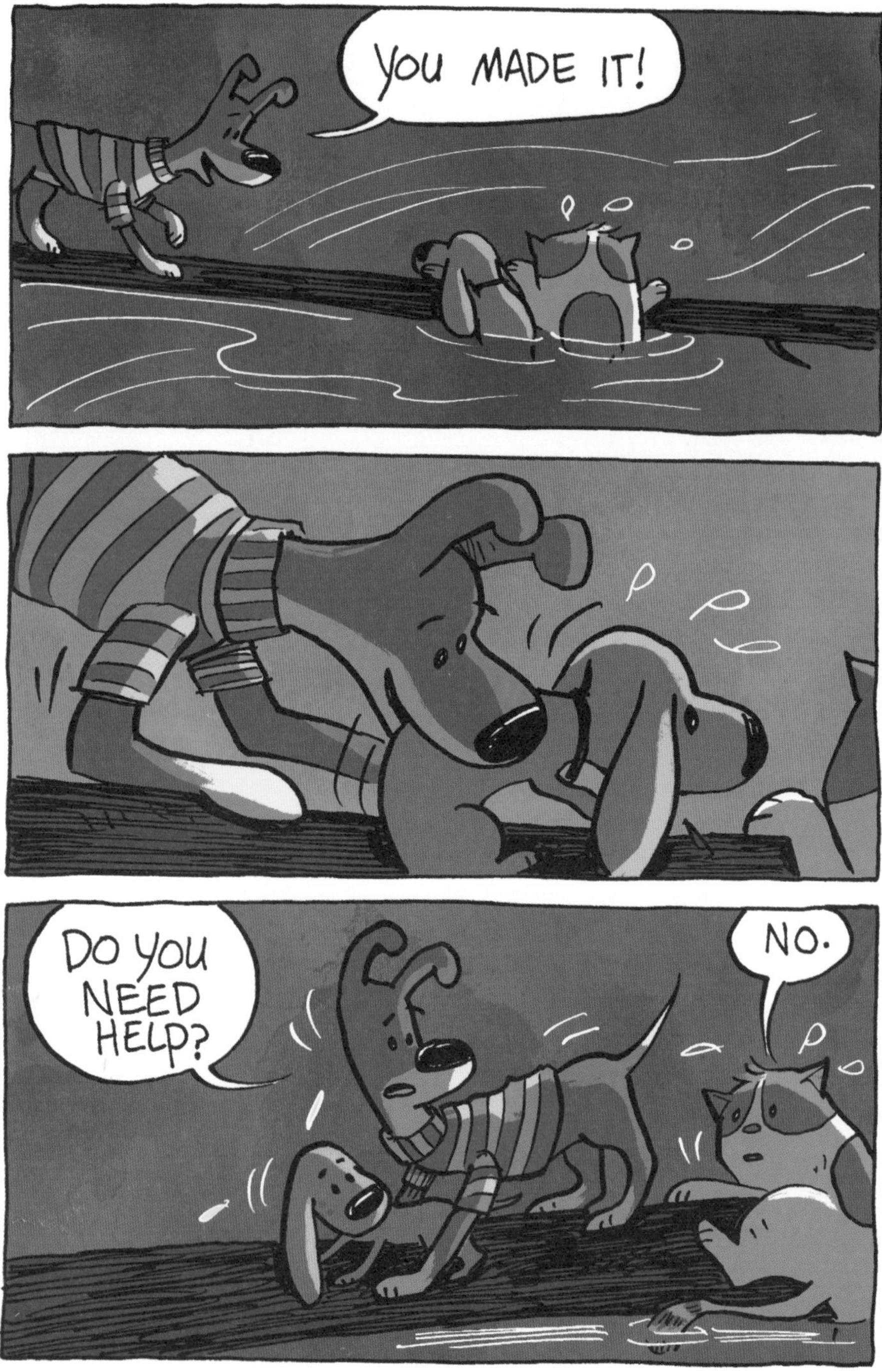
YOU MADE IT!
DO YOU NEED HELP?
NO.

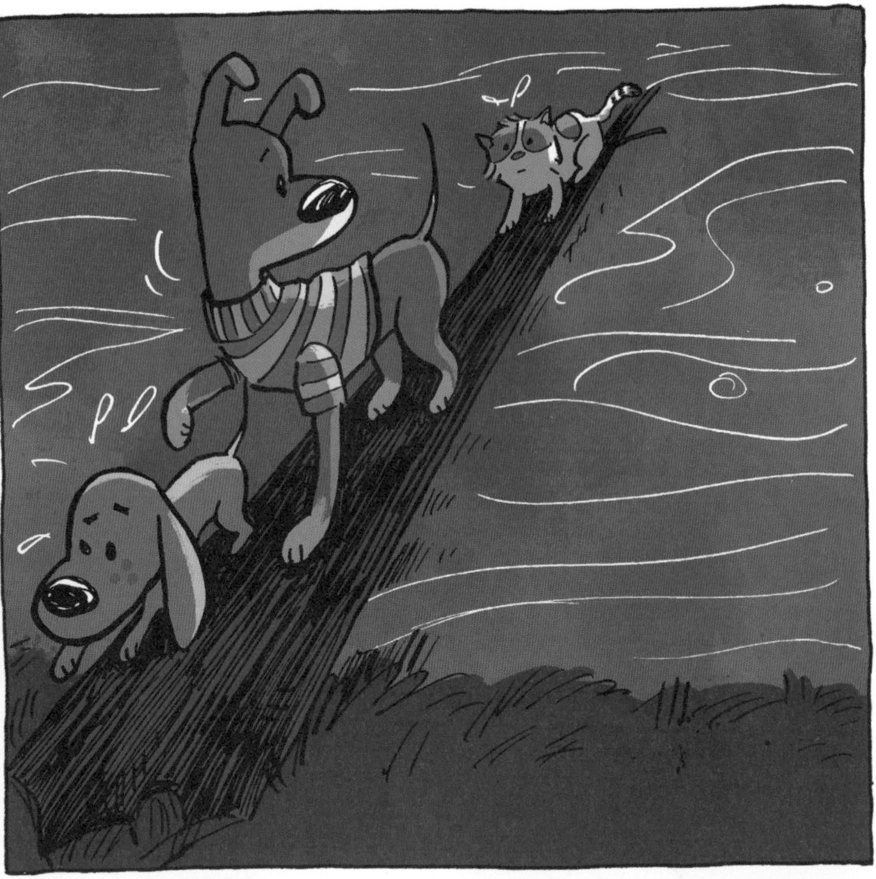

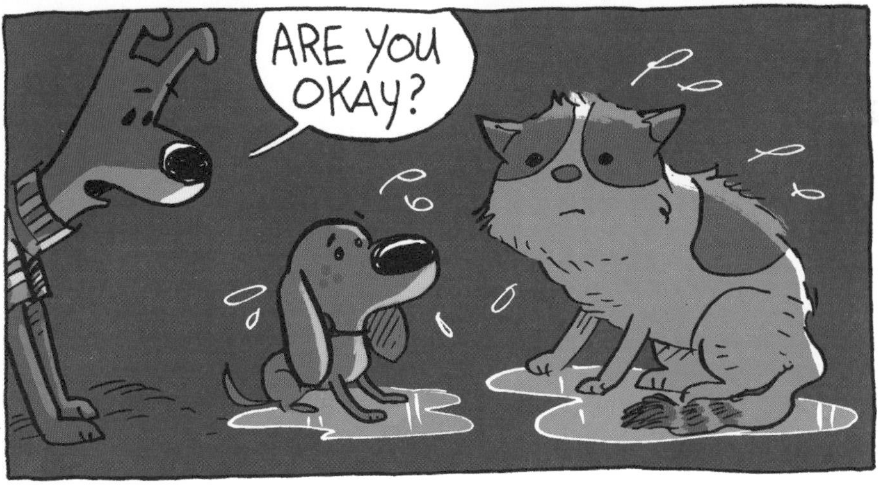
ARE YOU OKAY?

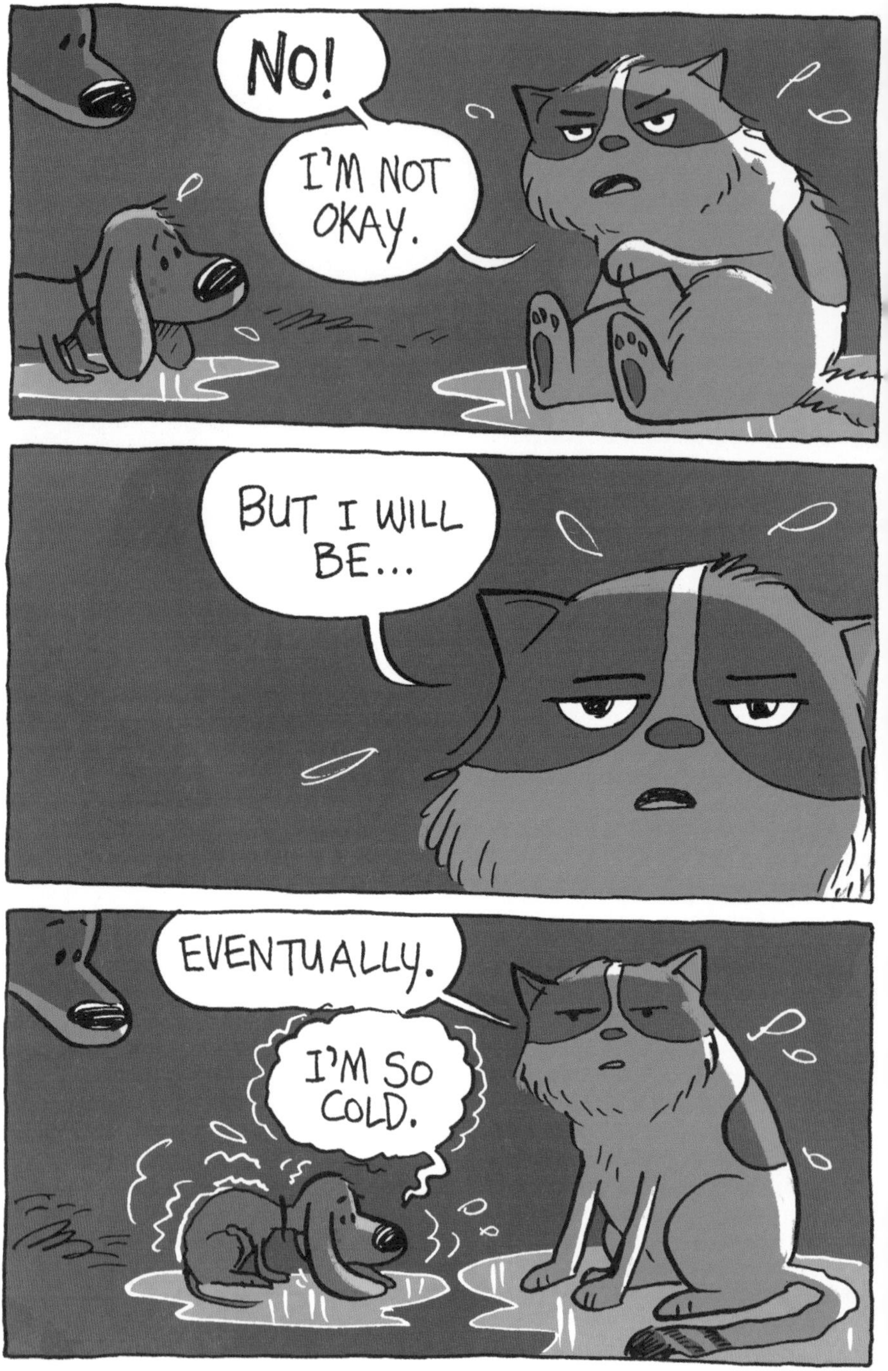
NO!
I'M NOT OKAY.
BUT I WILL BE...
EVENTUALLY.
I'M SO COLD.

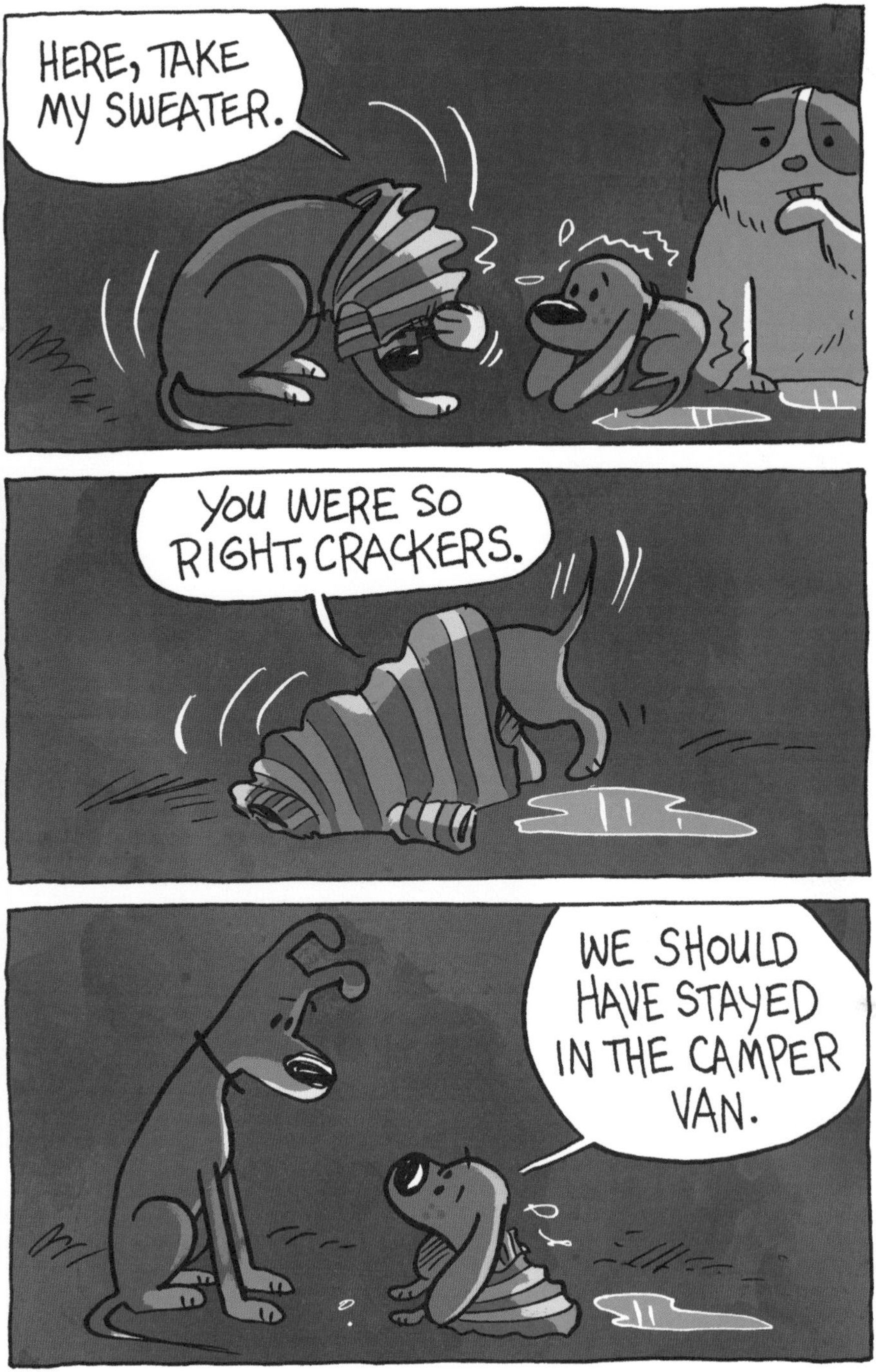
HERE, TAKE MY SWEATER.
YOU WERE SO RIGHT, CRACKERS.
WE SHOULD HAVE STAYED IN THE CAMPER VAN.

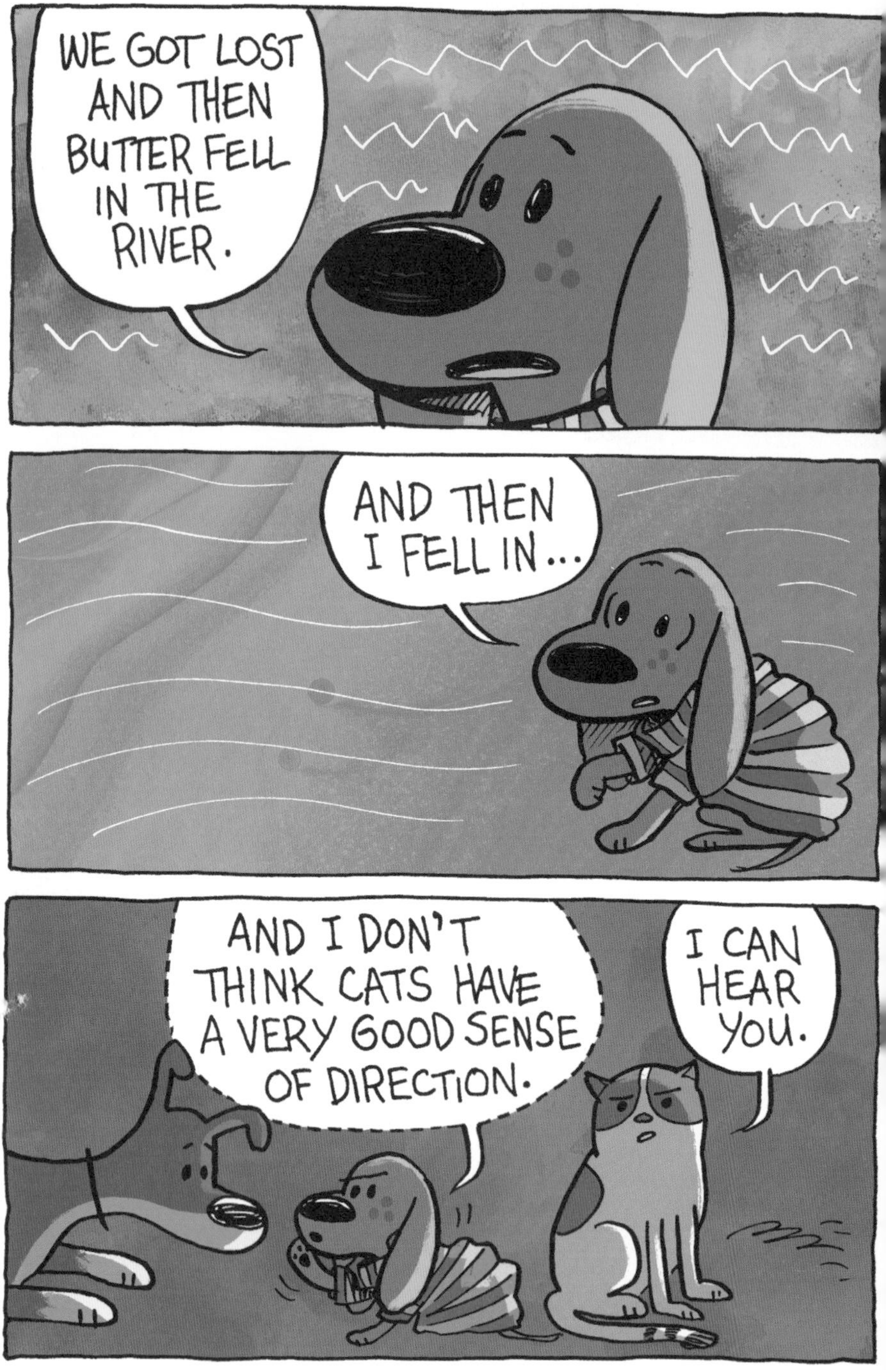
WE GOT LOST AND THEN BUTTER FELL IN THE RIVER.
AND THEN I FELL IN...
AND I DON'T THINK CATS HAVE A VERY GOOD SENSE OF DIRECTION.
I CAN HEAR YOU.

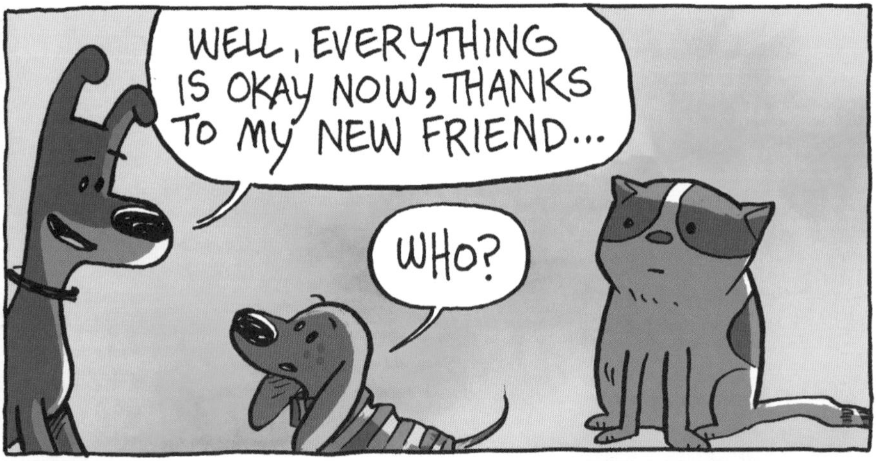
WELL, EVERYTHING IS OKAY NOW, THANKS TO MY NEW FRIEND...
WHO?

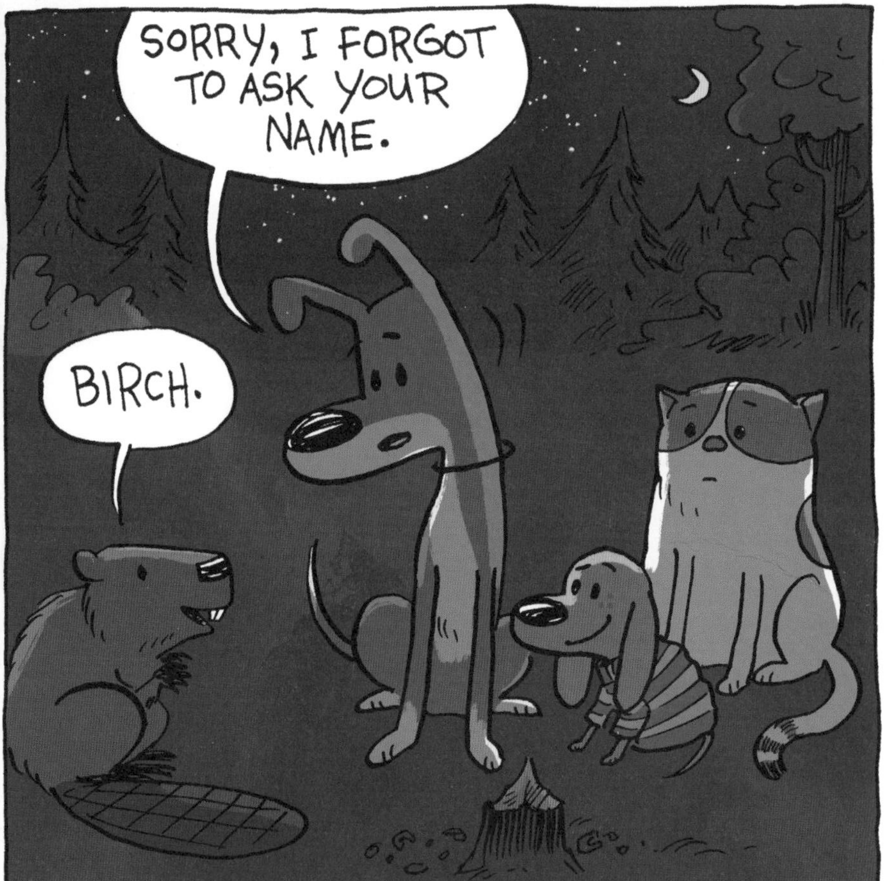
SORRY, I FORGOT TO ASK YOUR NAME.
BIRCH.

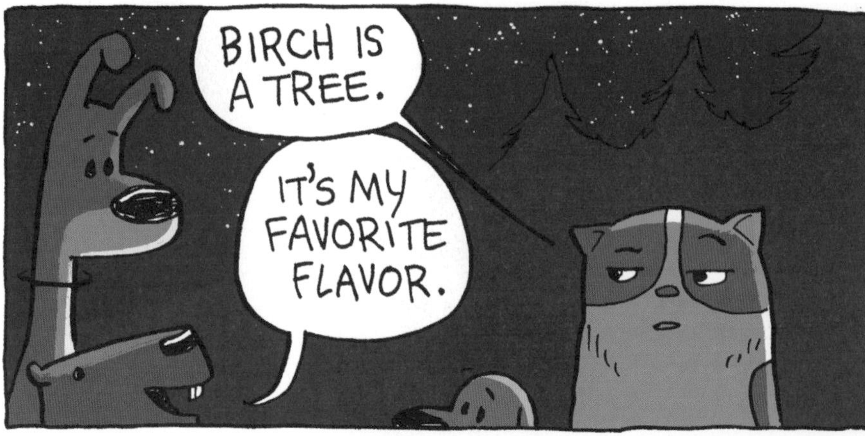
BIRCH IS A TREE.
IT'S MY FAVORITE FLAVOR.

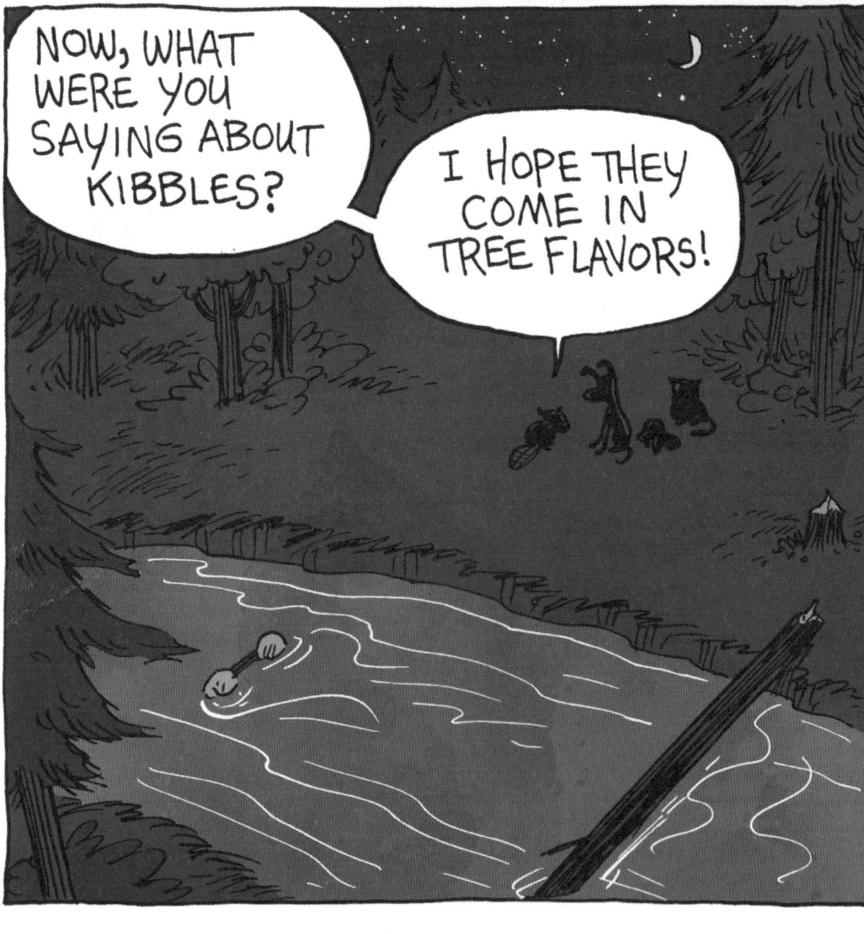
NOW, WHAT WERE YOU SAYING ABOUT KIBBLES?
I HOPE THEY COME IN TREE FLAVORS!

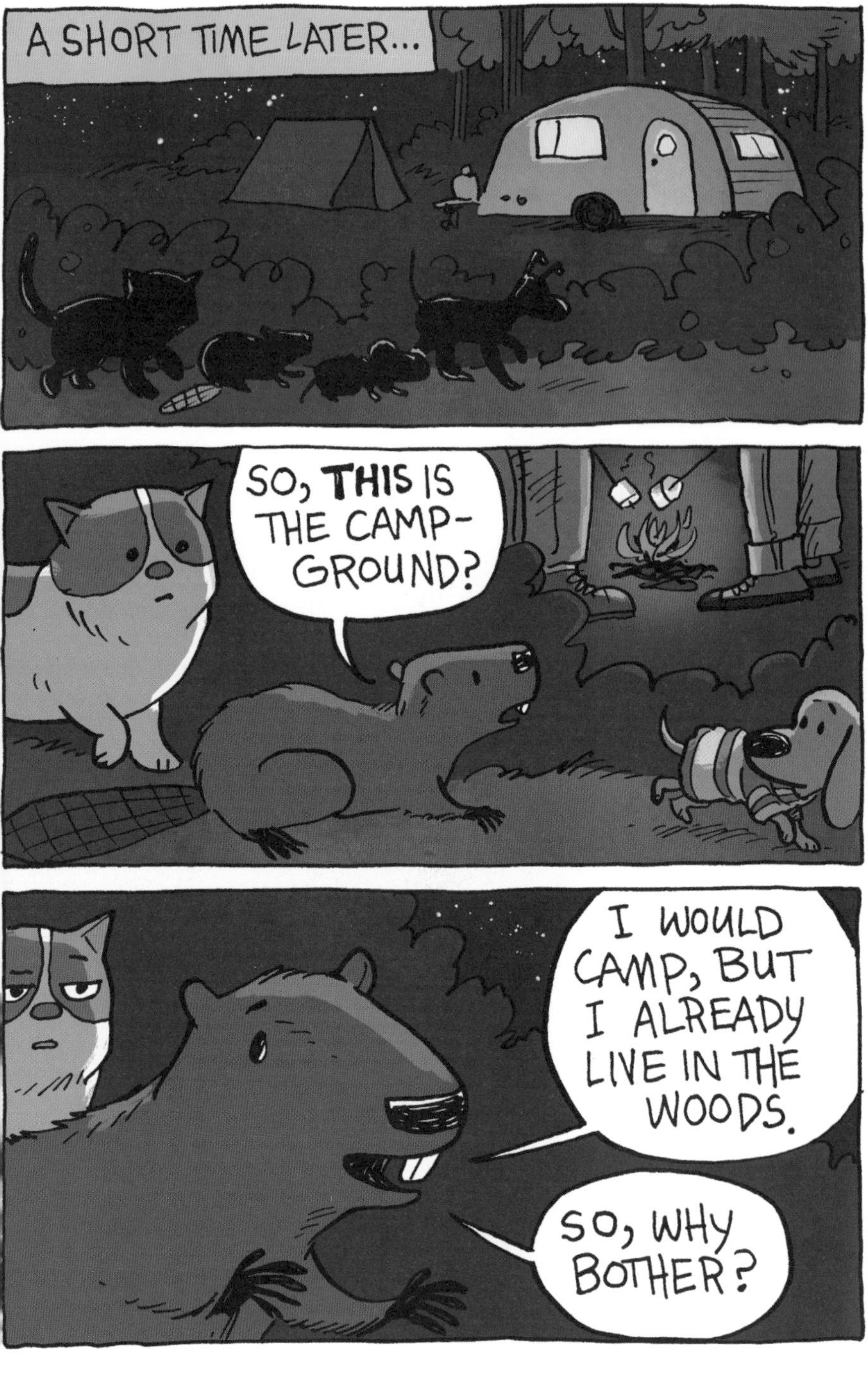
A SHORT TIME LATER...
SO, THIS IS THE CAMP-GROUND?
I WOULD CAMP, BUT I ALREADY LIVE IN THE WOODS.
SO, WHY BOTHER?

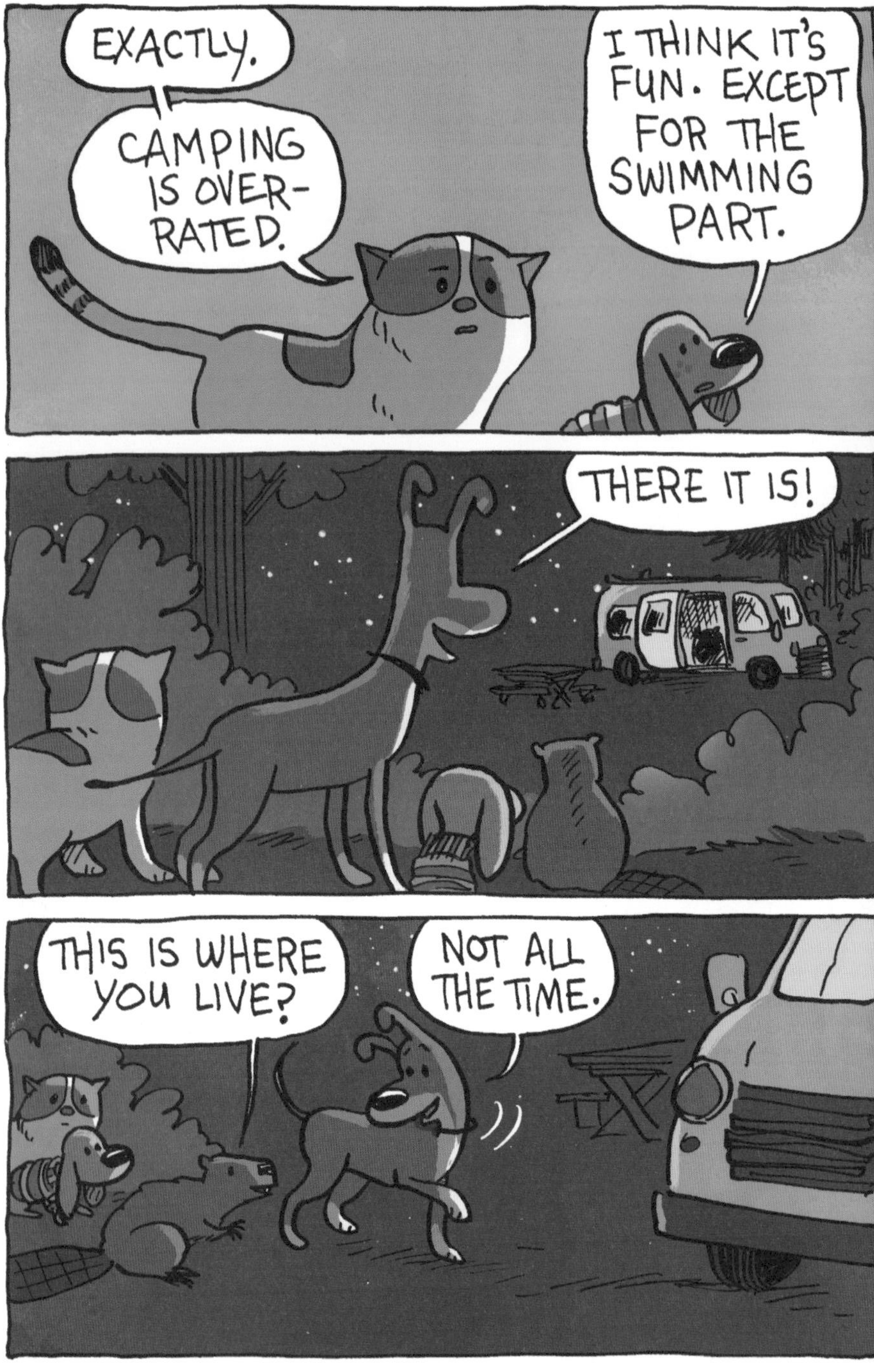
EXACTLY.
CAMPING IS OVER-RATED.
I THINK IT'S FUN. EXCEPT FOR THE SWIMMING PART.
THERE IT IS!
THIS IS WHERE YOU LIVE?
NOT ALL THE TIME.

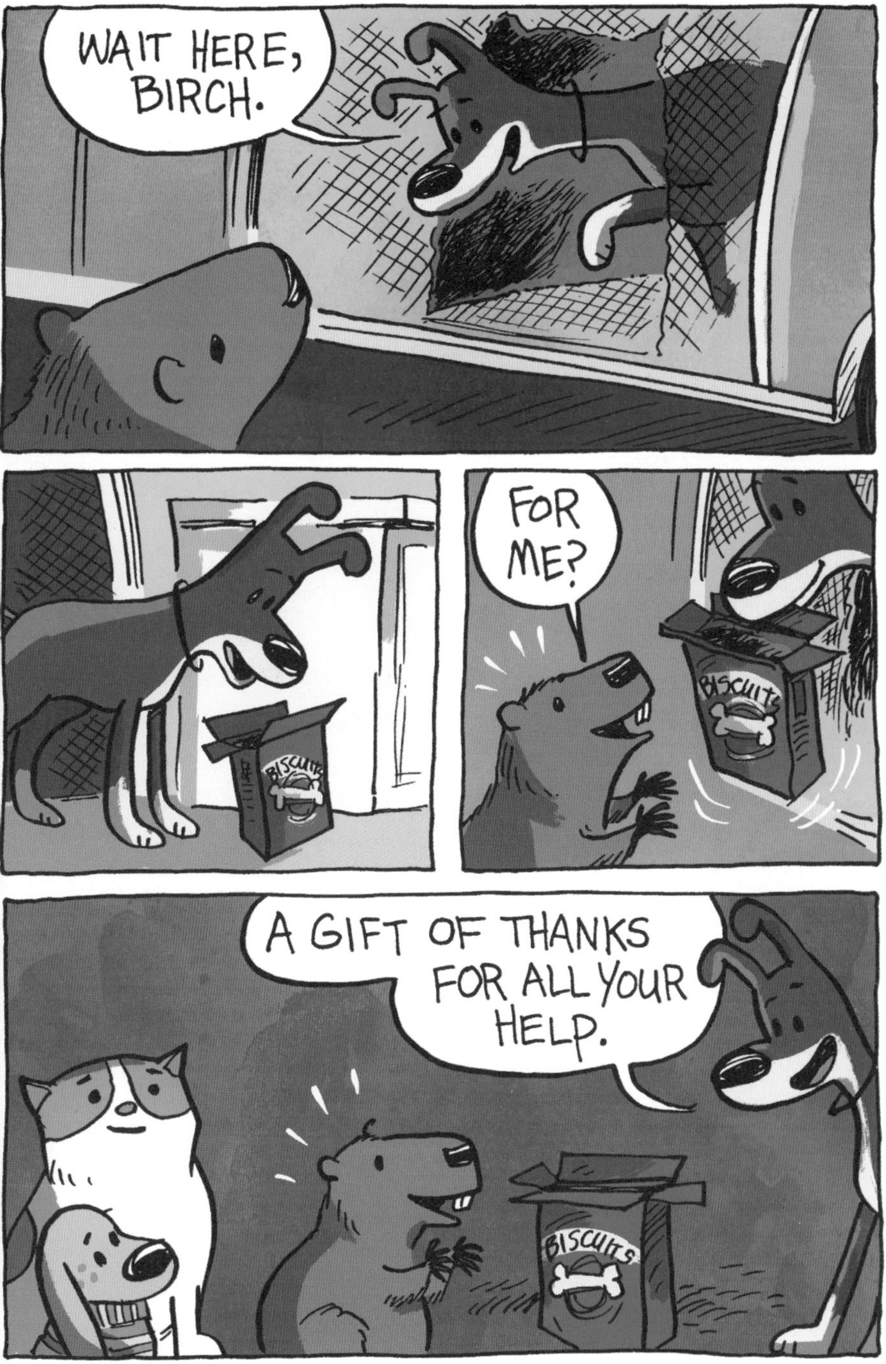
WAIT HERE, BIRCH.
FOR ME?
BISCUITS
BISCUITS
A GIFT OF THANKS FOR ALL YOUR HELP.
BISCUITS

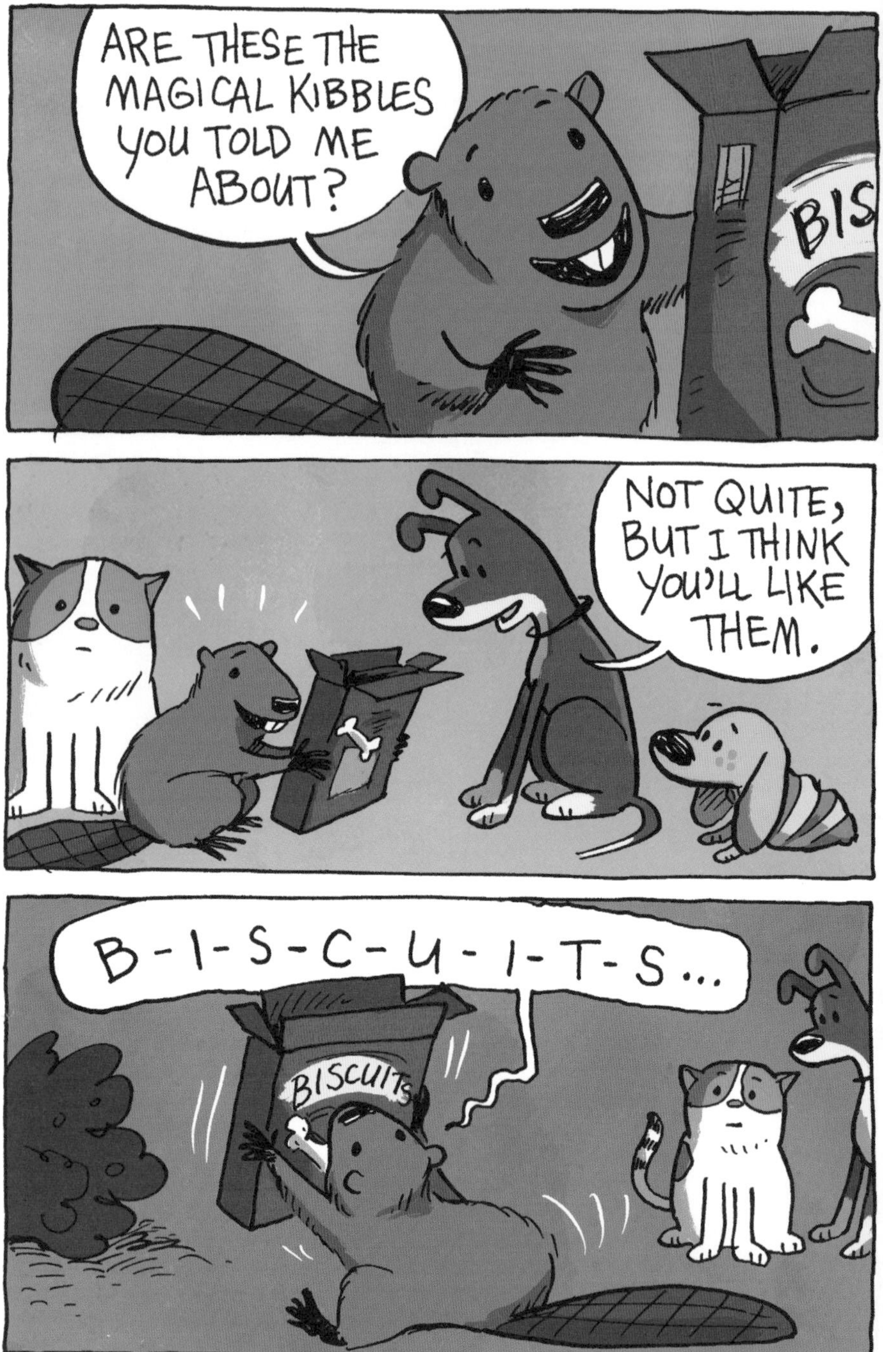
ARE THESE THE MAGICAL KIBBLES YOU TOLD ME ABOUT?
BIS
NOT QUITE, BUT I THINK YOU'LL LIKE THEM.
B-I-S-C-U-I-T-S...
BISCUITS

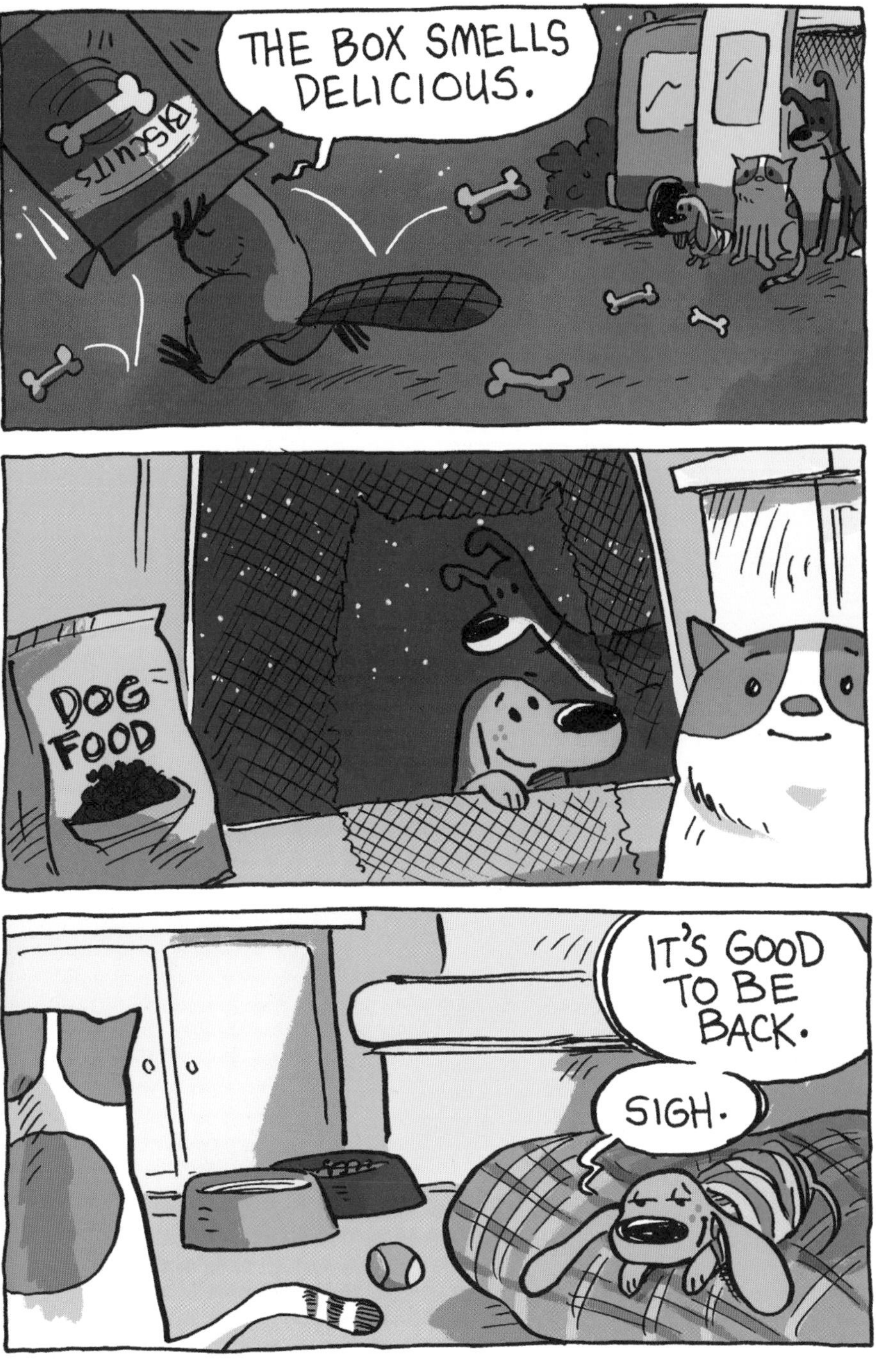
BISCUITS
THE BOX SMELLS DELICIOUS.
DOG FOOD
IT'S GOOD TO BE BACK.
SIGH.

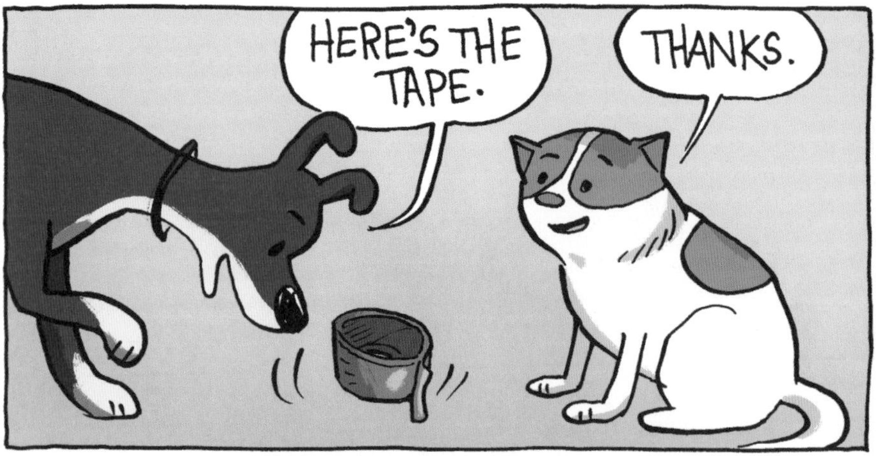
HERE'S THE TAPE.
THANKS.

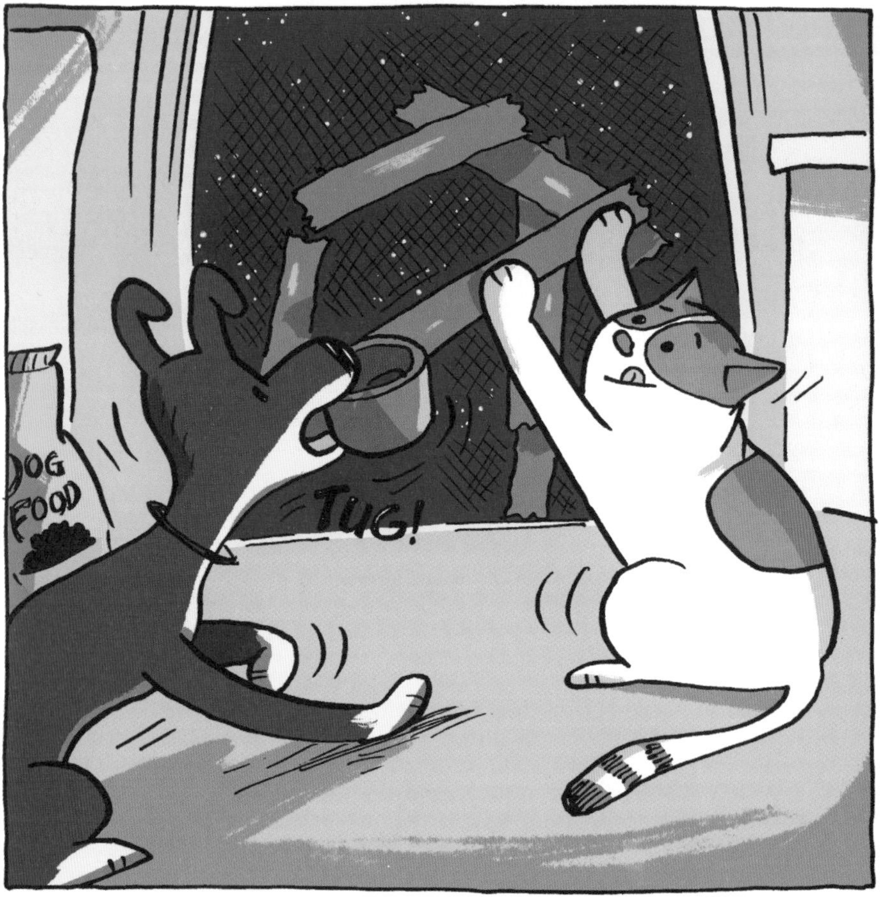
DOG FOOD
TUG!

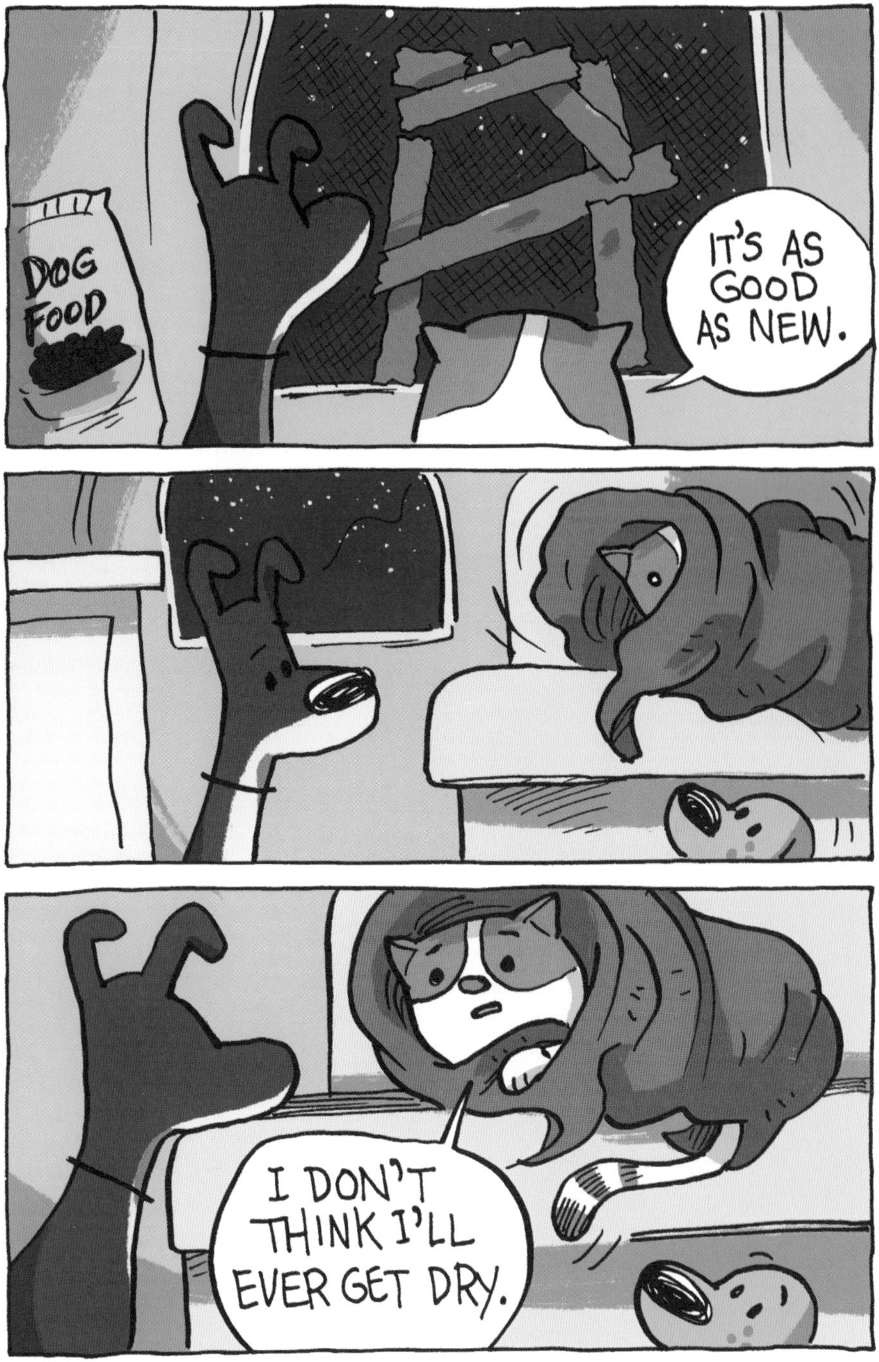
DOG FOOD
IT'S AS GOOD AS NEW.
I DON'T THINK I'LL EVER GET DRY.

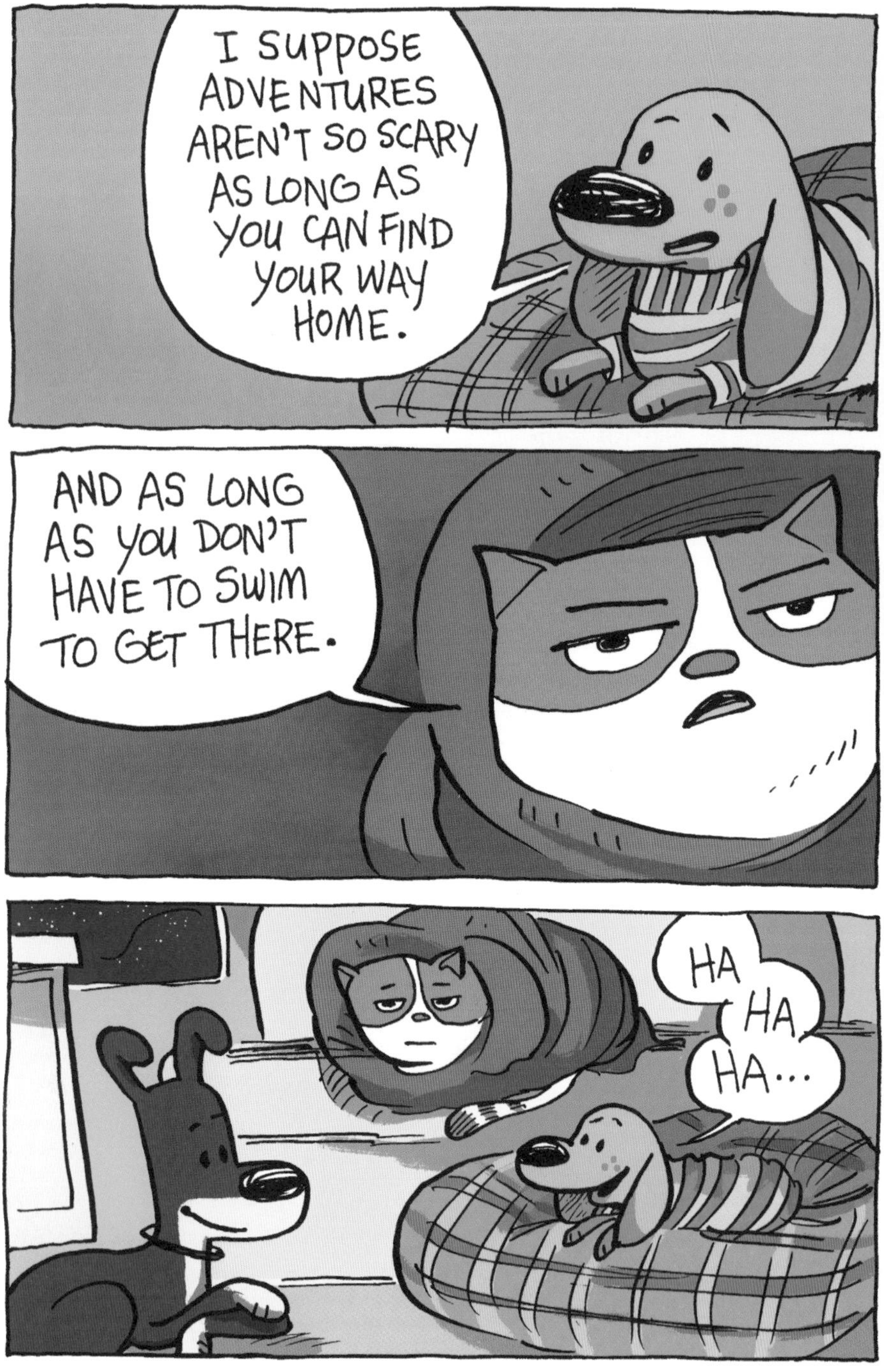
I SUPPOSE ADVENTURES AREN'T SO SCARY AS LONG AS YOU CAN FIND YOUR WAY HOME.
AND AS LONG AS YOU DON'T HAVE TO SWIM TO GET THERE.
HA HA HA...

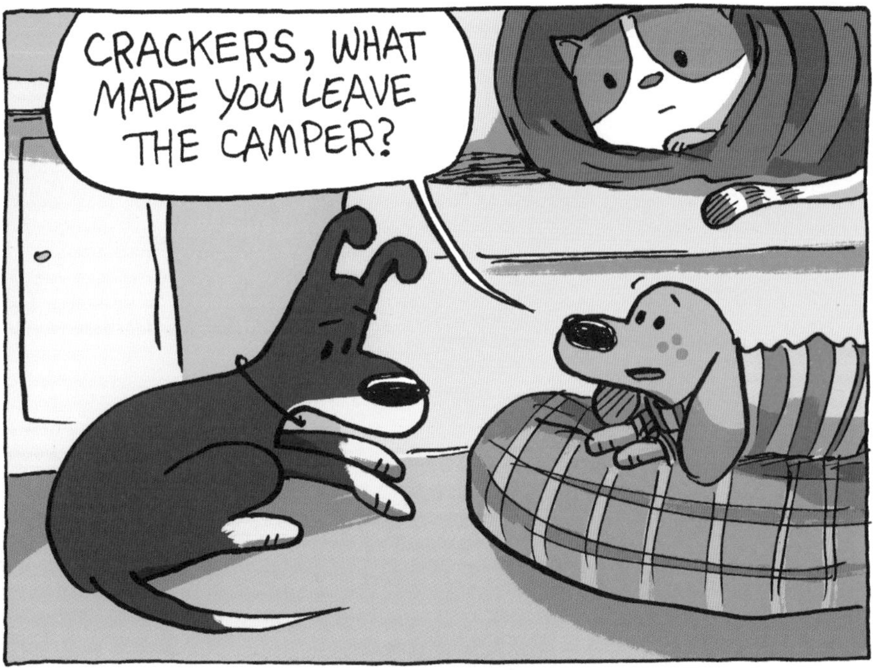
CRACKERS, WHAT MADE YOU LEAVE THE CAMPER?

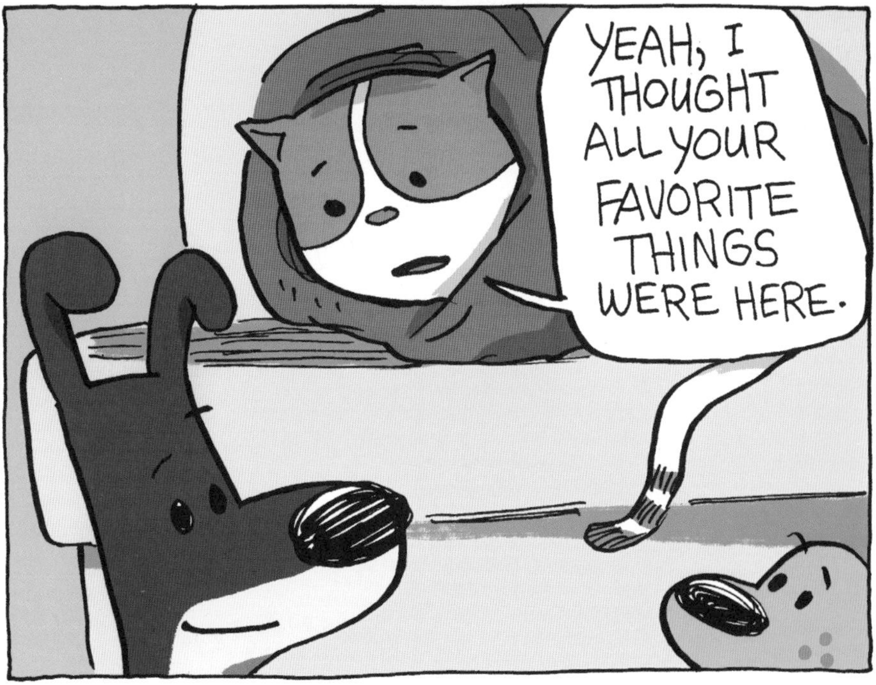
YEAH, I THOUGHT ALL YOUR FAVORITE THINGS WERE HERE.

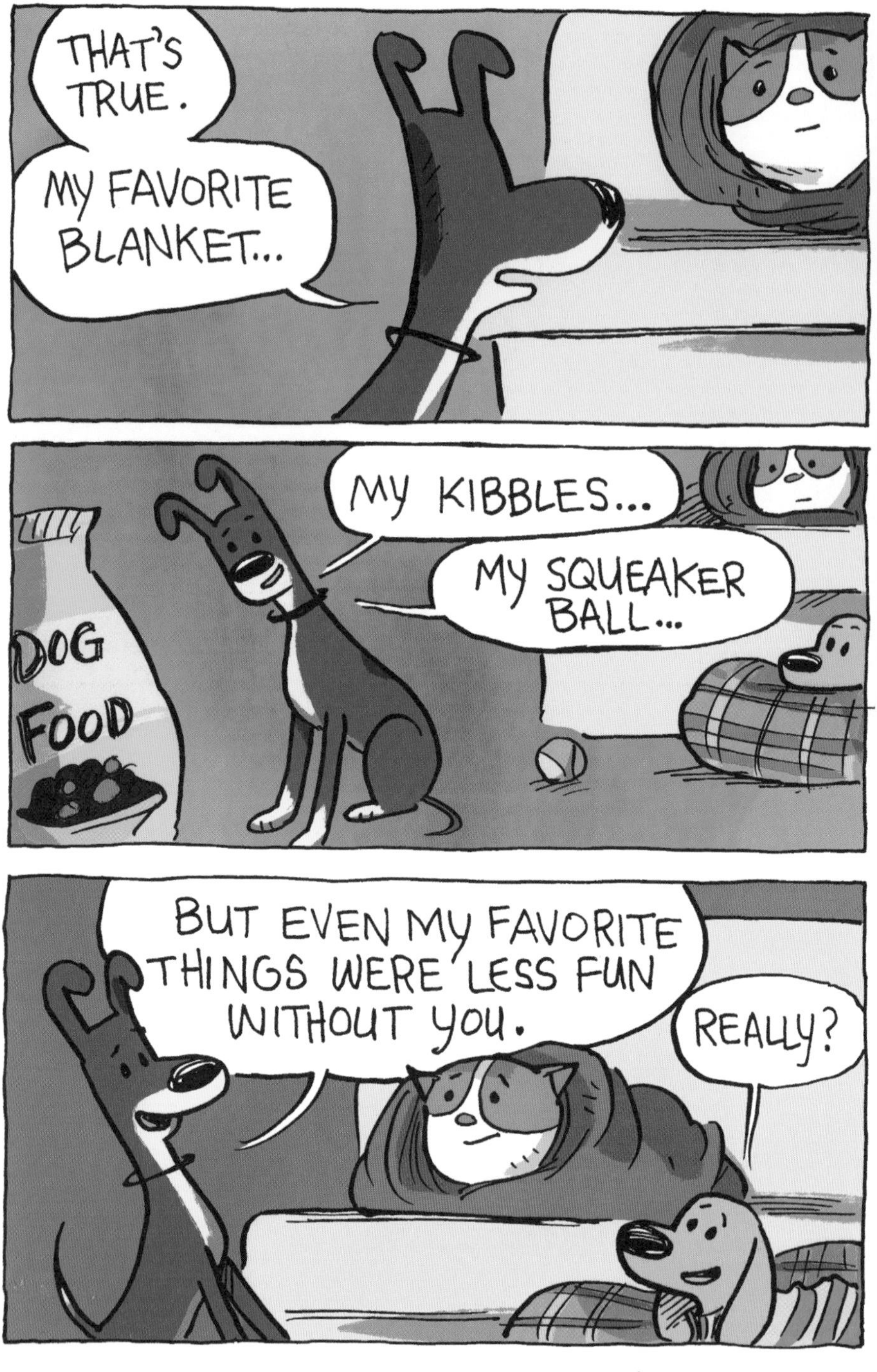
THAT'S TRUE.
MY FAVORITE BLANKET...
MY KIBBLES...
MY SQUEAKER BALL...
DOG FOOD
BUT EVEN MY FAVORITE THINGS WERE LESS FUN WITHOUT YOU.
REALLY?

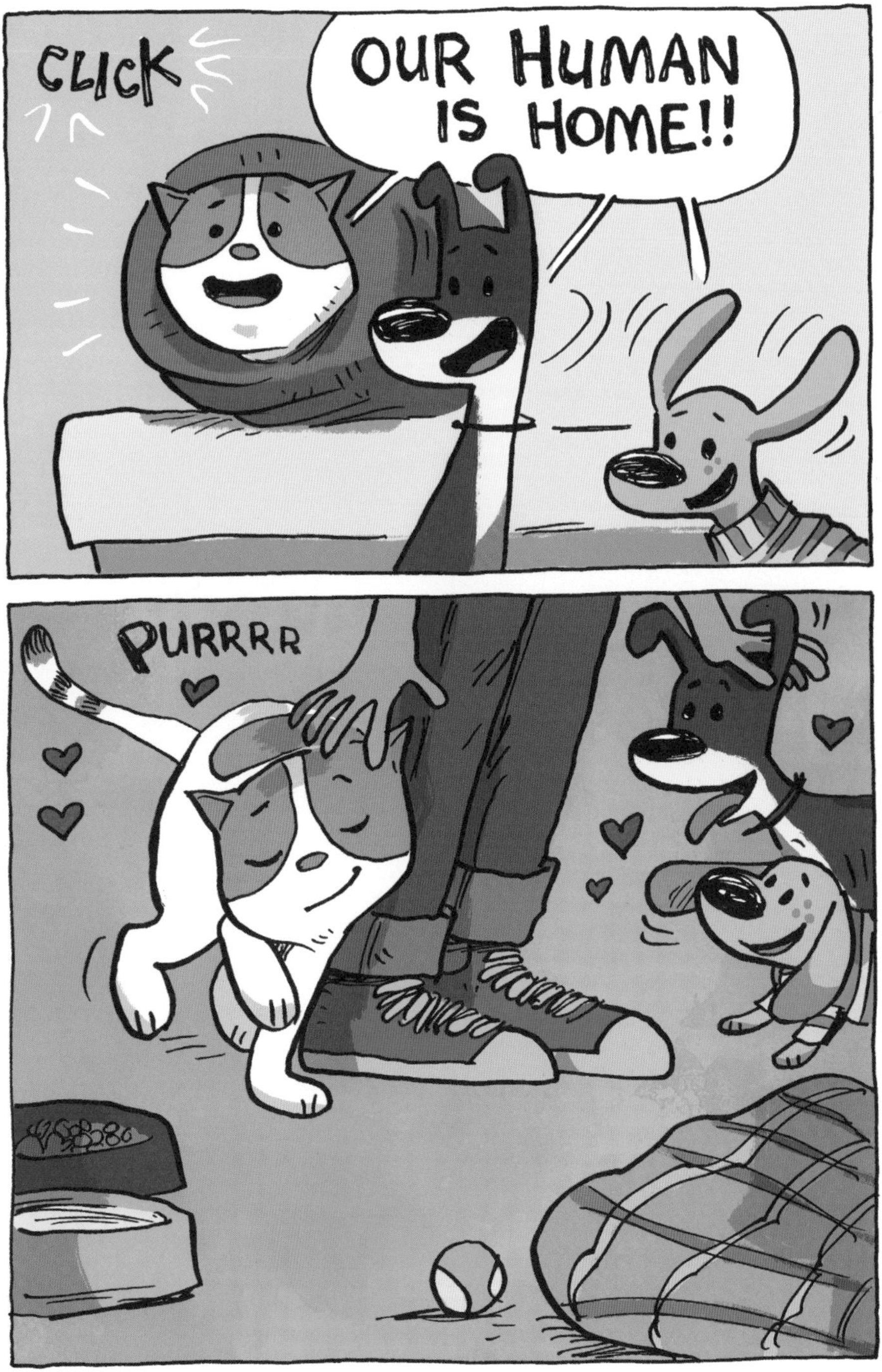
CLICK
OUR HUMAN IS HOME!!
PURRRR

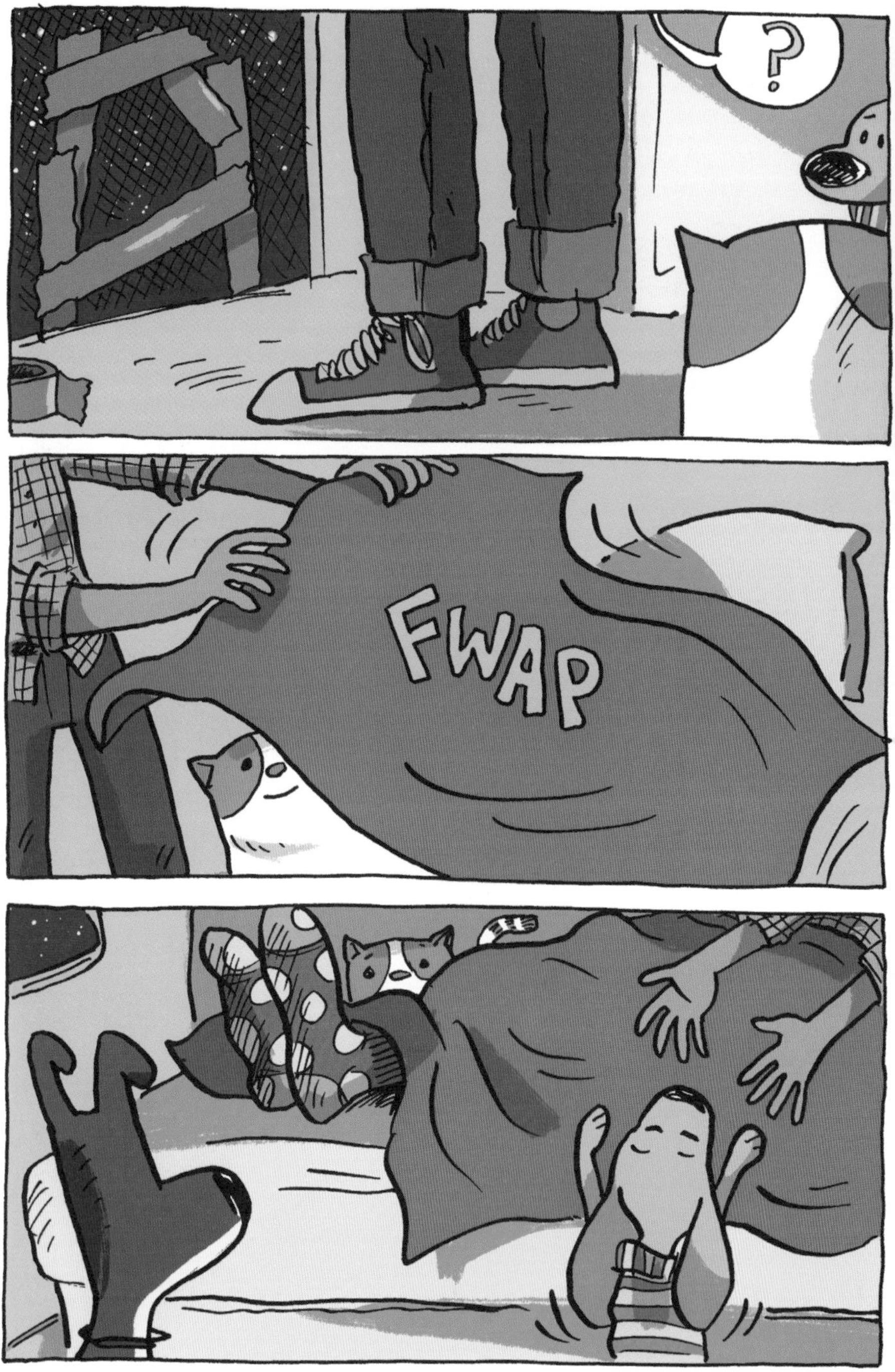
?
FWAP

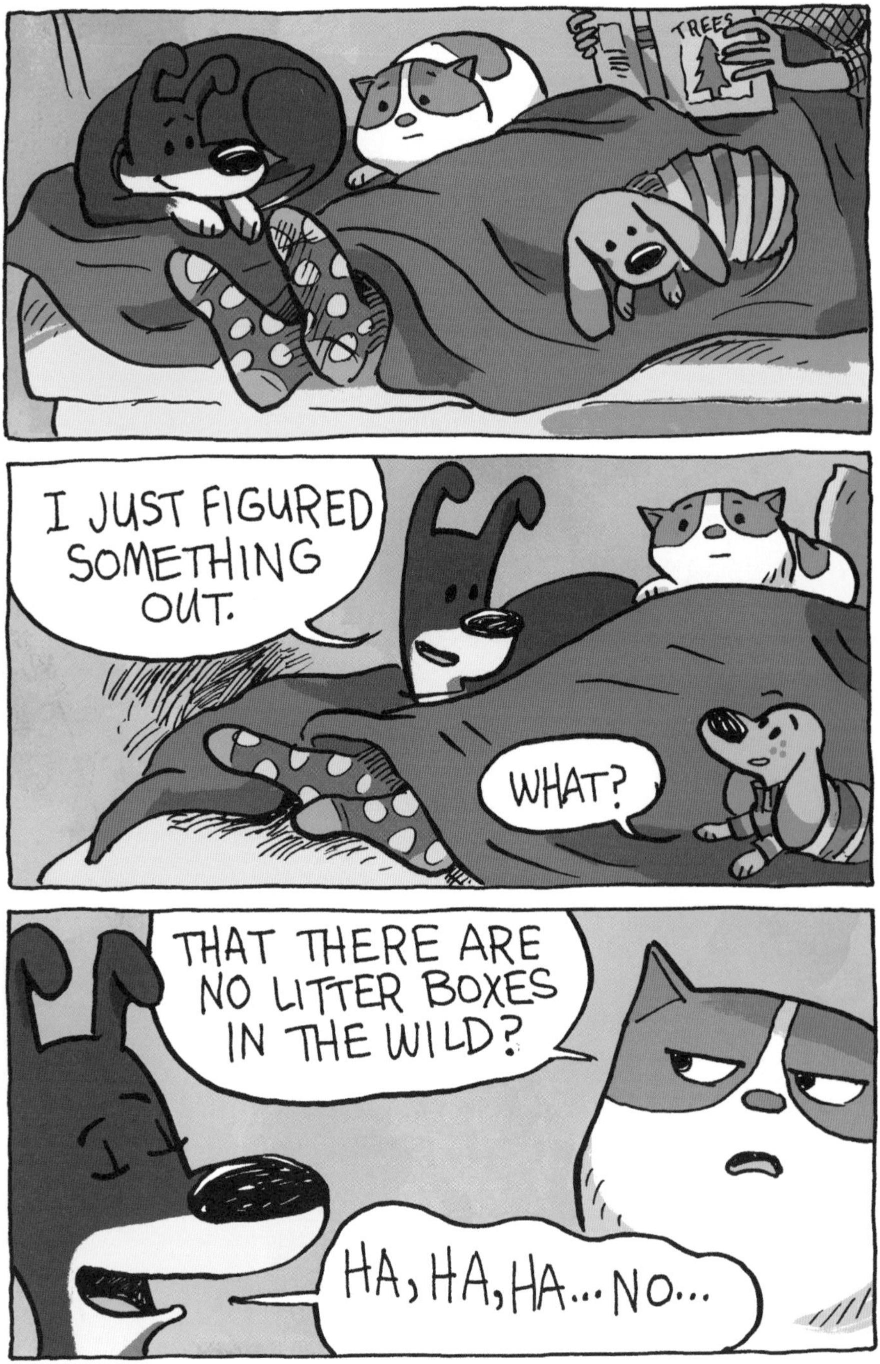
TREES
I JUST FIGURED SOMETHING OUT.
WHAT?
THAT THERE ARE NO LITTER BOXES IN THE WILD?
HA, HA, HA... NO...

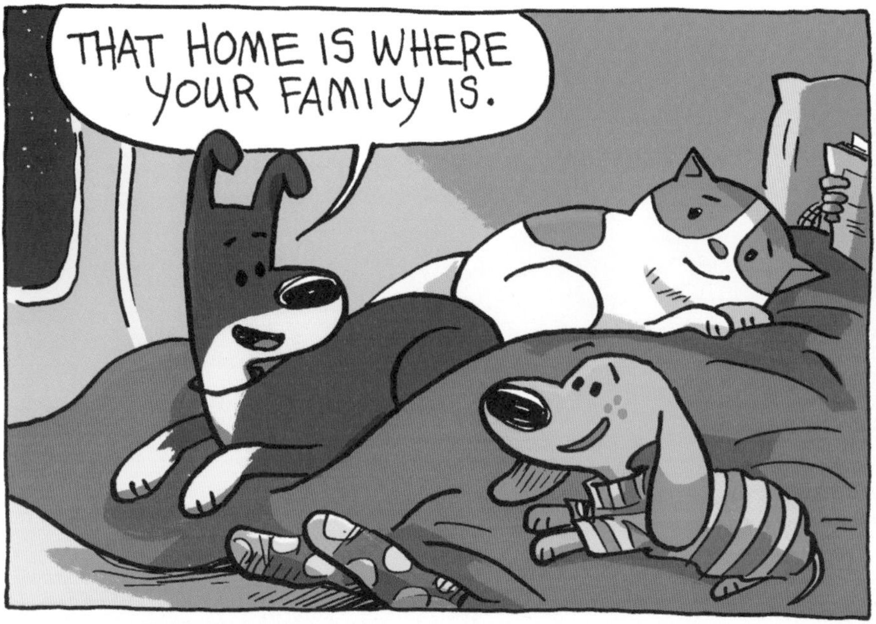
THAT HOME IS WHERE YOUR FAMILY IS.

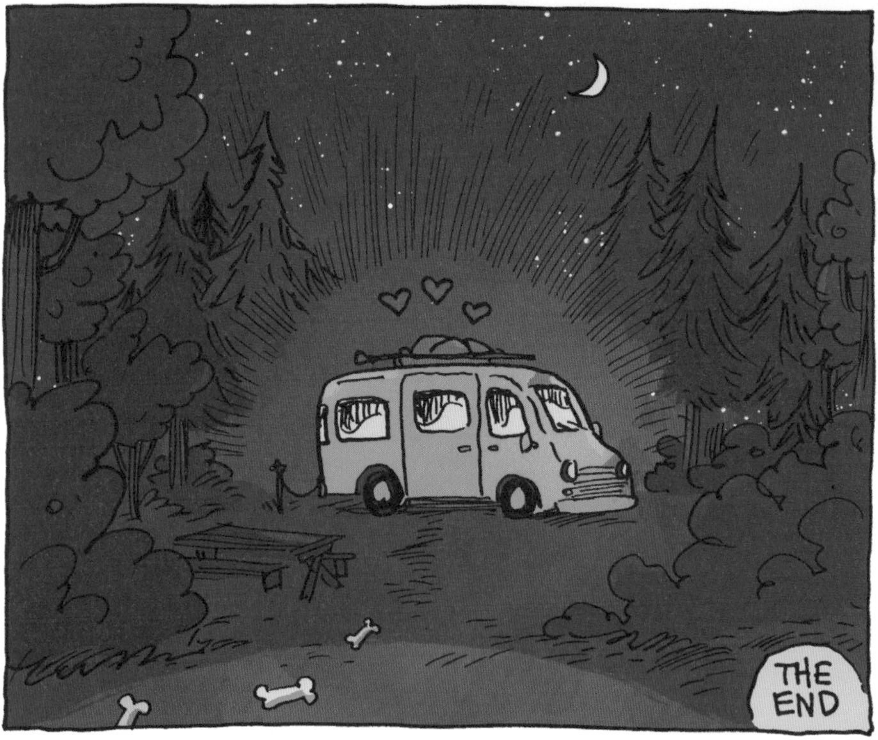
THE END

MEET **PAIGE BRADDOCK**

I started drawing comics when I was seven years old. Wiggins, Mississippi, the town I grew up in, was very small. Wiggins didn't have a comic shop or a bookstore. Mostly, I learned about comics by reading the Sunday funnies in the newspaper. My favorite characters to draw were Snoopy, Popeye, and Beetle Bailey. It wasn't long before I started creating my own characters. *Captain Lightning* was the first comics story I wrote and drew. It starred a very clumsy superhero whose cape was always getting snagged on fences and bushes.

Comics have always been one of my favorite things. I majored in illustration in college at the University of Tennessee and later worked as an illustrator for several newspapers. Then I got my dream job: working with Charles M. Schulz at his studio in California. He was the creator of Charlie Brown, Snoopy, and the whole *Peanuts* gang. It's funny how things work out sometimes. Snoopy was one of my all-time favorite characters and now I get to work with him every day.

I've always loved to draw dogs, but when our pet Buddy Barker came to live with us, I started drawing dogs even more often. Buddy was one of the main inspirations for the Peanut, Butter, & Crackers series. Of course, I can't leave out our cat, Otis—who once ate a *whole stick* of butter—and when we added our little dachshund, Charlie, to the mix, we really did begin an even bigger adventure!

It's important as artists and writers to figure out what inspires us and to make that part of our story—and *everybody* has a story to tell!

ACKNOWLEDGMENTS

I'd like to offer special thanks to the colorist for this book, Kat Fraser. Her colors really took this adventure story to the next level. And thanks to our flatter, Jewel Jackson. A big thank-you to my editor, Meriam, and the team at Penguin—Jim and Lucia! To my wife, Evelyn, whose sense of humor inspires me to be funnier all the time. And lastly, I'd like to say thank you to all my readers. Without you, creating stories wouldn't be possible.

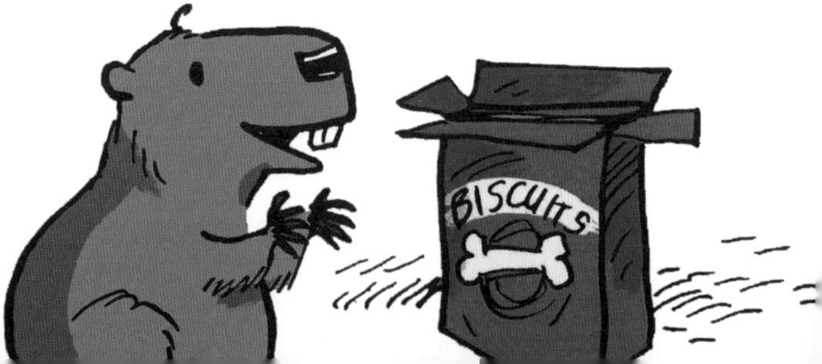
BISCUITS